FUR AND FURY

FUR AND FURY

REG RAWLINS, PSYCHIC INVESTIGATOR
BOOK TWENTY-FOUR

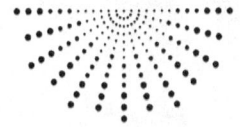

P.D. WORKMAN

ISBN: 9781774687635 (KDP Paperback)
ISBN: 9781774687642 (KDP Hardcover)
ISBN: 9781774687666 (Lulu Paperback)
ISBN: 9781774687659 (Large Print)
ISBN: 9781774687673 (Digital)
ISBN: 9781774687680 (Auto-narrated audiobook)

ALSO BY P.D. WORKMAN

FIND MORE BOOKS AT PDWORKMAN.COM

Reg Rawlins, Psychic Detective

Paranormal Mystery & Adventure

What the Cat Knew

A Psychic with Catitude

A Catastrophic Theft

Night of Nine Tails

The Immortal's Key

Yule's Sinister Spell

Fairy Blade Unmade

Web of Nightmares

A Whisker's Breadth

Skunk Man Swamp

Magic Ain't A Game

Without Foresight

Careful of Thy Wishes

Time to Your Elf

Undiscovered Tomb

Missing Powers

Thrice Spared

Cloaked Campaign

Sleepwalker's Sanctuary

Cat Tales in the Swamp (Short Story)

Tainted Truffle Treachery

A Fowl Play on Christmas Day (Christmas crossover story)

Lunar Lies

X Marks the Past

Spellbound Statues

Fur and Fury

Parks Pat Mysteries

Police Procedural Set in Canada

Out with the Sunset

Long Climb to the Top

Dark Water Under the Bridge

Immersed in the View

Skimming Over the Lake

Hazard of the Hills

Knows the Hills

Spanning the Creek

Sanctuary in the Stream

Echoes of the Engine

Bench with a View

Beneath the Icy Depths

Grounded in the Wind (Coming Soon)

Reservoir of Secrets (Coming Soon)

Peril in the Blooms (Coming Soon)

Stand Alone Suspense Novels

Looking Over Your Shoulder

Lion Within

Pursued by the Past

In the Tick of Time

Loose the Dogs

AND MORE AT PDWORKMAN.COM

To loyal friends
who will not be shaken

* * *

CHAPTER ONE

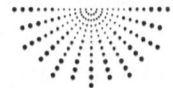

*R*eg had not expected to have to pose for the camera when she arrived at City Hall. Several of the attendees had encouraged her to go to the summit meeting between the warlocks and the werewolves, though she didn't exactly feel qualified to be there. Who was she? She didn't have any standing in the negotiations between the two factions.

"But don't you see, that's just the point?" Sarah asked. She was Reg's landlord and one of the witches who would be attending the so-called peace talks. "We need people there who are impartial third parties who can help to come to an acceptable solution for both sides. We must find some way to de-escalate the violence between the coven and the pack before further harm is done."

Eventually, Reg had let herself be talked into attending. She had to admit that she was curious to listen in on what was being done. She could go and just keep quiet and listen to what everyone else had to say. Attending didn't mean she had to stand up in front of everyone and give them her opinion or try to personally mediate peace between the two sides. She would just go and watch.

She had pictured a room full of chairs, maybe forty or fifty of them, with all kinds of people from around town who wanted to sit in and hear what was going on. She was not expecting the security check she had to go through when she got to City Hall. She needed to show her identification and have her picture taken for the security badge she was issued before entering the community room where the debate would occur.

She tried to tidy herself up for the picture. She gathered up her skinny red box braids and pushed them all behind her shoulders, made sure that her blouse and headscarf were straight, and smoothed her colorful, voluminous skirts, even though she knew that they probably wouldn't make it into the picture. It was a lot more attention than she had expected to get.

"What is your position?" the security guard asked her after taking her picture.

Reg wondered if he was a troll. He was quite tall, and his face did not show what he was thinking. She was clearly just another person to be processed, not of any real interest to him. He wanted to classify her, put her into the system, and get on to the next person. The rigidity of his process reminded her of Skippy, the supervisor at the Cyclone Tower.

"I don't have a position," Reg explained, shaking her head. "I'm a psychic here in Black Sands."

"You are part of the coven?"

"No. I'm not—"

Reg stopped herself from saying that she wasn't a witch. She had never seen herself that way, even though Sarah and others had repeatedly told her that her powers were very well-developed and she had a number of gifts that were quite rare. Even more surprising was that she had learned to exercise them as she had when she had been forced to repress them for her entire childhood. She hadn't even been aware of them until she had moved to Black Sands just a couple of years before.

Reg still didn't consider herself a witch. She had chosen to be known as a psychic, back when she thought she was just really good at cold-reading people and didn't know that she could read thoughts or auras and hear the actual voices of the dead. She had been told that the voices in her head were not real and she needed to shut them out and pretend that they didn't exist if she didn't want people to think that she was crazy.

She might also be part siren and part immortal, but she chose not to spread those tidbits around. They made her a target of the people who feared those races and she preferred not to find more smashed eggs on her car or door, mystical graffiti, or remnants of curses in the yard.

The guard looked at her, scowling. "Are you a member of the pack?"

"No, I'm not a wolf."

"So you're just… independent."

Reg nodded. "Yeah. I just wanted to see what was going on, what everybody has to say…"

He tapped whatever information he needed into the computer and printed her security badge onto a white plastic card, to which he attached a lanyard and handed it to her. Reg looked at the unflattering picture on the badge and shook her head. She didn't think she looked that bad. Somehow, the government always seemed to produce the ugliest identity pictures. It was like they did it on purpose.

Reg hung the lanyard around her neck and adjusted the length, trying to center the badge and position it so that it didn't sit in such an awkward position. She wished it had been on a pin instead of a lanyard.

"Move along," the security man encouraged, "I need to get everyone processed."

It wasn't like there were a lot of people behind Reg, and they had three officers checking people in.

The halls had wood paneling and tile floors. Smudgy beige paintings hung at intervals down the corridor.

The room was much smaller than Reg had expected. A large boardroom table with chairs around it rather than a podium at the front of the room and mostly anonymous people observing from rows of chairs.

Sarah was talking to Davyn and turned around when Reg walked in.

"Oh, Reg, I'm glad you made it!"

She made it sound like she hadn't just talked to Reg about it a couple of hours earlier and might have thought Reg was still in bed, even though it was afternoon, and Reg was always up by noon.

Almost always.

"I thought there would be more people," Reg said. There was a quiet murmur of voices. Reg looked around at the people who had assembled so far. She recognized most of them. Davyn was her mentor in helping her to hone her firecasting ability. Letticia, the old crone who led the witches' coven. Mayor Nichols, whom Reg had only ever seen on TV and never in person. Jake, Reg's ex-boyfriend who had accidentally been transformed into a werewolf while he had been conducting heinous experiments on them.

John, the son of Corvin, the absent leader of the warlock coven. Reg had not seen Julian, initially. Julian Sabat was an investigator with the Magical Investigations Endangered Species Division. Reg supposed he was there because of the involvement of the werewolves.

And Aleph, the alpha of the werewolf pack was there. Reg had rarely encountered him in his human guise. He had a rugged appearance, with shaggy blond hair and a gaunt, wary expression.

Aleph saw Reg examining him and frowned. But his eyes did not linger on her for long. She was clearly not a person he needed to be worried about.

"We would like to call the meeting to order," the mayor said pompously. "If everyone would please take their seats."

Reg looked for the chair where she would be the least visible. She was regretting that she had listened to Sarah. She didn't belong there with the community leaders.

"Come sit over here," Sarah tugged on Reg's arm and guided her toward a seat. There wasn't really anywhere for Reg to hide around the oval table. Everyone had the same visibility. It wasn't Arthur's round table, where everyone had an equal place, but it was pretty close. Reg sat down as instructed. The poofy seat squeaked as she settled in. The rest of the attendees sat down. Bending down to talk in his ear, the mayor's PA asked in a loud whisper whether he needed anything else. He motioned her away, and she drifted out of the room, pulling the door shut quietly behind her.

As soon as it closed, Aleph shot out of his seat. He wrenched the door back open, startling the PA so that she shrieked and jumped back.

"This door is not to be closed," Aleph said fiercely. "There will be no closed doors."

"I'm sorry!" The woman looked past him, through the doorway to her boss, for confirmation.

Mayor Nichols gave a little wave. "It's fine, Chelsea."

She put a hand over her heart, trying to calm herself. "I'm sorry, Mr. Aleph, I didn't know."

He looked around, alert for the approach of any enemy. Eventually, he gave a nod and retreated to his seat in the meeting room.

CHAPTER TWO

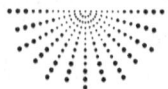

*M*ayor Nichols looked around the table as everyone settled in. He repositioned the yellow legal pad on the table in front of him, and his eyes moved slowly around the table, evaluating each person present.

"Should we start with introductions?"

"I think everyone here knows everyone else," Letticia observed. "I suggest we get right into it."

There were a couple of faces that Reg did not know, but she was not going to argue Letticia's suggestion. She preferred not to introduce herself to everyone when she knew she had no standing there and should have just stayed home. Sarah and Davyn could have filled her in on anything she needed to know.

The mayor looked around the table. "Is everyone okay with that?"

There were no objections. The mayor didn't have a gavel, but he gave a brisk, official nod. "Moved by Letticia Adams, I will second. No objections."

He looked at the scrawny, ferret-like man seated to his right, who scribbled something in the thick, hardcover black book that must be the official minutes of such meetings.

"I don't see the need for your human rules of order," Aleph

barked. "We do not follow them in our gatherings. They're just the humans' way of trying to assert dominance."

The mayor raised his eyebrows. He looked at his recorder as if he didn't know whether a change in procedure were even allowed.

The recorder shrugged his narrow shoulders. The mayor looked around the table. "Are there any objections?"

Aleph's expression was a snarl. If anyone had thought to object, they were probably dissuaded by his long canines. Reg swallowed. She was on good terms with the werewolves but, even as a friend of the pack, she would not want to argue with that snarl. No one in the room raised any objections.

"Fine, then," the mayor said slowly, "I'm not sure how to proceed without our usual order of functions... the purpose of this meeting is an open discussion of... the tensions between the were-wolves and other practitioners. There are concerns about an escalation in violence. As various community leaders, we wanted to gather together to discuss possible solutions."

"There is no need for any outside interference," Jake asserted. "There is no need for the municipal government or anyone else to get involved in something that is none of their business."

"If our citizens are being targeted by these attacks, the municipality can't just look the other way," the mayor disagreed. "We need to deal with it before it escalates and more people are hurt."

"The reason for attacks on humans is that they have been targeting wolves," Aleph said. His voice was a low growl. "They will soon learn that doing so is a dangerous proposition, and they will stop." He gave a cold smile. "It is what we call a natural consequence. Wolves find using natural consequences to be a very effective way to train our cubs."

"Why are the wolves even coming into Black Sands?" John challenged. "After their unprovoked attack on the coven in the midst of our spring equinox ritual, they are not welcome here. I thought they had agreed to move out of the area. Maybe even out of Florida."

"The attack was perpetrated by a small number of wolves," Aleph pointed out, "not the entire pack. They have moved on.

There is still talk about moving the full pack, but this is a big decision when we have just gotten established here. We have one litter of cubs only half-grown, and two more expected in the next couple of weeks. Even humans can understand the difficulty of disrupting so many infants. Such a move would put both the mothers and the pups at considerable risk."

"Maybe the wolves should have considered that before attacking the coven," John shot back.

"The actions of a few rogue wolves do not constitute a decision of the pack."

"We all know about the attack at the Temple Orange Grove," Sarah interposed, "and if October and the other wolves involved in that attack have left, then that doesn't enter into today's discussion."

There were a few nods from around the table.

"What we are talking about today is something quite different. There is ongoing friction between the warlocks and the wolves even though the wolves involved in the attack have left," Sarah went on. "That is what we need to address."

Reg had heard only rumors and half stories about what had been happening around town. She listened with interest, wanting to get all the details of what had happened.

"There have been more unprovoked werewolf attacks," John spoke up. He absently rubbed a long, red scar on his forearm that he had sustained in the equinox attack, his movement drawing it to everybody's attention. "The attack at the temple was not the only one. Either the perpetrators of that attack have not left the area, or more are willing to take up the cause."

"There have been no unprovoked attacks," Aleph argued. "Not since the one October led. You have been misinformed."

"There have been attacks," John repeated, raising his voice to a shout. "Why do you think we are fighting back? We have been living in peace for decades. Why would that suddenly change? You need to leave here and take all of the pack with you. You say that October is gone, but he is obviously still here, being hidden and protected by the pack, or else others have taken up his cause."

Jake stood up. While he had some of the wildness of Aleph, he still retained the beauty that he'd had before his transformation. Even without the spell that Jake had used to bind Reg to him, she found herself irresistibly drawn to him, yearning for the closeness they once shared. The spark in his blue eyes and the chiseled contours of his biceps and pecs, reminiscent of a statue carved from marble, made her heart race. His strong jawline, framed by either a short beard or a rugged stubble, only added to his allure.

"The warlocks have been harassing the wolves," he accused. "Every time someone from the pack comes into town, they are bullied and harassed until they are goaded into taking action or have to return to the pack without completing their errands. Does it amuse you to tease and taunt women and children? To keep up a constant stream of pressure until we are all forced to either fight back or leave?"

"It's not that long since you were a warlock yourself," John said with a smirk. "You're pretty new to the shifter scene. Exactly how did *you* treat the wolves before you were turned?"

Jake reddened at the accusation. Reg was sure he did not like to be reminded of how he had caged the wolves, keeping them in tiny kennels in deplorable conditions while he performed his abominable experiments on them. Not only on adult wolves but also on embryos. Things that were forbidden by the human authorities, not just by unwritten moral or ethical standards. He had not cared about the wolves' human characteristics, claiming that they were not sentient. He had told many other lies to justify what he had done.

In the end, it had been a blessing that he had been bitten and turned by one of the newborn werewolves he was tormenting. It had been a kind of justice that no one had expected. Now, it would appear he was a full member of the pack with no sentimental ties to the warlocks he had once been aligned with.

"There must be some independent reports of what has been going on," Reg murmured to Sarah. "Have the wolves been harassed and provoked? Where are they now?"

John heard Reg, even though she was speaking quietly. "Whether they have been confronted or not doesn't make any difference. There is no excuse for the werewolves attacking humans in the town. They are in human territory. They are expected to abide by human laws."

"Wolves are an endangered magical species," Julian spoke up. "All of Florida is their territory. Any violence toward wolves, any kind of harassment, is punishable by fines and possible jail sentences."

"Nobody wants to hear from you," John snapped. "Who invited you here, anyway?"

"Magical investigations has every right to be present at this meeting. We must do everything within our power to preserve this endangered species." His eyes flicked toward Aleph. "Especially when there are actively breeding pairs in the area. One litter of cubs already born and two more on the way! They cannot be moved now. They must remain here."

"You think that because they're pregnant they can't be moved? Women move while they're pregnant all the time. Are the werewolves so delicate that their women drop their litters at the least disturbance? Are they like other animals that will eat their young if the babies have been touched by humans?"

Aleph leaped to his feet with a roar. His chair crashed to the floor. There was chaos for a few minutes while everyone tried to keep Aleph and Jake away from John and the others. Eventually, everyone was seated again and, when Reg looked around the room, it didn't appear that anyone had sustained any injuries. No bloody noses or split lips. It was a good thing no one was drinking, or it would have been a good old barroom brawl.

"Everyone sit," the mayor said belatedly. "Everyone must remain in their seats. Keep your hands to yourselves. This is a discussion; there will be no physical contact."

He looked around at everybody, pausing on each person individually until he got a nod or word of acknowledgment from them.

CHAPTER THREE

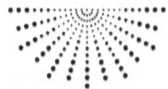

*T*he accusations being thrown around here are not helping anyone," Letticia said, her expression severe, frown lines creasing her forehead. "We know that there have been incidents in town. That is not in doubt. So what can we do to eliminate the friction and reduce the violence? What can we do in a peaceful, constructive way that befits the residents of Black Sands? We have lived here in harmony with many different magical races and practitioners for hundreds of years. Let's not throw that out the window now."

"It's quite simple," John said in a measured tone. "Keep the wolves out of town. There will be no so-called harassment. There will be no retaliation. Any attacks by the wolves will be considered unprovoked aggression, and they can be put down like the vicious dogs they are."

This provoked more shouting from Jake and Aleph, but everyone stayed in their seats this time. The mayor held his hand up tiredly.

"There is no need for that kind of talk. We are here to find solutions. That is not helpful."

John sat back, arms crossed and a self-satisfied smirk on his face. Reg tilted her head, attempting to shake off the whispers of

Verity that lingered in her mind. It was unsettling to hear the voice of John's deceased mother whenever Reg drew near him. Verity had been a powerful witch, instilling in her son a disregard for the strict boundaries set for power drinkers like him. Their bond had been intense and, even in death, she clung to him, refusing to let go.

They are nothing, Verity whispered. *The inferior try to set limits on the most powerful and promising practitioners. You do not have to accept their authority over you.*

"Perhaps we can arrange for the wolves to be given safe passage when they come into town," Julian suggested. "A vanguard to assure their security while they run their errands. I'm sure there are companies in town that could be hired for this purpose."

Reg thought of Damon, who had a security company. Would he be assigned to ensure that the wolves were safe while they were in town? She couldn't imagine the wolves allowing themselves to be restricted even by those measures.

"How about they just stay where they are supposed to?" countered another warlock, whose name Reg did not know. "They stay on the land they are granted and don't leave it and come into town. If they need something, they can order it to be delivered, just like anyone else."

"Our territory is all of Florida," Aleph reasserted, "we will not be confined to a postage stamp."

The warlock's face was flushing red. "There is plenty of wild territory out there. If you want wilderness, why do you need to come into town at all? Other animals do not need to come into town to do their business. You hunt out there, live out there, *breed* out there, and leave Black Sands alone."

Aleph's golden eyes blazed. "We have commerce like any of you. We don't stop humans from making homes outside the town. We don't stop humans from traveling as they wish. Why must you put restrictions on us?"

"Because you cannot get along with human society. How long have humans and werewolves been fighting each other? Wolves are predators, and we do not wish to be hunted!"

"The loup-garou are as civilized as any humans," Aleph

declared. "We are not animals living out an existence with no self-awareness. We have homes, families, other relationships. We use technology, transportation, and other tools. We are fully capable of carrying on commerce with humans. Without them even knowing that they are dealing with someone other than human."

"And you are capable of going feral and attacking another species without provocation and without any regard for whether they are a sentient species."

Jake stood up. Everyone turned to him, tense, ready for a physical confrontation.

"I think we are finished," Jake said calmly. "It is clear that no one here has any interest in hearing what is really going on in town. You just want to paint us all with the same brush. But we are not all October Phoenix. And we are not all the kind who would attack humans, provoked or otherwise. We just want to live our own lives and be left alone, treated with the respect you would give any other sentient being."

He looked around. Aleph stood up, giving a curt nod, and headed for the door. Jake waited and followed him out. Reg watched them go, disappointed that no one had been able to come up with anything that might help to address the current situation.

CHAPTER FOUR

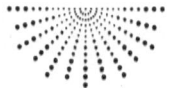

That's it?" Reg asked Sarah and Letticia. "There isn't anything that can be done to improve relations? What about—I don't know—mediation or something like that. Can't someone talk to both sides and work things out?"

Sarah sighed. "We'll keep trying, but you can see what we're up against. Neither side is particularly eager to talk to the other or make any concessions. They are both sure they are in the right and that if they back off, they are betraying their own."

Reg turned and looked at Davyn, who had remained curiously quiet through the whole meeting.

Davyn held his palms up in mute appeal. "I don't have the authority to make anyone do anything they don't want to," he reminded her. "The leader of the coven has no authority or power over the coven members. It is a position—"

"It is a position of service," Reg recited. "Yeah, I know, so I've been told. Are you the coven's leader again, since Corvin is…" she hesitated, unsure what to say about his condition, "unable to act as the coven's leader right now?"

"He could still continue to act. In fact, he has not resigned his position so, technically, he is still the leader of the coven. Unless the coven chooses to elect someone else. And I don't see them doing that anytime soon; they are still loyal to Corvin and are not ready to replace him."

"But he's not doing anything right now."

"No. Corvin has not left his house in a few weeks, as far as I can tell."

"So, who is leading the coven while he sulks in his study? You? Or John?" Reg shot a look toward John Saunders, who was talking to the mayor and a couple of his staff members. "He seems to be pretty vocal."

"He is. I am sure he would probably like to lead the coven, but that is just one of the things that shows he is not ready for such a position. Besides, he just barely joined the coven and needs to work his way up the ranks. No one would trust him to take over the leadership of the coven right now."

"But he is Corvin's son. So if Corvin can't lead... can it fall to his heir?"

"We don't follow a patriarchal line of leadership. It has always been an entirely democratic process. As you know, we are one of the longest-surviving covens on the continent. That is no coincidence. For us to change our procedures now and start to allow patriarchal succession..." He shook his head. "It's not going to happen that way."

"Well, that's good, at least. And you don't think they would elect him?"

"Not without a lot more campaigning by John. He can certainly play off the fact that his father was the leader, had it stolen from him, wants John to take over in his absence..."

"Does Corvin want him to take over?" Reg asked, interrupting. "I didn't think he did."

"No one knows what Corvin wants, because Corvin is not talking to anyone. John can say whatever he wants and no one will contradict him."

Reg scowled and shook her head. "I'll talk to Corvin. He won't want to let John run around telling everyone that he's got Corvin's endorsement as the new leader of the coven."

"Well, you're welcome to try. Corvin hasn't been talking to anyone else, and I thought you were still on the outs with him."

"Well…" Reg shrugged uncomfortably. "He hasn't exactly been sending me flowers. But he usually lets me in if I go over there." She didn't say that she hadn't gone over since Corvin had decided he was angry with her about the use of his library. But it had probably been long enough that his anger had waned. He didn't normally stay angry for very long.

"Do what you want. I don't know if it will make any difference. I think everyone in the coven knows that Corvin and John don't exactly see eye to eye. Corvin tried to take John under his wing, but I think the idea was that John would be… pliable. And John turns out to be pretty strong-minded. There has been a certain amount of friction between them from the start. John isn't quite the long-lost son that Corvin hoped he would be. The son of his one great love, and all that. It turns out that John is too much like his mother for Corvin to get along with him."

Reg nodded. "And he still has Verity whispering in his ear. So even if he planned to go his own way… I think she might have something to say about that. She wants him to gain power, the same as she would have if she had lived."

"You really think… that she still has that much control over him?"

Reg nodded. "I know she does. I can hear her."

Davyn gave a little shudder. "I am thankful that I do not need to experience that."

John finished talking to the mayor and drifted across the room toward Reg. She assumed that he wanted to talk to Davyn or one of the witches, and looked for the chance to slip through the remaining attendees and get out of there, but John walked directly up to her and blocked her escape route.

"Reg Rawlins." He gave a handsome smile. He got his good looks and charm from Corvin, and she knew from experience that he was nearly as adept as Corvin at using those magical charms and pulling her in. She braced herself mentally and raised a psychic shield against him. Surely, he wouldn't try to charm her and steal her powers in front of everyone else there. But she couldn't assume anything. John was, as far as she was concerned, just the kind of crazy that might attempt something like that.

"John," she acknowledged him politely. "How are you?"

"I would be better if we didn't have to worry about werewolf attacks right in the middle of Black Sands. I assume you would support any measures we could put into place to regulate their movements and make sure that the populace of Black Sands is kept safe?"

"Uh… no," Reg said slowly. "Why would you think that?"

"You don't want your friends to be hurt in unprovoked attacks. You know how Corvin was hurt. I know you have been seeing him during his… convalescence."

Just how closely was he monitoring her movements? Or was he monitoring his father and who was seeing Corvin?

Reg nodded. "Yes… but I also know some of the wolf pack, and I know that they are not just attacking random people. I don't know what has happened with the people who have been injured since the attack on Corvin, but Aleph said it was because they were harassing the wolves, so I assume that's what happened. I don't think any of my friends are in danger… as long as they are behaving themselves and not harassing the wolves."

John scoffed. "No one is doing anything to harass the wolves. Why would anyone do that? You can bet that if they came to town, they came looking for trouble, and they took the first opportunity they could get to attack someone. We are lucky no one has been put in the hospital yet. Werewolf bites can be very serious."

"Well, maybe that tells you they weren't actual attacks."

John rolled his eyes. "I thought you were smarter than that, Miss Rawlins." He leaned toward her, infringing on her personal space. "You and I should get together over dinner to discuss it. I think I could explain things to you much better in a quiet, intimate atmosphere."

Reg's heart sped. She could smell John's pheromones. The intoxicating smell of baking brownies. Corvin smelled like roses, which were also romantic and alluring but didn't have quite the draw of brownies fresh out of the oven. Reg hadn't realized the first time that John was a power drinker like Corvin, and that pheromones could smell different from one to the next, and she had been taken in by his charms. It had been a close thing, though not as close as some of her encounters with Corvin.

"Back off, John," she told him sweetly. "I don't see any reason for the two of us to get together for dinner. I don't need to be educated by you, thank you very much. I know more about how the wolf pack operates than you do."

John drew back slightly, wrinkling his nose in distaste. "You should be careful of who you associate with," he declared. "There are certain people or *creatures* you do not want to get too close to."

Reg wasn't sure how to respond to that. She enjoyed being with Zora and her pups, now half-grown cubs, but she was not as comfortable around some of the other wolves. Even though she had rescued them from Jake's clutches, some still viewed her suspiciously and didn't think she should hang around with the pack.

October was the first wolf Reg had met and she had felt very close to him, but she didn't understand how he could have attacked Corvin like he did and still thought that it was the right action for him to have taken.

And Aleph... he had never said a mean word to her or made any kind of threat, but when she was around him, she felt very intimidated. That same feeling she'd had as a child growing up in foster care when she had ended up with a parent who was a strict disciplinarian. That feeling that he was just waiting for her to step over the line or break some rule, and then the hammer would fall.

Of course it was silly. Aleph was not Reg's parent and had no authority over her. She wasn't required to do anything he said. And he would not attack or punish someone outside the pack for something she had done.

But knowing this logically did not take away the uneasiness she had around him, recognizing that he was dangerous and could do her harm if he chose to and didn't follow the same rules of society that most people in the community did. He came from a completely different culture, one that she didn't know all the rules of.

"I think it's time for us to go," Reg said, pulling out her phone to check the time and nudging Sarah. "Don't we have to be at home for that thing?"

Sarah looked blankly at her for half a second and then nodded. "Yes, of course. The thing. Yes, we'd better get on our way."

CHAPTER FIVE

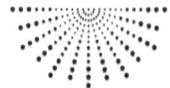

*I*t took a while for Corvin to come to the door. Reg rang the bell a couple of times, letting him know that she wasn't just going to go away because he hadn't answered it the first time. She knew he was home, after all. Not just because his car was visible in the garage. Not just because he hadn't left the house since the werewolf attack. She could also feel his presence there. She knew he was there just as surely as she would have known if she had heard his voice.

Eventually, Corvin opened the door. He stared at her balefully, looking older than she had ever seen him before. Without magic to keep up his appearances, his beauty and youthfulness were waning. Yes, he was still much younger-looking than his several centuries, but he looked *old* for the first time since she had met him. He had dark circles under his eyes that told her he was still not sleeping well. The smell and his slightly disheveled appearance told her that he was still drinking as a way to manage the pain that any accidental use of his powers caused him and the mental pain of having lost the use of his powers.

Corvin looked at her for a few seconds, then shrugged. "Come in." he swung the door open to admit her.

In thinking about the pain that the loss of his powers brought him, Reg had initially thought that it must be the first time that he had ever been left without powers. That it would be a big shock to his system that he had no access to the power that had been so central to his life.

But that wasn't true. It was Corvin's nature to take powers from others. Those powers didn't last forever, but degraded over time. Corvin fed a constant hunger for more. Most practitioners had only one or two gifts, and they could nurture and grow their gifts through practice, increasing their knowledge, and working under a mentor. But Corvin's kind had the ability to steal powers from other practitioners and constantly add new gifts and strength.

Corvin's affliction—or gift—had been inherited. His father had also been a power drinker, and Corvin had once related to Reg how his father used to come home hungry and would steal his powers, leaving his young son weak with hunger and pain, bereft of any powers.

So, it was not the first time Corvin had been faced with the loss of his powers. And maybe that brought back the traumatic memories of his childhood on top of everything else.

"Why are you looking at me like that?" Corvin demanded.

"Like what?"

He settled into his usual chair in the living room and poured them each a drink without asking. She noticed that he was still favoring his injured arm. She would have to try to heal it some more. Maybe because it was cursed, it would never be fully healed. Or maybe she just didn't have the skills necessary to heal him. She was not a healer by nature, but had nominal healing power due to her gift as a firecaster.

"Like you have something to say but are afraid to say it."

Reg shook her head. "Why would I be afraid to say something to you?"

"I don't know. Were I to use our connection to read your mind, what would I find? It wouldn't be the first thought you've tried to keep from me?"

"I think my thoughts should be my own," Reg told him tartly. She didn't think there was any point in revealing to him that she had been thinking about the way his father had abused him as a child. Corvin would not be happy knowing she felt sorry for him. He wanted to be strong, even if he was injured and cursed. He wouldn't want her to feel sorry for him. At least, not consciously. Subconsciously, it might be exactly what he wanted. Someone to care about him and look after him. Someone who didn't care that he wasn't the warlock he had once been.

She pushed these thoughts away. Just because Corvin would be in pain if he were to use his powers to read her, that didn't mean he was unable to do so. He might decide it was worth the pain he would feel, or he might just be too curious and exercise the gift accidentally. If he did, she didn't want him to discover any tender feelings toward him. Or any pity.

"How have you been?" Reg asked, forcing a casual tone. No anxiety over his condition. No worry about what was going on in Black Sands or the coven. Just a natural conversation between two acquaintances when one of them had been sick.

"I think you know how I have been." Corvin scowled into his tumbler. "Nothing has changed."

"I thought maybe you might be seeing some improvement. It has been a few weeks."

"Do you think I don't know how long it has been? You can see that it is not improved."

"Oh." Reg nodded. She looked around the living room for some way to bring up the coven without forcing an obvious conversation shift. "I was hoping that you might have seen some changes... Have you... had many visitors?"

"Most are not as persistent as you. They go away if I don't answer the door. Or don't come back when I tell them not to bother to visit me anymore."

Reg shrugged. "I don't see why that would stop anyone," she said with a smile.

Corvin shook his head. But he did look slightly amused at this, which was progress.

"Maybe they don't care about me as much as you do," he said, lowering his lids and giving her a sultry look.

"Nah, I don't think that's it," Reg offered. She took a sip of her drink, then examined the glass. "Are you going out at all? Or just getting everything delivered here?"

"I still have plenty in my stores. Why? Is there something wrong with that?"

"No, nothing. I'm just wondering whether you plan to live as a recluse for the rest of your life. Don't you want to get out and do things? See people?"

He scowled. "I have no desire to be seen in this condition."

"Drunk?"

"No. Powerless. Vulnerable. Cursed." He hissed the final word.

"Well, it isn't your fault. I don't think anyone would think less of you for it."

"You have no idea how people would treat me. Do you know how many people would be delighted to take me down a peg? I have no desire to be made a mockery of. Or to have to listen to the derision and see their scorn." He shook his head. "I have work to do here. And that is what I will continue to do until I am healed from this curse and able to return to normal."

"Do you think..." Reg bit her lip. "Are you close?"

"The answer could be in any book in my library, and you saw how large that is. It isn't like it is all indexed and searchable like an online database. I have to sift through each volume, trace leads, and endure all the dead ends and misleading information along the way. It demands immense time and effort. But I will find the answer." His jaw clenched as he spoke, resolution etched on his face.

Reg was cheered by this thought. "Why don't we ask Theodore?" she suggested. "Since he read your library, he could answer questions for you. It would be much faster."

"Theodore, your homunculus. I don't think so. I have already told you not only what I think of you using such a dangerous piece of magic, but also one that you clearly do not understand. And you know how I feel about you letting him read all the books in my library—"

"There was no other way to find out how to unpetrify you.

23

Would you rather we left you that way until recovering you became impossible?"

"Perhaps that would have been kinder. More so than this living torment."

Reg swallowed. She didn't like hearing him talk that way. It was one thing for him to be angry with her over the violation of his library. She could deal with that. She still didn't understand why he had such a problem with her using Theodore or with her having set him the task of reading Corvin's library for a solution to Corvin's petrifaction.

Theodore had been able to give her a way to save Corvin from that fate. Why couldn't he give them a way to reverse the curse that October had put on Corvin? If it was so important for Corvin to find a cure, why wouldn't he use all the resources at his disposal, including Reg's homunculus?

"Besides that, you know that the homunculus is unreliable," Corvin pointed out. "You know that he gets confused and that he makes things up. It is dangerous to believe anything that he says. It could make things worse."

"But if you're that desperate for a solution... couldn't you just double-check any answer he gives you?"

"That is not always possible. If he makes something up, there is no way to know whether it will work, make things worse, or have unintended consequences."

Reg thought about her experiences with magic since coming to Black Sands. It was true of many of the situations she had found herself in. Maybe a spell or power would work, and maybe it wouldn't, and, either way, there were often unexpected results. Fairy magic was particularly well-known for causing a negative effect to counter every positive result. The "no free lunch" saying seemed to apply. There seemed to always be a cost to either the spell-caster or the person on the receiving end of the magic.

"Isn't that true of any magic?" she suggested.

Corvin shook his head. "You are taking far more risk with a creature like the homunculus. You don't even know under what power he operates. Or what other instructions he has been given that countermand yours? You know that if he doesn't know the answer or has conflicting sources, he'll just make something up. He won't tell you that he doesn't know."

"I could tell him to."

"That doesn't alleviate all the risks. I'm not going to trust my life to your plaything, Reg."

CHAPTER SIX

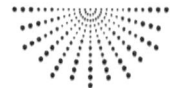

*R*eg sighed. She leaned back in her chair and rolled her head, stretching out her neck and trying to relax the muscles she had been holding tense since the meeting at City Hall.

"Why didn't you go to the meeting?" she asked.

At Corvin's blank look, she clarified.

"The meeting at City Hall about what to do about the... warlock-werewolf friction in town."

"Friction? Is that what they are calling it?"

"Friction... incidents... the 'situation,' yeah."

Corvin gave a humorless laugh. "The situation. Of course. Well, I'll let everyone else take care of the *situation*. I don't have the ability to do anything about it myself, including protecting myself. What is to stop the wolves from making another attack on the coven? They will be more careful now, but you still leave yourself vulnerable when participating in a group ritual that opens you up to others. The coven is supposed to be a place of peace and balance. We can't exactly have guards stationed around it. That defeats the whole purpose of having a sacred space."

"But I thought you would want to be part of the discussion about what to do about it, suggesting possible solutions, all of that...?"

"Did you find it to be a productive meeting?"

"Well... no," Reg admitted.

"No. Councils and town hall meetings rarely are. Everybody gets together, beats the topic to death, surrounds it with red tape and bureaucratic roadblocks, and no one can do anything to move forward because nothing has been approved." Corvin turned his glass on the side table, looking mesmerized by it. "While I may not agree with all October's methods, there is something undeniably attractive about taking action rather than waiting for permission."

Like October had done when he had convinced other werewolves to go with him to attack the coven at the equinox ceremony? Like he had done when he tried to free the rest of the werewolves from Jake's lab himself and had lost control of the situation? Reg, too, was impulsive and preferred action over contemplation, but October had made more than one mistake lately. He was too reckless even for Reg.

"So you don't care what they do or how they handle it?"

"I am relatively safe in my own home. Jumping into the fray between the coven and the pack would not be particularly safe. I think everybody already knows my position." He fixed Reg with an unwavering gaze. "The pack should not be here. Anything that can be done to... encourage them to move on... is fine by me."

"They have just as much right to be here as anyone else. Not October and the wolves who attacked you; I mean, they shouldn't be here to cause any more trouble. But the rest of the pack, why not?"

"You've seen why not. You were just at a meeting about the *situation*."

"But the wolves say they are being harassed. That isn't their fault. They should be able to live here, to be here in whatever form they like. Why can't they run errands, go to the grocery store, see a dentist here in Black Sands? How is that hurting anyone? It certainly doesn't hurt you while you sit here in your house day after day."

"We tolerated them when they were released from Jake's lab because they were the victims. Because there used to be wolves here,

27

who are long since gone. We thought that they would integrate into their native land, which would help balance the ecosystem. But it didn't turn out that way. They have been a thorn in our side ever since we helped them to escape. You remember that I was there, Reg. I played a part in that rescue."

Reg nodded. "I know. I remember."

"You can't say that I was prejudiced against the wolves from the start. You can see that wasn't the case. They were the ones who attacked us without provocation. And who continue to be an irritant to the magical community and to perpetuate more violence. It's time for them to go."

"If they are being bullied and harassed, then it isn't their fault."

"That may be one side of the story, to excuse their behavior. But do you really believe that is all that is going on here? That they are fully innocent, just trying to go to the grocery store?"

Corvin let Reg think about that for a few seconds.

Reg's heart sank, because she couldn't convince herself that the pack members were completely innocent. Did they need to come into town at all? If they were wolves, didn't they have everything they needed to survive in the wilds? Why would they need to go to the grocery store instead of hunting? Did they require professionals like accountants and lawyers?

They didn't need to come into town at all, did they?

Corvin nodded. "They are just causing trouble by coming into Black Sands. If they are not going to go away to somewhere else in the state or the country, can't they at least stay out of Black Sands?"

"Maybe… I don't know."

"We have been here for years. They have not. They were brought here against their will, I understand that. But there was no need for them to stay. No need at all."

Reg kept the excuse about them not being able to move with the cubs and pregnant wolves to herself. She knew what kind of a response she would get.

Reg drained her drink, setting the empty tumbler down with a dull thud. Corvin eyed it for a minute, then turned his gaze back to her. "Is that it, then? You just wanted to plead the case for the wolves?"

"No." Reg massaged the muscles around her eyes. "I actually wanted to talk to you about the coven."

"What about it?"

"Well, about… you are still the leader of the coven, right?"

Corvin blinked slowly. His eyes glittered. "Why would you ask me that?"

"Because, well, if you're never leaving the house again, how will you lead the coven?"

"I didn't say I am never going to leave the house again," Corvin growled. "Just that for the moment, I am going to stay here, doing my work, until I figure out how to reverse the curse that October put on me."

"But how long is that going to take? And in the meantime, who is leading the coven? You've just left them in the lurch."

"That's between me and the other warlocks in the coven. Not you."

"What are they supposed to do while you're closeted up here and haven't told them anything about your plans or how they should go on without you?"

"It isn't any of your business, Reg. What I do or don't say to the others has nothing to do with you."

"Did you know that John thinks he should be able to take over the coven while you aren't able to? Since he is your son?"

Corvin's eyes blazed. He sat forward in his chair. "Being my son doesn't give him any rights over the coven. He hasn't been elected. No one has any right to step in unless they have been elected."

"And you don't think he's campaigning for votes? Based on the fact that he's your son and the most powerful warlock in the coven?"

"There is no need for anyone to take over leadership of the coven right now. They can operate for a few weeks without electing a new leader."

"How much longer do you think it will be before they decide

that you're not coming back and they need to choose someone else? They won't go forever, you know."

"They can go a little longer," Corvin sneered.

"Have you told them that? Why don't you appoint Davyn to take over in your absence, or something like that? Tell everyone to go to him if they have any questions?" Reg shook her head. "Because John will take over if you don't do anything to stop him. I can promise you that."

"You can promise me that?" Corvin's voice was slightly mocking. "Is that a psychic prediction?"

"I..." Reg thought about it. Where was her certainty coming from? From listening to what John and Davyn had to say at the Town Hall? Because she had read them? Or because she sensed what was unfolding in the future, including the fate of the warlock coven? She closed her eyes and built a picture in her head, imagining the timeline and events and trying to explore other branches. "I don't know... maybe? But you don't want John to be the next leader of the coven, to wrest it from you while you're afraid to leave the house."

"I'm not afraid."

"Do you want him to take over?"

"He is my son. So, after I have served... yes, I think he would be a good choice for the next leader of the coven. Once he's had the chance to be properly trained and mentored as to what that means."

"You don't think he should just do whatever Verity tells him to? He shouldn't just continue to follow the path she led him in?"

"Whatever she *tells* him to?" Corvin shook his head. "You mean whatever she *told* him to."

Reg chewed on her lip. She hadn't talked to Corvin about Verity whispering in John's ear. Corvin was too close to his son and Reg did not want to tell him anything he did not already know about John's personality, nature, and... sanity.

"Sure, whatever she told him to. When she was alive."

Corvin narrowed his eyes at her, not liking how quickly she had capitulated. "What do you know about John?"

"I don't know anything other than what you know. You know

John wasn't brought up the same way as you were. Not trained to follow the rules that are supposed to govern your kind. And probably not anything about warlock ethics, either. Do you think he follows the maxim 'an' it do no harm'? Like you said, he needs to be mentored before he's ready to take over the coven leadership."

Corvin nodded slowly. "Yes."

"But he's ready to take over now. In his mind. And you're giving him the perfect opportunity by hiding out here and not taking your responsibilities seriously."

Corvin's eyes went to a stack of thick, old books on his side table. "When I have finished researching the matter of my curse and how to reverse it, I will be able to resume my responsibilities as the leader of the coven."

"That sounds like something that will take more than a couple of days."

He shrugged.

"I don't think the coven will wait that long."

Corvin shook his head. "The coven will wait. They will be loyal."

CHAPTER SEVEN

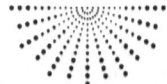

*R*eg left Corvin's house wondering why she had bothered to go in the first place. Had she really thought that Corvin would do anything? He had been sitting in his house doing nothing but drink and study since the equinox attack. All that would change just because she told him that John wanted to be the new leader of the coven and he should step forward and do something about it?

The thought had been pure fantasy.

More likely, she had wanted to go to his house because she had been increasingly drawn to Corvin in his difficult circumstances. She had never considered herself the nurturing type, but something in her wanted to help him. She wanted to use her healing powers to make him better, even though she knew that using her fire would be unlikely to have any effect on a curse.

Before leaving, Corvin had asked her not for her to give him some of her healing power, but for her to take some of his own power.

It was not the first time he had made this request, so it didn't come as a shock to her this time. She didn't understand how it worked, but taking power from Corvin, rather than increasing his hunger as it normally would have, or making him feel weaker, seemed to soothe him and make him more comfortable, taking away the pain he suffered just by holding his gifts, trying not to use them.

After she had taken the power that Corvin offered, careful not to take more than he demanded, she left him dozing in his chair, peaceful at last. She hoped that it would take away some of the bags under his eyes and give him the energy he needed to complete his task.

She was full to bursting with energy, like she'd just had a dozen cups of coffee. She felt ready to run a marathon, paint the house, cook a feast, or maybe all three. She drove home with focus and lightning-fast reflexes and, instead of needing a nap before her evening filled with client consultations, she had her second wind and was ready to take on the day.

Her clients seemed exceptionally easy to connect with, and she was able to provide them with the experience they were looking for. They all left happy. Usually, there was at least one who did not get exactly the experience they were looking for and left with some measure of disappointment. She couldn't be expected to give everyone the answers they sought. People didn't like to be told "no," and Reg couldn't always find a way to spin the answers she received for them in a positive way.

After the last client went home, Reg was not ready to go to bed. As she cleaned up, she spoke to Starlight. The tuxedo cat with a splash of white on his forehead and mismatched green and blue eyes watched her uncharacteristic cleaning spree.

"I wish I knew exactly what was going on with the werewolves and the warlocks," she told him as she picked up garbage and wiped down the counters. "I don't know what to think of the reports of what is going on between them. They each blame the others, of course."

She sprayed down the counter again and wiped it down, scrubbing at the sticky spots with great vigor until she was able to break them down and produce a shining, reflective surface. The finish had never looked so good.

"I guess I would have to see it myself to know who was in the wrong. But I'm not a member of either group, so that isn't going to happen."

Starlight meowed as if engaged with the conversation, encouraging Reg to continue.

Just how much did he understand of what she said to him? Reg knew Starlight was pretty smart. And maybe had stronger powers than hers. But he chose to remain in cat form most of his time with her, so she tried to forget about the times he had transformed to help her, and just think of him as her furry confidante. Just like any other cat she could have brought home from the shelter that day a couple of years ago when she had decided that a cat would improve her image as a woman with psychic powers. She had known nothing about the problems she would get into and the adventures she would have in Black Sands as she learned more and more about her heritage and true abilities.

"I don't like to think of anyone in either of the factions doing anything wrong," Reg sighed. "I know that October did. He should never have attacked and cursed Corvin. But he has left. The other wolves who are still here are the ones who will follow the rules and who are innocent of any wrongdoing in the attack on the coven. So why would they choose to hurt anyone in the town? It doesn't make any sense. They don't have any reason to attack any of the townspeople."

Reg decided to tackle the sink. She put everything that was clean away in the cupboard, something that she never did. She just took whatever was drying on the rack and used it without putting anything away where it belonged. But she attacked the job with vigor, putting all the dishes and cutlery away, scrubbing the drying rack and leaving it draining in the sink so it would dry out properly.

"The wolves say that people in the town are harassing them. I guess that's not the same as denying that they had anything to do with any attacks. But if they're being harassed, is it to the level that they are justified in protecting themselves physically? Can't they just walk away? And what are they being harassed about?"

Starlight didn't appear to have any insight on the matter. He decided to have a bath, sitting back and licking his splayed-out back legs vigorously, appearing to ignore Reg and her running commentary.

"Why can't everyone just get along?" Reg demanded.

CHAPTER EIGHT

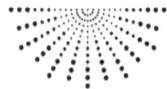

$\mathcal{R}$eg was stirring up a storm of dust when Theodore appeared.

In the beginning, Reg had needed to throw a handful of soil and recite an incantation to get Theodore to re-form and appear to her. She had been careful never to do it in her house, which was the guest cottage behind Sarah's house. She knew inviting entities into her home could have far-reaching negative effects, allowing them to take advantage of her in ways she had not foreseen. She had formed Theodore in the garden to be on the safe side.

But she had summoned him to Corvin's house without any negative consequences and, after a while, it seemed silly to go outside whenever she wanted to ask him questions. He had never stolen anything from her or given any indication that he would do anything to harm her, Starlight, or any of her possessions.

So she had started calling him to the house instead. And she didn't need to actually throw dirt and recite the incantation to bring him back again; she could just call on him or form the intention to call on him, and he would take shape.

Despite anything Sarah or Corvin might have to say about her homunculus, Theodore was pretty handy to have around, and for more than just party tricks. He had consumed all of the library of

Sma Firea, the ancient witch he had been attached to. And then, in an effort to reverse the petrifaction spells on Corvin and several others, Reg had assigned him to read all Corvin's books too, which was what had aggravated Corvin despite her attempts to heal him and help him out.

Theodore was like one of those AI computer programs that could answer any question. As Corvin had said, he occasionally made mistakes, but far fewer than anyone else Reg knew. And no one she knew possessed the deep knowledge of all things magical that Theodore did.

Lately, Theodore had begun to appear without being specifically called. Reg figured he had been called to the cottage enough times that he felt comfortable forming there without an invitation. He was, after all, bonded to Reg now rather than to Sma.

Despite his vast stores of knowledge, Theodore looked like a child, a boy with tattered clothing, a dirty face, and flat black eyes like a shark's.

"Bound by craft and ancient lore,
    In service, I arise once more—"

"Forget the formal greeting," Reg told Theodore, waving away the recitation of the verse as usual. "I don't need all that."

Theodore stood there for a moment, looking at her as if he didn't know what to do next. But they were getting used to each other, and Theodore got back on track again quickly.

"It is late," he observed. "You are not asleep?"

"No, I wasn't tired and there was a lot of work to be done around here, so…"

Theodore looked around and didn't comment on the amount of work there was to do or whether he considered what Reg had already done to be enough. He tilted his head and gave the peculiar click he made when calculating an answer.

"I am still working on the curse of the werewolf on Corvin Hunter," he announced.

Reg nodded. She had set him this task a few weeks ago, and

Corvin had rejected all Theodore's initial suggestions. While Reg knew that homunculi were not supposed to have any feelings of their own, she thought that she detected Theodore's disappointment in his initial answers not being accepted. He wanted to help. So he had kept searching for answers, in whatever plane he existed on when he was not visible to Reg. She didn't know whether he was tracking down additional ancient knowledge about reversing curses or if he was somehow grinding away at the wisdom he had already collected, calculating other permutations, or adding in other facts as they were revealed. He had seemed excited when Reg told him that the potion used in the curse had included mandrake.

But eventually, his ideas on how to counteract mandrake petered out as well.

"Have you discovered something new about how to reverse Corvin's curse?" she asked Theodore.

"October's curse," Theodore corrected. "October cast the curse and Corvin was the target."

"Right," Reg agreed. "Sorry. Did you find out something new?"

"Rumors of an artifact that might be used in cases just such as this," Theodore told her. "It was created in ancient times by a werewolf matriarch and a warlock whose power was unmatched. The artifact bound their clans together and symbolized their commitment to peaceful coexistence."

Reg stopped cleaning.

She looked at Theodore, repeating his words in her head. "Wow. That sounds... really promising. That sounds like something that could heal the rift between the pack and the coven. Almost like that was exactly what it was created to do."

Theodore nodded seriously. "It is said to have great powers to break curses, unify the factions, and bind together those who access its power with a bond that cannot be broken by mistrust or betrayal."

"What is it? What kind of artifact?"

"There is much work left to do. Only fragments of the original records are still in existence, and I must fill in the rest. This means examining and reexamining the fragments, seeing how they fit together, what is missing, and what would fit in that space."

Reg nodded. She could see how it would take a computer a long time to analyze and construct all the different permutations. And Theodore was not a computer. She didn't know what he was, but he wasn't mechanical or electrical.

She knew he had been created by alchemy, but didn't know what that meant with regard to his brainpower or where that information was stored. Did he cease to exist when he disappeared from her sight? Were his atoms rearranged? Did he exist on some other plane?

The questions were too deep for Reg. She wasn't even sure of her own existence, let alone how and where a homunculus existed. Especially Theodore, who should have ceased to exist when Sma had died, and yet he hadn't. He said that she had not left the forest where he was created. Reg took this to mean that her spirit had chosen to stay there and not go on to whatever place it was meant to progress to. And as long as her spirit remained in that world, Theodore remained there with her. And with Reg, now that she had taken him in hand.

She couldn't just leave him wandering around the forest alone for eternity, could she?

Sarah and the others seemed to think she should have, but Reg couldn't see how that would have been the right thing to do. Theodore might not be a child, even though he looked like one, but there was still something vulnerable about him that she couldn't ignore.

"So, do you think that you'll be able to figure it out? What the artifact was and where it might be now? It wasn't destroyed, was it?"

"According to rumor, it is not far from this place," Theodore told her proudly. "Once I have all the information I need, we may be able to retrieve it and use it for its intended purpose."

"Near here? Near Black Sands?" Reg asked.

"Yes. There is an ancient werewolf territory near here, and that is the last known location of the artifact."

Reg thought it odd that he would know *where* the artifact was without knowing *what* it was. But sometimes information was uncovered in strange, unpredictable ways. Her heart pumped hard at the thought of recovering a relic that might be able to reverse Corvin's curse—October's curse—and somehow unify the were- wolves and warlocks so that they could live in harmony instead of the fighting and friction they were going through now.

"Will we be able to find it?"

"The artifact is hidden and protected," Theodore revealed. "Only those who are worthy may approach it and access its powers."

Hidden and protected in ancient werewolf territory. Reg exhaled slowly. "Where exactly is this ancient werewolf territory? Is that where the wolves are living now?"

Theodore cocked his head, clicking and calculating. Then he looked at Reg, meeting her eyes and nodding. "Yes. It is in the current werewolf territory," he agreed. "The territory that is occu- pied by Aleph's pack."

Reg swore under her breath.

How was she going to retrieve an ancient artifact from Aleph's territory? Something that Theodore already confirmed was under some kind of protection spell or guardian. Having recently retrieved a series of relics that bound a group of four rogue elemen- tals, Reg really wasn't looking forward to hunting down yet another. Wasn't it someone else's turn?

She felt once again the anxiety she had felt when Aleph looked at her. How was she going to get past his watchful eye or, worse yet, convince him to let her access the relic? Why hadn't he already offered its use to heal Corvin from the curse and to unite the warring factions? If such a thing existed, wouldn't it be in his best benefit to use it?

"Great," Reg muttered. "That's just what I needed."

CHAPTER NINE

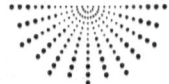

$\mathcal{T}$heodore left, but Reg was still too wired to go to sleep. She had cleaned pretty much everything that there was to clean in the cottage and was not ready for bed. Having everything so tidy was strange, and it made her too restless to stay in the cottage. It was too distracting to have everything sorted and put away where it should be. She felt like she had walked into someone else's house. Or that someone had come into her house and moved everything around while she was away.

Starlight kept meowing for her to join him in the bedroom, where he was watching out the window as usual. But Reg was not ready to settle down and could not force herself to relax. After receiving so much power from Corvin, she might not sleep for three days.

"I'm going to go out," she told Starlight. "Just for a little while, then I'll be home, I promise. Right now, I just can't sit still. If I tried to go to bed, I would toss and turn all night."

Starlight kept encouraging Reg to stay, coaxing her to go to sleep like she was supposed to, but Reg just couldn't do it. She firmly said goodbye once more and then left.

She didn't have a destination in mind. She wasn't one who usually wandered around the town at night, but her heart sang as she left the cottage behind and ventured out. The moon was bright in the sky, and she could see a few stars despite the light from the streetlights. It was a warm, clear night, and she felt the excitement of being up after the rest of the world had gone to bed.

The witching hour.

There were still people up and around like she was. Those who practiced hidden arts. Those with secret powers. Those who saw and heard things like she did, the voices that foster parents, case workers, and doctors had told her didn't exist. But they were wrong. She wasn't just hearing things. She wasn't imagining them, and they were not hallucinations that needed to be controlled and suppressed with drugs.

She stretched out her senses, feeling for the other people and creatures out there, prowling the streets as she was. There were cats and smaller animals investigating the garbage cans or sniffing each other out. Restless minds and worried hearts. Those who simply enjoyed the velvety darkness and being alone in the vast world.

Reg strolled to Main Street, but The Crystal Bowl, her usual haunt, was closed for the night. It would not reopen until midmorning when the breakfast crowd was on the prowl.

Of course, most of Main Street was closed. It was too late for any business to be conducted.

But there was music coming out of a bar down the street Reg had only been in once or twice. The Hexed Hogshead wasn't really her kind of place. She enjoyed the ambiance of The Crystal Bowl. The Hexed Hogshead was darker and catered to a seedier crowd. A lot of people were there alone instead of with family or friends. People who were not interested in striking up a conversation with a stranger sitting at the bar. People who were there to conduct the type of business that was conducted under cover of darkness rather than out in the open.

But it was the only place open at the moment, and Reg wanted to go somewhere there were people, even if she didn't have anyone to talk to.

The chords of recorded music washed over her as she opened the door. It was a little too loud to stay in the background. It would be a strain to hold a conversation. But maybe the point was to cover up the conversations of other tables so that people had more privacy. The steel notes of an electric guitar seemed angry and sharp.

Eyes turned toward Reg as she entered. Hooded faces in some cases. People who valued their privacy and remaining anonymous. Not her crowd at all, but they would have to do. Reg was able to protect herself if violence broke out. She knew how to cast a psychic shield that none, including Corvin, had managed to break. She could transport herself to another location, right back into her own living room, if she felt threatened and wanted to get out of there.

She approached the bar. The female bartender was a hard-looking woman with an angry, set jaw, tattoos, and hair that was spiked and teased into a fright wig. Her makeup was dark and emphasized her angry eyes.

"You lost, sweetheart?"

Reg grinned. "No, I'm not lost. Just out looking for a drink and somewhere to sit and you're the only place open."

"Everyone else has gone home to bed."

"I know. That's where I should be, but since when did I ever go to bed when I was supposed to?"

The woman gave a nod and an acknowledging smile that did not reach her eyes. "Then this is the place to be. What will you have?"

"Whiskey."

She didn't give any other instructions, and the bartender didn't ask. She poured a couple of fingers into a tumbler for Reg and placed it on a square napkin in front of her.

Reg was left to her own thoughts. She took a sip of the whiskey, and it burned all the way down. She let her eyes wander around the room, using the mirror behind the bar to assess the other customers of the bar without attracting their attention.

Mostly men. Mostly alone. There were a couple of other women, but neither was alone. There were a few murmured conversations going on, men with cloaks on and heads close together.

Reg's eyes fastened on a couple of men in a shadowy corner. They were vaguely familiar, but the cloaks and their positions made it impossible to make out their faces. Reg probed closer to them, using her psychic senses rather than her eyes.

She was shocked when she realized who they were. She took a sip of her drink to fortify herself and keep from showing her surprise to the bartender or anyone else looking in her direction.

They were just two men sitting in a bar. And she was just a woman sitting by herself. Their business was their own; it had nothing to do with her. She tried to ignore them, pretending she didn't know who they were. She scrolled through content on her phone, trying to distract her mind. But she was drawn back to look at them again, to reach out and verify who they were. She didn't want to listen to their conversation, but she couldn't help wondering what they were saying. It was impossible to believe they were sitting together, yet there they were.

She supposed it was inevitable that they would see her. She wasn't cloaked as they were, not hiding in a corner, but right out in the open, sitting on a bar stool, her face visible to them in the mirror. If she could see them using the mirror, they could see her.

Reg glanced into the mirror to find one of them staring at her. He crooked a finger for her to join them. Reg shook her head and looked away.

She felt drawn to them. Her body warmed, and she knew they were looking at her, trying to figure out why she was there. When she glanced in the mirror again, they were both looking at her, and one motioned again for her to join them.

She could go home. She could get off the bar stool, walk out of the bar, and go home. No one would follow her. No one could if she transported herself directly home. And no one could enter the garden or the cottage, protected as they were by wards. When had she last strengthened the wards? She knew it had been a few days. She had been lazy, not motivated to do it when there were no obvious threats. The biggest danger in the past had been Corvin, who had eventually grown in strength enough to get past them if she and Sarah did not combine their powers to prevent him.

But now Corvin couldn't use his powers anymore. She hadn't really been concerned about anyone else.

That had been a mistake. Reg would have to remedy it immediately.

They continued to stare at her and, eventually, Reg got up. But she didn't head out the door and run for home. She walked over to the dark table in the corner and looked down at the two men.

One warlock, one werewolf. Sitting together, having a serious talk over drinks, their faces mostly covered.

But Reg knew the body and the profile of the werewolf. She had been intimately familiar with him before he had been turned. And the warlock... even without seeing him, she knew the voice still whispering in his ear.

Verity was there in spirit now, warning John that Reg was not to be trusted. Of course, John would not have trusted her anyway.

And Jake? He was the one who had motioned for Reg to come over. She slid into the booth beside him, uncomfortable, but the only other free seat was beside John, and she wasn't about to sit beside him. It was bad enough being across the table from him. She could immediately smell the baking brownie pheromones and the warmth she was familiar with from her interactions with Corvin. She put up a shield against him immediately, reflecting back any heat directed at her, so that he shifted uncomfortably and quickly withdrew it.

"What are you doing here, Reg?" Jake demanded. "You should be home in bed."

"I'm a big girl. I can go out if I want to."

"But why are you here? This isn't the kind of place you go."

"It's the only place open right now. What does it matter? I wasn't doing anything to bother you. I was just sitting there by myself."

"Yeah," his tone was suspicious. Maybe he didn't know whether she could read him from across the room and listen in on their conversation. "But why are you here?"

"For a drink."

He glanced at her glass, which she had brought over with her.

She'd consumed about half of it so far. Slow and steady, that was the best way to do it.

"Did you follow us here?"

Reg shook her head.

"We were here long before she came in," John pointed out. "She couldn't have followed us."

Jake still looked suspicious. He scratched behind his ear. "I've never seen you here before, and then you suddenly show up like this. Who told you to come here?"

"No one."

"Who are you spying for?"

Reg looked from Jake to John and back again. "No one."

She didn't suppose that either the pack or the coven would be happy that the two of them were meeting together.

"What are you doing here?" she turned the tables. "Why would the two of you be drinking together?"

"It's just casual," Jake said dismissively. "We happened to run into one another."

Reg rolled her eyes. "Do you expect me to believe that? Both of you cloaked, with your heads together? That didn't look like a casual conversation."

"It was," Jake insisted. "I don't know what you think you saw or heard. We are just here as… acquaintances."

It took him a long time to come up with the word. Not friends. Not colleagues. Acquaintances. Two men who just happened to know each other.

But Reg knew better. They were not two men who would have run into each other and chosen to drink together. She shook her head. "You didn't just both happen to be here," she told him with certainty. "I know better than that. You are talking about the warlock-werewolf war."

"It isn't very becoming to eavesdrop on someone else's conversation," Jake told her with a scowl.

Every time he opened his mouth, she was reminded of how he had behaved when they were together, constantly criticizing her, telling her what she needed to do to please him, and ignoring anything she had to say. She had been steadfastly in love with him, not just because she was attracted to his incredible physique and brilliant mind, but also because of the binding spell he had put on her without her realizing it. When she first met him, she hadn't even known he had powers. She hadn't known about hers, either. But Jake had known all along and had taken advantage of her.

But Reg wasn't under his spell anymore, and she was reminded by every cutting comment why she would never go back to him or anyone like him. Never again would she let herself be dominated and patronized by a man.

"And it is doubly bad form to listen in on other people's conversations using psychic powers," John said, his eyes drilling into Reg. "You know that."

"I wasn't listening in on your conversation. Maybe if you are having secret conversations, you shouldn't be doing it in a public place. All I was doing was sitting at the bar, having a nice drink by myself. How was I to know that you would be here? I didn't even see you at first, sitting here with your cloaks half covering your faces. You look like you are ashamed of yourselves."

John's face flushed red. "What we are doing here and discussing is none of your business."

Jake was the one who was a wolf, who Reg would have expected to react with rage and perhaps to try to hurt her without even thinking about where he was. Instead, he spoke up in a calm, reasonable tone. "Of course we're talking about the warlock-were-wolf... situation," he admitted. "I'm sure that everyone who has any knowledge of what has been going on in Black Sands lately is just as concerned about it as we are."

"Concerned about it," Reg repeated. That seemed like a pretty shallow way to describe how anyone close to those who had been attacked must feel about it. *Concerned* was not what Reg had seen at the Town Hall meeting.

Jake and John exchanged looks. "Of course we are," Jake assured her. "It is our highest priority. We are very concerned with the safety of our people. Both the wolves and the warlocks. It is only by working together that we are going to be able to find a way to put a stop to the violence."

It sounded completely reasonable. It was too bad Reg knew Jake to be a totally unreasonable person, therefore she knew that it was just what he thought she wanted to hear.

Jake gave John a look that clearly indicated John was to agree, and John stumbled over himself expressing his agreement.

"It's a terrible thing," he agreed. "The only way we are going to be able to put a stop to it is to talk to each other but, as I'm sure you know, the members of our groups are... less than eager to do so. Hence..." He made a motion indicating their surroundings, "the need to meet in an... informal setting."

"So you're meeting here to try to come to an understanding. To broker some kind of peace accord for the pack and the coven."

Both men nodded in agreement. Reg shook her head slowly. Did they really think she was that stupid? "Why you?"

Jake and John both looked at her blankly.

"Why you?" Reg repeated. "You aren't the leader of the coven. Wouldn't it make more sense for the leaders of the factions to be talking to each other?"

"They wouldn't exactly be able to meet secretly," Jake pointed out. "Aleph can't come into town without everyone knowing about it. And Corvin..." Jake looked at John and shrugged. "He is still... recovering from his injuries. He isn't exactly in a position to lead the coven any longer."

"And you think you're in line to get the coven's leadership?"

His lips pressed together into a thin line. "I do not aspire to the position," he lied, voice and jaw tight. "Whoever is next elected to the position will lead the coven. I can't tell you for sure who that would be. I am simply providing what service I can to the coven."

"Under whose authority?"

There was silence for a few seconds. John swallowed and considered his reply. Reg could clearly hear Verity hissing her advice to John, between bursts of curses aimed at Reg. She was glad that Verity was no longer in any position to do anything to harm Reg physically.

John could, but Reg was maintaining her psychic shield and did not believe he would be able to break her concentration or overpower her spell.

"I'm sure you know that no one has authority over the members of a coven. We gather together for worship and ritual. There is no line of authority over individuals. We are free to do what we wish." He looked Reg in the eye. "And I wish to do whatever is in my power to put an end to the... current unrest."

"And the two of you are just going to get together and talk it out and come up with a solution that both sides will be happy with. And then the conflict will be over and you will live together in harmony."

Jake smiled. John was earnest. "Yes," he agreed. "There have been conflicts between werewolves and other practitioners before, and we know that coming to a peaceful accord can be done. We just need to put aside our differences, really listen to each other, and we will be able to find a peaceful solution."

He said it like he believed it, but the feeling Reg was getting from him was not of sincerity and a desire for peace. There was something much deeper and darker behind that ardent expression.

She swallowed, looking back and forth between the two of them.

"Well... good luck to you. I hope that you can work things out. The way things are right now... well, they're not very good. I don't want to see anyone else hurt, warlock or wolf, or anyone else."

"Neither do we," Jake assured her. He shot a look at John, and put his hand on Reg's knee.

It was warm and might have been comforting if Reg still had feelings toward him. But she had to push aside those old, confusing emotions. She wanted to pull her leg away from him and tell him not to touch her again, but she was trying hard to stay calm and friendly.

"There's just one thing," Jake went on. "You can't tell anyone that you saw us together. It would be very detrimental to the talks if people were to find out too soon. You don't want to derail everything before we even get started."

Reg had a mental image of two little boys with their hands caught in the cookie jar. They weren't doing anything wrong, just *checking* on the cookies. And if she wouldn't tell anyone, maybe she could have a cookie for her silence.

"And what do I get for staying quiet?"

John opened his mouth, but Jake motioned him to silence, and Jake knew Reg far better than he had any right to.

"What you get," he told her encouragingly, "is that warm feeling that you helped to broker peace in this difficult situation."

John chuckled softly. When Reg turned her eyes to his face, there was no hint of humor in his expression.

CHAPTER TEN

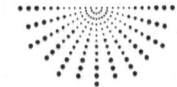

*R*eg left the bar with a strong sense of disquiet. She couldn't attribute her feelings to any one thing that had happened at the bar, but her emotions were a mixed-up hot mess.

On the surface, she had seen nothing wrong. There was no evidence that Jake and John's meeting was anything other than what they had said. An attempt to find a peaceful solution to the problem. A warlock and a wolf putting aside their differences to try to broker peace between their factions. Reg would have been very happy if it had been true.

But she knew it wasn't. Whatever Jake and John were up to, they weren't trying to find peace for the community.

A dark figure crossed Main Street, disappearing into the shadows a block ahead. She thought nothing of it until she saw another figure following close behind him, moving stealthily from shadow to shadow. Reg followed quickly, keeping them both in sight. She drew closer to them while trying to avoid making any noise or getting out in the open where she might be seen.

The first figure was tall and lithe with a peculiar loping gait. While Reg was pretty sure he was male, he had long shaggy hair. The following figure was blockier, solidly built, with a jacket or cloak that billowed when he walked.

The loping figure turned and looked around, hearing or sensing his pursuer. There were words Reg couldn't make out exchanged between them. She got closer, trying to flank them in a way that they would not see or hear her, engaged with each other.

"Your kind is not wanted here," the blocky warlock growled. "We don't need your kind of trash littering the streets."

"Begone," barked the shaggy-haired figure, "our presence does nothing to hurt you. No one is bothering you."

"Things were fine before you showed up. You're not wanted here, with your howling, your messes, unkempt children running around in the street. Do you think anyone wants to look out the window and see your kind?"

"We have as much right to be here as you do. There has been wolf territory here since before the human settlement."

"You haven't been here since then. You left, and now you think you have some kind of right to the land, and you don't. That's not the way it works."

"It is our land," the wolf argued. Reg thought she recognized him as a lieutenant of Aleph's. High in the structure of the leadership of the pack.

It was fascinating that the pack had such a structured leadership, and the coven was the opposite, with no one taking up the leadership of the coven during Corvin's absence.

"You gave up rights to that land decades ago. You're squatters, and we want you out of there."

The figures drew closer to each other, sizing one another up. Reg tensed. She didn't like the way they were moving as they circled one another. She felt the anger growing and multiplying. They were surrounded by a smoky red aura.

"You are nothing but animals, and if you remain, we will hunt you down and kill you, just as we did the last time," the warlock threatened.

"It is our land. We have women and children. You cannot drive us out."

"We can and we will. And you can do nothing to stop us. You think your claws and fangs are any match to our weapons? How do you think we extincted your kind the first time? It's too bad you were stupid enough to come back for more."

The werewolf growled. Reg could feel his conflicting thoughts and emotions. He knew he was being baited, yet he couldn't seem to stop reacting.

"Nobody wants animals like you in town. Get out while you still can, because we're coming after your puppies and your bi—"

With a snarl of rage, the werewolf threw himself at his tormentor. With the dim lighting and dramatic shadows thrown by the streetlights spaced too far apart, All Reg could see was a tangle of bodies. Arms and legs at first, and then fur and paws emerging as the werewolf transformed mid-fight. There was a cry of pain from the warlock, then a boom and a rush of air as he cast some spell that threw the werewolf off of him. He got up onto one knee and started firing off spells at the werewolf, a wand extended, flashes of light punctuating the casting of each spell.

The wolf did not respond with any spells of his own. Not all werewolves had any magical gifts or were tutored in using them. October had cursed Corvin, and Reg was aware of other magical work he had done, but he had never performed any magic before her. Perhaps he needed privacy, time and space, herbs, potions, and incantations. There were many different ways to perform magic, and not everyone had the same gifts.

Faced with the magic being wielded by the unknown warlock, the werewolf ran, quickly disappearing into the shadows. Reg could sense him nearby for a few minutes as he worked his way back toward the werewolf territory, and then he was beyond her reach.

She turned back to the warlock and tried to identify who it was. She didn't know everyone but could recognize most of the warlocks in Davyn and Corvin's coven. The warlock wore a hooded cloak, which prevented her from recognizing him.

Reg reached for her phone to take a picture of him, then thought better of it. He was too far away, and if he saw the light from the screen or it was set to flash, she could end up in deep trouble. She didn't know his motives, but he was not a very nice person, and she would prefer it if he didn't know who she was or that she had seen him.

She watched him after the flight of the werewolf. He laughed in satisfaction and looked around to see if anyone had observed the fight. He did not spot Reg, and she stayed absolutely still so as not to attract his attention. He fist-pumped the air and continued to walk down the street. Reg watched him until he was nearly out of sight, and then walked the opposite direction.

She could have transported herself home instantly, but chose instead to walk back. After witnessing the fight, she was more hyped-up than ever, and needed to work off some of the energy before trying to go to sleep.

And she wanted to see if there were anything else going on nearby. She had seen Jake and John together, and she had seen an open conflict in the street. Either there was a lot more going on than she had realized, or the "friction" between the wolves and the warlocks was getting rapidly worse. She hadn't realized how bad it really was.

CHAPTER ELEVEN

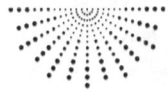

*E*ventually, Reg returned home. She spent some time sitting on the bench in the garden, listening to the trickling water of the waterfall, the cool air tickling over her skin. That was something that would often help her to calm herself down when she was having a bad night. Something about the sound of the water trickling was very peaceful and sleep-inducing.

But it didn't work this time.

She was still wide awake and her brain was going a mile a minute as she reviewed what had happened in the past twenty-four hours. It seemed like everything had changed, with the situation escalating from the occasional friction between the warlocks and the werewolves to a real conflict. After hearing the news of the attack on Corvin and the coven, Sarah had said that it could be seen as a declaration of war, and Reg had hoped that she was exaggerating.

But now it seemed as if Sarah's words were coming true. The conflict was escalating. More innocents would be hurt or exposed to traumatic situations. Some of the warlocks were intent on ousting the werewolves without any regard for them having women and children in the pack. They would drive them out by whatever means they could.

Sooner or later, the wolves would be forced to leave. Reg couldn't see any way around it unless they found the artifact that Theodore had spoken of.

Back in the cottage, Reg changed for bed, hoping that doing so would help convince her brain that it was time for sleep. She pulled on the ratty old T-shirt and shorts and decided she wanted a snack. Starlight followed her into the kitchen to see what was on offer.

"You're getting too fat," Reg told him. "We're going to have to put you on a diet. The vet said that I need to stop feeding you so much. And not every time you decide you want to eat."

Starlight yowled at her crossly. If Reg was getting a snack, why couldn't he have one too? It was only fair. She was putting on weight herself and hadn't put herself on a diet.

"I'm trying to eat better, though," Reg told him.

She knew that none of the skirts she had arrived in Black Sands with fit her anymore. She had been pretty skinny, though. She'd lived hand-to-mouth for a long time. Most of the time since she had aged out of foster care, other than when she had been with Jake. She'd had many jobs, some of which had even paid well, but never for long. And if they provided room and board, then when she was fired, she lost her home as well. It had not been an easy life.

Life in Black Sands was better. Cheap rent paid to Sarah, who probably would have let her live there for free if times were bad. But Reg could usually find enough clients to keep her bank account happy, and Sarah also helped by referring people. And then there were certain valuable gifts she had been given as well. All in all, she was more comfortable than she had ever been in her life, and that showed in her waistline.

"I *am* trying to eat better," Reg insisted, as if the repetition would make it true. She might have thought that eating better was a good idea, but putting the thought into action was a bit more difficult than it should be. She could buy herself healthy food, make plans to eat it, even look up cooking videos but, in the end she would end up ordering takeout or discover that a chocolate cake had mysteriously appeared in her fridge.

Her mouth watered at the thought.

Reg opened the fridge now. Starlight wouldn't leave her alone until she gave him something, no matter how small. "You see? I have carrots, an apple, and one of those bagged salads. I even have salad dressing."

She had *planned* to switch to salad and vegetables for lunch. One meal a day would not be so bad, and then, as she got used to it, she could eat more healthy food.

But so far, she had not had a salad for lunch. To be fair, lunch was really her breakfast, and breakfast was usually a couple of cups of coffee. Sometimes a cup of tea and a muffin with Sarah. Sarah made the most delicious baking—always more than she needed.

She put some casserole Sarah had left in the fridge into Starlight's dish. "You see, if you would eat the dry kibble, it would satisfy your tummy and be good for you. The vet says that people food is not good for you. Too high in sodium and other stuff that's bad for cats."

Starlight snarfed the casserole down with such gusto that Reg considered trying some herself. Starlight made it look delicious.

Reg thought of Theodore again. He didn't immediately appear, and she considered saying the incantation to make him re-form, but decided to give it some time. What if he were busy with some important homunculus duties, and she interrupted his train of thought or stopped him from being able to find out more about the ancient artifact?

She found a pint of ice cream in the fridge that looked like it had been there for a long time. She decided she'd better eat it before it went bad. The salad would have to wait.

When she turned around to get a spoon for it, Theodore was standing on the other side of the island, waiting for her attention.

"Oh, there you are. How's the research going?"

He cocked his head. "Greetings. The research is going fine."

"Good…" Theodore's answers were usually more detailed than that, so she waited a moment to see if he had anything to add but, when he didn't say anything else, she went on. "I think it is becoming more urgent that we find out about that artifact. The violence between the warlocks and werewolves is increasing. I'm worried about the number of people who might be hurt."

Theodore looked at her blankly.

"Have you made any progress on finding out what it is and how we can find this artifact?" Reg prompted.

"I believe it is a stone. But there are conflicting stories, and I need to find out more."

"A stone? That doesn't sound too scary."

Depending on how it was protected or guarded, of course. There would be some kind of challenge or quest to get it.

Reg's mind went back to Jake and John meeting in the bar. Was it possible that they had already found the stone, and that was why they were conducting peace talks? She hadn't believed that they were both being honest with her, but what if they had found the stone and, with it, they would be successful in sorting everything out? Maybe their deception was only in not telling her about the artifact they had found.

She took in a deep breath and exhaled. Somehow, she didn't think that was likely to be the case. If the stone had been lying in the werewolf territory since they had last been driven out of Florida by overhunting, then what were the chances they had known where to look and how to retrieve it when they escaped Jake's lab and re-established themselves in their old territory?

CHAPTER TWELVE

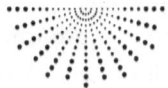

 ave you found anything about John Saunders in your research?" Reg asked him. "Maybe in Corvin's study?"

She had never intended to spy on Corvin or his son. That wasn't why she'd had Theodore read everything in Corvin's library (other than the locked books). It had been a dire situation and she had been justified in having Theodore look into Corvin's private library to see if he could find the solution to unpetrifying Corvin.

"John Saunders is Corvin's son," Theodore said promptly.

"Yeah, he is. And Verity's."

"A powerful witch," Theodore offered, and then went into a long spiel about her genealogy, history, and powers. Reg tried to stop him.

"It's John I am interested in. Verity is dead."

"She is dead," Theodore repeated. "But John Saunders lives on, the thirty-seventh in his line—"

"What are John's powers? Would he be good at negotiation? Brokering peace?"

Theodore clicked and cocked his head and clicked again. "That is not supported by the documents I have read."

"Yeah, that's what I thought. So why is he meeting with Jake

Bosco and what are they trying to do? Is Jake trying to make peace between the wolves and the warlocks?"

"I have little information on Jake Bosco."

"He was a warlock and a scientist performing experiments on werewolves, but now he is a werewolf himself."

"Irony!" Theodore seemed pleased with this piece of information. "A fitting consequence for his crimes."

"Yes," Reg agreed, suppressing a smile. "I thought so too. Do you think you could find out more information about him? And speculate on what he and John are up to? I don't believe they are just looking for a peaceful solution to the conflict. I think they are up to no good."

"They are up to no good," Theodore agreed. "They are not doing what they said they would."

"Did you just make that up?"

Theodore looked at her for a moment. "Yes," he admitted. "I apologize. I do not have enough information to draw a conclusion."

"Can you get more information?"

"I have heard of the public library, where much information is stored."

"Yes, but not that kind of information."

"I would like to go to the library."

"Well, maybe you could do that as a reward if you can find me the information I need about John."

Theodore nodded slowly. He seemed to have developed a genuine love for reading. He never asked to return to the forest where he had guarded Sma's home from intruders, but he had always been eager when she offered him new books to read.

"Can you watch someone without allowing them to see you?"

Theodore cocked his head. "I am not invisible."

"Could you be?"

He clicked, looked down at his body, and raised his hands in front of his face.

"I am not."

"What happens when you leave me? Can you still… see and

move around this world without me seeing you? Where do you go when you don't exist for me?"

"I am... not here."

"So you can't see me unless you appear to me?"

"Yes." He considered his answer. "I can see you if I am here. But if you close your eyes..." He gestured at Reg to do so.

Feeling silly, Reg closed her eyes.

"Now you cannot," Theodore declared.

"Right. So can you... be sneaky? Watch John when he is not looking at you and stay quiet and blend into your surroundings so he doesn't notice you?"

"Perhaps. I would be a spy?"

Reg nodded, smiling. "Yeah. You would be a spy. Would you like that?"

"In disguise?"

"Well, it probably wouldn't hurt if you... had some sunglasses to hide your eyes. And clothing that is... like the clothing of the other children around here. Can you change your appearance? Do I need to buy you different clothes, or can you change them yourself?"

Theodore looked down at his dirty, tattered clothing. He pinched the fabric of his shirt between his fingers, examining it. "This is what Sma gave me in the beginning when I was first formed."

"Well, let's get you something else, then." Reg looked at the time on her phone. It was still too early for any children's clothing or department stores to open.

But if she could make food appear in her fridge or cupboards when she wanted it—usually by accident, as she hadn't known she had this power until just recently—then why not clothing? She pushed away her consciousness of the fact that when the food appeared in her cottage, it was actually disappearing from some-where else. She was transporting the food rather than creating it.

It wasn't her fault that was the way her gift worked.

She envisioned other clothing for Theodore. A fresh T-shirt and blue jeans. A jacket. A pair of kid's sunglasses with red plastic frames. She picked them up off of the counter and offered them to Theodore.

"Do you want to… go into the bathroom and try these on?"

Theodore took them eagerly from her hands. Reg watched him go into the bathroom and dug into her ice cream. She was trying to figure out how it would all work. Was she really going to set a naive homunculus on John Saunders to follow him around and report back to Reg on his activities? He wasn't exactly 007.

But what could it hurt? John couldn't do anything to harm the homunculus. He wasn't a human being. Theodore could dissolve and re-form somewhere else. He didn't have a body of flesh and blood like Reg's.

It didn't take long for Theodore to return from the bathroom with the new clothes on. He sported the red-framed sunglasses and had even scrubbed his face while he'd been in there. He looked completely transformed from the dirty, ragged child she had grown used to.

Theodore turned his head away slightly, looking self-conscious. "Is it good? What do you think?"

"I think you look great. I wouldn't even know you were a homunculus. Not if you keep the sunglasses on."

Theodore pulled on the shirt, looking at it with dissatisfaction. It was a plain blue T-shirt that appeared to fit well enough, so she wasn't sure why Theodore was looking at it the way he was.

"What's wrong with the shirt?"

"Well…" he pulled on it some more, looking down at it. "Do you think you could make one with Spider-Man?"

Reg laughed. "Spider-Man? How do you know about Spider-Man?"

"There were newspapers at Corvin's house, and I read them, and there were articles and advertisements about Spider-Man. He is very popular."

"Yes, he is."

"I have seen him on shirts."

"Yes, okay…" Reg focused on a T-shirt with Spider-Man on it and, after a moment, handed the new shirt to Theodore. He raced to the bathroom even more eagerly this time and returned seconds later, sporting the Spider-Man T-shirt proudly.

"Wow, that looks great," Reg obliged. And it did. He would fit in much better with the licensed tee than the plain one.

She looked down at his feet, still shod with dirty, scuffed tennis shoes, and decided they looked right and did not need to be changed. Kids walking around with clothes so dirty and tattered they looked like they should be incinerated stood out. Kids with well-kept, casual clothing and dirty, worn shoes did not.

"You'll blend in much better now. I don't know if John goes out much to places you could hang around and not be noticed. You'll just have to see. If it isn't a place where there are other kids, you should probably avoid it. We don't want him to notice you because you don't belong, and we don't want other people calling Family Services because they think you are at risk."

Theodore nodded.

"You can't go in places like bars. That's where I saw him last. Do you think you can do that?"

"You cannot perform an invisibility spell?" Theodore asked.

"I wouldn't even know where to start."

"If you don't have photonic crystals or metamaterials, you could make a potion of juniper berries and nightshade, mixed with—"

"I haven't made any potions before and I'm not going to start now," Reg spoke over him, "and isn't nightshade poisonous?"

"Very," he agreed, "you must be very careful to use only a few drops of the juice of the nightshade berry, but it is invaluable for—"

"I'm not going to experiment with poisons."

"—light wave manipulation so that the object appears to be—"

"Theodore!"

He kept talking.

"Theodore, we are not going to make you invisible."

By nightshade's touch and juniper's grace,
Bend the light, erase thy trace.

"Theodore," Reg interrupted the incantation. "We are not going to make an invisibility potion."

He stopped chanting and looked at her, disappointment clear on his face. He shook his head. "I would be able to see more and be a better spy if I was invisible."

"You are going to have to be very smart and use good spycraft instead. Some people can still see the shadows of what should be invisible, you know."

He looked solemn at this. "I did not know that."

Reg nodded. "I can still see pixies when they are in the world of shades, and Davyn when he is supposed to be invisible. Not clearly, but I can still see them, and it would not be good to expose yourself like that. Besides, if you used too much deadly nightshade... I wouldn't want something to happen to you."

"I am a homunculus," he pointed out. "I am not susceptible to human weaknesses like poison."

"Oh. Right. Well, I still think it's best if we don't start potion-making with something so complex and possibly deadly. If you can find out if John is up to something..."

Theodore sighed. He smoothed his Spider-Man shirt. "I will be a good spy," he promised. "I will not get caught. I will be like Spider-Man."

"Good," Reg pronounced. "You look great. You'll fit right in. Come back and let me know when you find something, okay?"

CHAPTER THIRTEEN

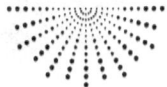

*W*ith Theodore venturing out to see if he could figure out what John was up to, Reg decided she would take the opposite side and see what she could find out about Jake and the werewolves.

Now that October was gone, the wolf she was closest to was Zora, the mother of the cubs she had rescued. It had been a difficult task, and Zora had been in pretty bad shape after her incarceration in Jake's lab and what Reg believed were multiple unsuccessful pregnancies before he had been able to produce the cubs. She had never asked Zora about any of the details. In Reg's experience, it was best not to have to relive traumatic experiences. The diabolical lab was in the past, and now Zora, the cubs, and the pack were free.

Since there had been difficulties in town between the warlocks and the wolves, Reg did not suggest meeting in a park as they had previously done, but drove partway out to the end of the werewolf territory where she knew the pack had been last and tried to reach out to Zora telepathically. Zora agreed to meet with her and sent her in the direction of a grassy hollow in the woods about a mile away.

She couldn't go all the way in the car, having to take the last leg

65

on foot. Reg reached the little clearing in the trees and found Zora alone. She was disappointed not to see the cubs.

Zora sat on a fallen tree in her human form, a mysterious dark-haired woman with haunted eyes. Reg approached slowly, trying to make it obvious that she was there on her own and that there was no danger of anyone being ambushed.

There was a movement in the trees. Reg turned her head and, out of the corner of her eye, she caught a fleeting flash of a long-haired blond boy of eight or nine before he disappeared out of sight.

"There's someone back there."

Zora nodded. "The cubs."

"I'd love to see them. But this was a boy. Is there a family living out here?"

"Fenris," Zora advised. "He is in biped form."

"Oh!" Reg knew that he had been transforming briefly, or only partially, for some weeks. But so far, she had only ever seen the cubs in wolf form. It was unusual for them to transform so young. Normally the transformation did not begin until adolescence. "Will he come talk to me?"

"He is very self-conscious." Zora considered what to tell Reg. "It is challenging to adjust to a new form. And especially for the cubs, transforming so young. They are precocious, and the other members of the pack do not always know how to take them. There are no other cubs yet. Mine will always be the oldest of the next generation, so they do not have role models."

"That would be tough."

"And even more so for them. We do not know all the effects of what Jake did and how it will affect their health, physically and mentally. There is a doctor in town, a geneticist, and he wants to document the cubs' development and how it tracks with the changes to their DNA. He is trying to help us."

"So you have to go into town? With all the tension right now?"

"Yes. And that makes the cubs even more self-conscious. Having to go into town and appear to be human children, when they are not and do not know how to behave. And they are not always able to hold their forms."

Reg could only imagine how difficult and possibly traumatic that might be for the cubs. No wonder Fenris was lurking about in the trees, even though he had always been the boldest of the cubs and the first to rush up to greet her.

"Are they okay? Did anything happen? What did the doctor say?"

Zora sighed, shaking her head. "It is not good, Reg. It is such a difficult time for the cubs, and to have to deal with all this trouble with the warlocks right now too... I wish that October had shown some restraint and not done what he did to Corvin. I know he had concerns about Corvin being dangerous, but now all the warlocks are a danger to us."

Reg knew why October had attacked Corvin and why he had picked the timing he had, but she felt bad that it had ended up being the worst possible time for the cubs, too. They needed to be nurtured and helped through the changes they were going through, and now everyone in town had turned against them. It wasn't the fault of the pups. They couldn't help when they had been born or the changes their bodies were going through. Too early because of Jake's monstrous experiments.

She sat with Zora, not knowing what to say or do. With a human friend, she might have taken Zora's hand or given her a hug to express her support and empathy for what they were going through. But there was a separation between Reg's instincts as a human and Zora's as a wolf. She wouldn't want to be touched without permission. Reg tried instead to feed Zora calming and supportive feelings.

Zora gave her a small smile. "You are always willing to give of yourself. You are like a wolf in that way."

Reg's cheeks warmed at the compliment. She didn't imagine Zora saw most humans in the same light.

"I am really sorry for what you and the cubs must be going through."

"I will tell you what happened." Zora began to tell her story. "We went into town to see the doctor..."

CHAPTER FOURTEEN

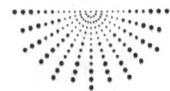

*Z*ora tried to keep the curious cubs at her side and prevent them from being too rambunctious and disturbing the townspeople. Humans did not tolerate differences well. People who did not adhere to expected behaviors were vilified and shunned. She did not want the youngsters to be exposed to disapproval and criticism from the humans in town. With all the friction between the warlocks and the werewolves right now, it was difficult enough to keep a positive attitude toward the humans.

She wanted her children to be able to choose their own paths as they grew to adulthood—whether they wanted to live with a pack, have commerce with the humans in their world, or both. If they had bad experiences with humans at a young age, they might never want to explore that world.

Fenris was wandering off, attracted by the window display of Witchell's Toys. "Fenris," Zora barked. "Come back."

He looked over his shoulder at her. She knew from the expression on his face and, of course, by his personality, which she knew well, that he would not comply. Of all her children, he was the least compliant. Always off on his own, doing his own thing, sniffing around danger. At some point, it would bring him a face full of skunk scent or porcupine quills. Or worse. But he was the cub that always had to see for himself. He always had to test the limits and see whether what she said was really true.

He would make a good leader one day. If he lived that long.

She didn't repeat the command, but kept walking, herding the other children toward their destination. Fenris would rejoin them again somewhere along the line. The experienced she-wolves in the pack had laughingly told her that her little lone wolf would come to her if she got out of sight. But that was never true of Fenris. He would hunt her down eventually, but only after he had satisfied his curiosity. Sometimes, that was hours later. But it couldn't be today. He needed to go to the doctor and it was not safe for him to be alone for long in town.

She worried about him, but she could not leave the others to chase after him. He would be safe at the toy store for a few minutes. Surely human children hung around the window at the toy store too. It would not be seen as aberrant behavior.

Adolpha stuck so close to Zora's side that she kept tripping over her. Even in canid form, Adolpha tended to be a needy child. Rather than calling her back like Fenris, Zora had to chase her away, tell her to go play or explore and to stay out from underfoot. In her biped form, Adolpha was even less sure of herself and had the most difficulty of the children in maintaining her shape. Of all of them, Zora wished that Adolpha had not started to transform so early. She would have been much more confident if she had been able to keep her canid form until late adolescence.

At least she didn't have friends to mock and tease her for transforming so early. The only cubs in the pack were her siblings and, while they tormented each other for other things, they didn't realize how unusual it was for them to transform so early. Adolpha had been the last to begin her transformation so, for her, it seemed like she was a late bloomer rather than an early one.

"Give me space," Zora told her, giving her a little nudge to get some breathing room. Adolpha separated by a couple of feet, and Zora sighed with relief, then turned to look for Fenris. He was not yet following them.

They reached the doctor's office. Zora took the three cubs in with her and checked in with the receptionist.

"I'm just going to leave them here for a moment," she said, her cheeks flushing in embarrassment. "I've got one straggler."

The receptionist looked wide-eyed at the three other children. She probably didn't know anything about them being wolves and thought they were human quadruplets.

"You stay here," Zora told the others. "Sit in chairs and don't move. Adolpha, you are in charge. The rest of you, listen to your sister."

Zora left the doctor's office and headed back toward the toy store. She kept a close eye out for Fenris, hoping he was already following her trail and had not been distracted by something that took him even farther away. She could not howl to call him, that would attract too much attention, and her mental connection had proven fruitless. He was very good at ignoring her when something else had attracted his attention.

When she drew within sight of the toy store, the hairs on the back of her neck stood up. Fenris stood facing a couple of men, his posture tense, hands up defensively. He gave no sign that he saw Zora returning.

"What are you doing here by yourself, dog?" one of the men demanded, instantly confirming Zora's fear that they knew he was a wolf and not just a human child playing truant.

"I can go where I want," Fenris snarled.

One of the others might have had the sense to show remorse or to say that his mother was close by, and that might have satisfied the men. But Fenris's haughty reply only served to increase their animosity. One of them struck out, shoving him back against the toy store window. Fenris was still growing accustomed to his biped form and was not as strong or well-coordinated as in his canid form. He had difficulty catching and steadying himself and still maintaining a defensive posture.

"Leave me alone!" he exploded, voice shrill.

"You'd better learn to mind your betters!" one of the men told him, touching his partner's arm and jerking his head in a way that meant it was time for them to move on. But his friend was not so easily deterred. He was determined to teach the young wolf a lesson.

Zora was in a quandary about how to react. Her instinct was to shift to wolf form and attack, to scatter her son's tormentors, to tear them to pieces if they reacted with violence. But she knew the problems they were already having in the town and did not want to make them even worse.

She could insert herself into the confrontation in her current form, tell them to leave her son alone, and to take him away from there, but that would be humiliating for a young wolf testing out the limits of his independence and might cause a deep rift between them.

She watched to see what would happen next, hoping the men would be satisfied with what they had done and move on, leaving Fenris alone.

The man who had pushed Fenris into the building grabbed the front of his shirt, lifting and twisting it so that Fenris was choking and standing on his tiptoes trying to relieve the pressure. His arms windmilled but he was unable to connect with anything. Zora gathered herself to attack.

"Hey!" a man came barreling out of the toy store. He was an older man, round and stocky, his hair graying. But he had powerful hands and arms, and he wasn't letting his age slow him down. "Leave him alone! Let go! You want me to call the police?"

Startled, the warlock released his grip on Fenris. Fenris lost control, transforming into canid form and lashing out, his teeth ripping into his tormentor's forearm, sending him reeling back, howling with pain. Fenris turned on the other warlock, who held his arms up to protect his face and throat. "No! No, stay back!"

Fenris turned to the third man, the one who had come out of the toy store to defend him. He held his hands toward Fenris, lowered, palms up to show he was unarmed and intended no harm. Zora held her breath, fearing that Fenris would attack anyway, too furious and panicked to recognize the gesture of surrender.

But Fenris backed slowly away, still snarling a warning. When he was a few feet away from them, he turned tail and ran, fleeing from the confrontation and the screaming, bleeding warlock.

CHAPTER FIFTEEN

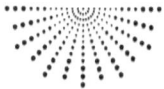

*R*eg covered her mouth, shocked at Zora's description. In the town council meeting, she had heard about the harassment of the wolves and the wolves attacking and injuring humans, but she hadn't really thought that it was that bad. She had pictured a drunken brawl. A couple of men mixing it up because they'd had a bit too much to drink, and neither really that much worse off.

But what Zora had described was much worse than that. "Oh, Zora! I'm so sorry! I really had no idea."

Zora nodded. "I know," she acknowledged. "It's nothing to do with you. I don't know of any witches that have been involved. But the warlocks... the amount of trouble they are causing for the wolves... I just don't understand it. Why would they behave that way? Why would they want to provoke such a violent reaction?"

"They probably didn't intend to," Reg said. "They probably didn't realize the damage a young wolf could do. They thought they were bullying someone who was helpless. Something they could get away with and laugh about later. Showing off how big and strong they were."

"But that isn't the only incident. It has been happening all over town, to all different wolves. Not just the cubs. That was the only run-in they've had with the young ones. But the same thing has been going on all over. To everyone."

"Well, I don't understand it," Reg shook her head regretfully. "I don't know why they would do that unless they actually want to incite a war."

"They think they can drive us off of our ancestral lands. If they bully and harass us and make it difficult enough, we will just get up and leave. Go somewhere else instead."

"Why would anyone care about that? It isn't like anyone else is living out there. It's your land, and you're outside of town and not disturbing anyone. You hardly ever come in for anything. And when you do… why on earth would anyone harass a child who had to come into town to see the doctor?"

Zora nodded her agreement over the ridiculousness of such an approach. But Reg couldn't help thinking about Julian and his talk about how to get the wolf pack to move on. Refusing them service. Spraying them with water. Making it too uncomfortable for them to come into town.

Julian had suggested it simply as a way to keep them out of town and prevent any more attacks like the one on Corvin. Not to run them off of their ancestral land. Quite the opposite; he wanted them to stay and repopulate Florida.

Reg looked over her shoulder to where she could feel Fenris watching her. She caught a glimpse of his face before he ducked back behind a tree.

Fenris, she called him in her mind. *It's just Reg. Come and say 'hi.'*

He stayed there, out of sight.

Are you afraid of Auntie Reg? She teased. *I brought some pepperoni sticks.*

He, of all the cubs, loved the spicy pepperoni sticks the most. She could feel his hesitation, but also his desire for the special treat.

Fenris was the type who could not be pushed into something. Tell him to do something or not do something, and he would dig in his heels and stubbornly resist. So she didn't push him; she just left him to think about the pepperoni sticks and continued talking to Zora.

"What about the warlock that Fenris bit?" she asked, thinking about the story. "Won't he turn into a werewolf now?"

Fenris turning Jake into a werewolf had turned out to be a positive thing. They were able to watch Jake and keep track of him telepathically. He tended to stay in his wolf form most often, and could no longer do any more secret experiments. He still had at least some of his magical gifts, so they needed to beware and not allow him to bind any of them again.

And he was a good hunter. Good at hunting with the pack, not just going out on his own when the need arose. But he was too confident in his own abilities, especially in his ability to replace Aleph and lead the pack. Reg didn't know how he thought he could lead the pack when he had so little experience as a wolf, but apparently he figured he could handle it, and do it better than the alpha.

"Not necessarily," Zora said, breaking in on Reg's thoughts with her answer. "All the right conditions need to be present to turn someone. Some people have strong resistance to the infection, while others are vulnerable. Reacting to a single bite is not as common as you might think."

"So Jake being turned by Fenris when he was still a newborn pup...?"

"Very unusual," Zora gave a little laugh. "Jake poisoned himself with all his experiments. Something that he did made him very vulnerable, whether it was just to Fenris or to any wolf. Normally, a newborn bite would be very unlikely to turn someone. Especially as quickly as it turned Jake."

"It was a full moon."

"That too. And close to the zenith. All those things make a difference." She frowned in concentration. "It was very... karmic." She looked at Reg. "Is that right? Is that how you would say it? He had... accumulated a lot of bad karma."

Reg nodded. "Yeah. It was karmic," she agreed.

There was the snapping of a branch nearby and, without thinking, Reg turned her head to look. Fenris froze mid-step.

Reg knew he would never have made a noise sneaking up on her as a wolf. If she were occupied with something else, he would probably have been able to sneak right up to her and steal the pepperoni sticks right out of her bag.

But he was still getting used to his new human form, and he was less stealthy.

Reg looked away from him, but he knew he had been seen.

"Hi, Fenris."

"You said you have treats."

"I do," Reg agreed. She pulled out a couple of pepperoni sticks and held them out to him. "You are the one who likes them the best."

Fenris took the last few steps to reach her side and took them from her eagerly.

"I love these."

Reg nodded. "I do too. I probably eat way too many of them."

As a wolf, he had to either get her to open them or chew them open. Now that he was in human form, he could use his fingers to split the plastic ends and peel the packages open. He grinned at his success and took the first bite.

"I'm sorry about what happened to you in town," Reg told him.

"I heard you talking to Mom about it."

"Some humans can be really mean. But we're not all like that."

"I know. *You're* not. It's not the women."

"Women can still do bad things too, but I'm glad they are not bothering you."

"I did not mean to shift." Fenris looked sideways at Zora. "We are not supposed to shift in town. We are only supposed to be biped. I did not mean to change."

Reg and Zora both nodded their understanding. Reg might not have much experience in shifting from one form to another, but she had definitely had the experience of losing control and doing something she later regretted or knew had been wrong.

"But that man deserved to be bitten," Fenris finished. "Maybe I should not have done it, but he deserved it."

Reg had to agree. She looked at Zora, suppressing a smile.

"We can't go around biting everyone who deserves it," Zora told him.

"I know," Fenris agreed. He looked down at the ground as he took another bite of his pepperoni. "That would be a lot of people."

Reg had difficulty not laughing, even though she knew it was a very serious topic. Fenris was right. There were a lot of people who deserved to be bitten.

CHAPTER SIXTEEN

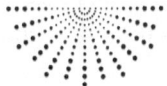

*I*t was a couple of days before Theodore returned. Reg was trying just to leave him alone and let him work. She didn't know where he was when he wasn't with her, or what plane he was on, or how or whether time was measured there, but it seemed like he needed time to complete his tasks just like anyone else, and she didn't imagine he liked to be interrupted any more than she did.

She had given Theodore more than one task to complete, and she didn't know how he prioritized them or if he could do that. Maybe when she gave him a new instruction, it overwrote the old one, and he would never get the first one done. They had never discussed what his parameters were. When she gave him more work, he just accepted it. She hoped she hadn't given him too much.

Reg was conducting a seance. A group of young women who had decided to include a seance in their friend's bridal send-off. Reg wasn't sure what had made them think of a seance for a bridal shower, but she was, of course, happy that they had. She hoped that people decided to have seances for any celebration of life or death. It would help to fill her coffers. *Whatever coffers were.*

The ladies had already had plenty of champagne to loosen them up. It was late at night and they were happy and in a very suggestible state. A good time to be holding a seance. Reg could make it a satisfying experience for them whether they were favored with the presence of a real ghost or not.

They were all holding hands—at least as much as she could get them to. They needed to let go to drink more champagne, and it seemed that drinking the champagne was very important to them. More important than keeping the circle unbroken.

Candles flickered around the room, contributing to the atmosphere. Reg was reading the bride, trying to find out what she hoped to see and if there were a spirit she was close to that Reg could reach out to. But Reg stopped talking or trying to read the bride when several women suddenly screamed, in long trilling, delighted anticipation, their eyes on something behind Reg. She turned to look behind her, unsure what ghost she would encounter, as she hadn't tried to make contact yet. She saw a short figure dressed in a Spider-Man shirt and red-rimmed glasses.

"Oh," she held up her hands to calm the women. "That's just my assistant. I'll need to take a break to talk to him. Theodore, can you wait a few minutes?"

Theodore gave a huge sigh and walked toward the living room.

"You could watch TV," Reg suggested. "Do you want to—"

Theodore picked up the remote control and turned on the TV. The volume was way too high, and Reg hurried over to turn it down so she could still converse with the bridal party.

"You have a ghost for an assistant?" asked Mandy, the woman who had arranged the seance with Reg.

"Uh, no, he's not a ghost," Reg assured them. "He's just a…" She paused, trying to think of how to explain the homunculus. She couldn't very well say that he was a regular child. Who would have a child for an assistant? Even a flaky medium was unlikely to do that. An adult with a growth disorder?

"I saw him materialize from thin air," Mandy interrupted. "Don't try to tell me that he isn't a ghost."

"Well, uh… I really can't discuss that due to our confidentiality agreement," Reg bluffed. "I'm sorry, I would like to tell you, but paranormal legal contracts are very strict and the consequences for breaking them are quite onerous."

The women were all nodding in agreement as if they had heard this very thing from other sources lately. Reg sighed in relief that she would not be required to explain Theodore's presence any further, and she tried to get the women focused on their own ghostly encounter.

"Now, if you want to get your money's worth before we run out of time, we can't be distracted by other visitors. Don't worry about Theodore. Marigold, you recently lost someone close to you, didn't you? I get the feeling that you are very disappointed that she will not be able to attend your wedding. You had always expected her to be there…"

"My aunt," Marigold agreed, her face brightening. "Is Auntie Clarice here? I was so disappointed that she passed before my wedding day. She was always very sick, you know. My mom said that she was just a hypochondriac and there was nothing wrong with her, but I guess she knows better now. I always expected her to be a big part of my wedding cele-brations."

"Why don't we all hold hands and be very quiet? Marigold, I want you to form a picture of your Auntie Clarice in your mind. I want it to be as detailed and clear as possible. As if she was sitting right here in front of us."

The ladies gradually settled, sipped their drinks, and finally put down their glasses to hold hands. Reg waited for them to close their eyes and focus on the job at hand. Then, she focused on Marigold and the picture she was forming in her mind.

"Clarice," she called, "Marigold's Auntie Clarice. We call you to join us tonight. Celebrate this joyful occasion with your niece. Share the good tidings with us all." Reg gave a long, low moan, waiting for an answer from the other side.

As always, when she was calling on the ghosts, there was a cacophony of voices in her head, and the difficult task was not in contacting the dead but in keeping the pathways open for the spirit she wanted to contact. There were so many voices vying for her attention, and she had to shut them all off and focus only on the one attached to her client.

"Auntie Clarice," she repeated, "Auntie Clarice."

I'm right here!

Reg gave a little start at the unexpected voice at her elbow. A very short old woman with wildly curly hair stood there. She wore a purple sweatshirt with a stylized dragon and diamond appliqués on her ample bosom.

"Oh! She is here," Reg informed the circle. "Marigold, your Auntie Clarice is here to talk to you. What did you want to tell her?"

"Oh, Auntie Clarice!" Marigold said excitedly. Then she dropped her voice to a whisper. "Is she really here? I can't see her. Where is she?"

"She's right beside me," Reg told her. "She is ready to hear what you have to say and has a message for you."

"Oh, this is so exciting!" Marigold was looking at the wrong side of Reg, staring intently as if she might be able to see Clarice if she just looked hard enough.

I don't have a message, Clarice argued.

"Well, you have two minutes to prepare something," Reg murmured to her. "Or I'll make something up, and you might not like what I say."

"This is just so exciting," Marigold said again. She seemed to be having just as much of a problem coming up with something significant to say as her dearly departed auntie was. "I love you, Auntie Clarice and I just miss you so much."

I miss you too, Clarice replied. *No more late-night pizza runs.*

Reg relayed this, and Marigold giggled. "She used to sneak out so we could go together," she confided. "My mom said that she was a bad influence and she should stay at the rest home and be a good example of how mature people should behave. But that would have been so boring. I loved it when she would show up in the middle of the night, tapping at my window, ready to go out on an adventure."

That's how a mature person should behave, Clarice declared.

Never get too old to surprise people and enjoy time with the ones you love. Even if it's in the middle of the night.

* * *

It was certainly longer than two minutes before Reg got back to Theodore to see why he had come. But he seemed to be happy sitting in front of the TV. So Reg concluded the seance and sent Marigold and her friends on their way before picking up with Theodore.

"Hey, Theodore, sorry to take so long." Reg sat down on the couch. "You wanted to tell me about something?"

Theodore continued to stare at the TV. He was still wearing his sunglasses and the reflection of the TV flickered in the lenses.

"If you want to watch TV, you can," Reg told him. "But if you want to talk to me about whatever you came here for, you'd better let me know what it is now. Otherwise, you will have to wait until I get up in the morning."

Theodore did not look away from the screen. "You are a very good medium."

"Oh. Well, thank you. I do try to provide a good service."

"Many mediums are just charlatans," he observed, "but you can really see spirits."

"Yes. Sometimes it can be too much, being able to see them all. Sometimes I wish that I couldn't see them. But I know what it is like not to be able to hear any voices anymore, and... I know I wouldn't like that, either. It would be too quiet."

Theodore finally looked away from the TV. Looking into the reflective lenses of his glasses was not much different from looking at his flat, black, expressionless eyes.

"What would it be like if you could never hear any voices again?"

Reg opened her mouth to respond that she had just said how she would feel about that.

"Living or dead," Theodore filled in. "What if you would never hear another voice again?"

"I would... I don't think I could stand that," Reg confessed. She didn't want to say that she would do something desperate or hurt herself, but she was certainly thinking of it. The silence in her head would be bad enough. Silence in the physical world too would be impossible.

"I wasn't supposed to stay here." Theodore pressed the button on the remote to shut the TV off. "I was supposed to go into the void, where there are no voices. There would never be anyone to talk to again."

"And... you didn't go?" Reg had never been able to nail down exactly how Theodore had been able to persist after Sma had died. Everything she heard or read about homunculi said that it was impossible. When the creator died, the creations died or were deactivated with her.

"So you... had a choice?" Reg asked.

Theodore shook his head. "No choice. But I did not want to go."

"Did someone tell you that you had to? Did you talk them out of it?"

Theodore looked down at his hands and turned them around, as if making sure that he was still there. "Nobody came. Sma was gone, and I was still there, and nobody took me away. And then you came."

"You said it was because Sma was still there. She had died, but her spirit was still there."

The homunculus shrugged. "I could not see or hear her. She *might* have still been there."

Reg laughed. Trust her to pick the disobedient little homunculus who did not disappear when he was supposed to and made up imaginary reasons for his ability to do so.

"And you are sure that Sma was really your creator?"

Theodore nodded. He looked at her sideways. "Of course."

CHAPTER SEVENTEEN

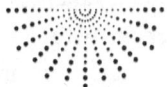

*R*eg sighed. She still had no idea why Theodore had survived the death of his creator or what that meant for either of them. But other things needed to be addressed more urgently. She trusted that someday, the mystery of Theodore's continued existence would unfold, and they would all understand it but, until then, there were other much more urgent problems to be tackled.

Namely, the warlock-werewolf war. They needed to find a way to overcome the tensions and friction between the two factions so that everyone, both the townspeople and the werewolves, would be safe. No more coming into town to see the doctor and being harassed or attacked for no reason. No more worrying about being driven out of the land they had established as their home. Just people doing their own thing and minding their own business, having free commerce with one another.

"Did you find out anything else about the artifact?" she asked Theodore.

"Yes." Theodore sat up straighter. "This is why I came to see you today."

"Great! What can you tell me?"

"There is an ancient legend about a stone," Theodore started, then paused, looking at her expectantly.

"You said that the artifact you were looking for might be a stone."

"Yes," he nodded, pleased that she remembered this point. "It was called Eidsstein or Oathstone."

Reg's breath caught in her throat, and her heart pounded harder. The name seemed to awaken an old memory in her. She couldn't quite put her finger on it, but it brought back echoes of a time she had once known, maybe in another life. She had often envied Ember his genetic memories and now felt like she finally had one of her own.

Eidsstein.

Oathstone.

It had to be the answer to their problems. There was no way she would react to it so strongly if it were not.

"That's it," she murmured. "Tell me about it. Where did it come from?"

"You know it?" Theodore asked, head cocked to one side slightly.

"I... no, I don't, but maybe I did once."

He continued to look at her, the image of the TV flickering on his sunglasses lenses.

"Something that I have forgotten," Reg explained. "Maybe... I saw it on a TV show once. But I can't remember any of the details."

Theodore glanced toward the TV, nodding. "I forget nothing."

"I wish I could remember everything."

But as soon as Reg said it, she knew it wasn't true. Did she truly want to be able to remember all the traumas of her childhood? The things that she had tried so hard to ignore and suppress? She wouldn't want them to all be crystal clear. She was glad to be able to forget much of what had happened to her and just put it behind her. The holes in her memory were much preferable to remembering with clarity what had happened during that time.

"So, tell me what I need to know," Reg urged. "What have you found out about the Oathstone?"

"In the hush of dusk, where shadows align,
  Eidsstein emerged from pact divine."

"Not in verse," Reg reminded him. "Just tell me in normal language."

"It is a legend," Theodore said sternly. "I am telling you what was written. It must be in verse. Just this part."

Reg sighed. "Okay, fine. Just for this part."

"Vargrena's wisdom and Drakskald's power,
  Bound by their oaths that fateful hour."

The skin on her arms goosebumped at the names Vargrena and Drakskald. They sounded like names right out of a vampire movie.

"Who are Vargrena and Drakskald?"

"Vargrena was a werewolf. The matriarch of her clan. Very wise and powerful."

"She was the alpha? I thought that only male wolves could be alphas."

"She was the matriarch of her pack. Of many packs. She was… greater than an alpha."

Reg tried to think of whether there was anything earlier or greater than an alpha, but couldn't come up with anything. *A matriarch greater than an alpha.* It was something she would have to think about.

"Okay, so if she was the leader of the werewolves, then I guess the other guy was the leader of the warlocks."

Theodore nodded. "Drakskald was a very great and powerful warlock. He was chosen out of the leaders of many covens to represent the warlocks in the pact with the wolves."

"So the two of them together represented all the wolves and all the warlocks, and they made some kind of agreement?"

"They created the Oathstone to bind their promise for all time. It would forever represent the will of the wolves and the warlocks to ally themselves, to put their differences aside and heal their clans."

"Wow." Reg breathed the word. "This is big. And the Oath-stone is still here? In the werewolf territory where Aleph's pack is?"

"Yes. Rumor has it that it is still there, though long forgotten. If it can be retrieved, it could once again bring peace to the two sides."

"That's amazing. That's just what we need. Good job in finding all that out!" As Reg started to get excited about it, her thoughts were suddenly dashed with cold water. She remembered the warnings from Davyn and the others. "This *is* stuff you found in your research, and not something you made up?"

He clicked and cocked his head, his expression still flat, not acting like she had offended him.

"Sma's library and Corvin's both speak of the Oathstone. It is very obscure, only a few short references."

"And you didn't add in any details of your own? Make anything up?"

"It is all in the ancient texts that I consulted. Even the verse."

Reg smiled, relieved. "Okay. I just had to make sure. I wouldn't want to go on a wild goose chase."

"A wild goose chase?" Theodore repeated. He cocked his head. "Why would you do that?"

"It's just an expression, it means..." Reg stopped. "I don't know exactly what it means. Trying to find something that isn't there."

"The Oathstone is there," he promised. "It is not a wild goose."

"Do you know exactly where it is? Or only that it is on the werewolf land?"

Theodore clicked and cocked his head, computing. "Not *exactly* where it is," he said finally. "But there are clues. And you have powers—can you *find?*"

"Sometimes," Reg admitted, "but it's a bit tricky. It's a lot easier if I've held the object before. And obviously... I haven't held the Oathstone before."

"No," Theodore shook his head sadly. He looked at her. "When will we retrieve it?"

"Uh... I don't know," Reg fumbled for an answer. Up until then, it had all been theoretical. Maybe there was an object that could help her. Maybe she could find it. She had recovered other hidden artifacts before, but it was always a challenge. "I guess we will have to put together a company and scout it out. And… you want to come?"

Theodore nodded. "Of course. I discovered the Oathstone. I must be on the quest to recover it."

It wouldn't make much sense to exclude him, especially since he was the only one who knew anything about where to find it. And if there were any problems, he was the one who had done the research and might know enough about the way it worked to get them out of trouble.

"Yeah. Okay. You know that it will be more than just you and me? You'll have to be able to work with others as well."

"I am bound to you," Theodore pointed out. "I do not know any others." He wrinkled his nose. "I will *not* work with the cursed Hunter."

Corvin would probably say the same of the homunculus. It was complicated trying to handle the relationships between the different magical factions. She would have thought that, with their powers and greater understanding of the unseen world, they would be able to get along with each other better. Especially those who had some degree of telepathy and could understand others' feelings and mental processes without words being spoken.

"You aren't actually bound to me. You are free to come and go as you like. I am not your creator."

"I am bound to you," Theodore insisted stubbornly.

"You help me, but you're not required to. We don't have any contract."

"I am bound to you."

"Okay. Anyway, you'll have to work with others. Even Corvin, if he agrees to come with us."

Theodore folded his arms and looked at Reg stubbornly. She shrugged. "Well, if you don't want to come along…"

"I do want to!" Theodore interrupted. "I will work for you. If I have to do something for the warlock, I will do what *you* tell me."

Reg supposed that was the most she could expect. If Theodore would do what she told him to and was willing to put up with the presence of the offensive warlock, then that was really all she could require from him. She nodded. "Okay. But I don't expect to have to put up with a bunch of whining about it."

"Fine," Theodore agreed.

CHAPTER EIGHTEEN

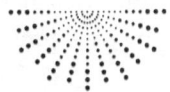

*R*eg was getting pretty good at putting together a company for a quest. It was not a talent she'd had the opportunity to develop as she was growing up but, after living in Black Sands for a couple of years, she'd needed to go on a few journeys to complete an objective. She didn't always know the exact skills that would be required for a particular journey, but she was getting better at guessing and, after working a few times with Davyn and Sarah, they were at the top of her list. They had several useful skills and were good at working things out, which was just as important as knowing what to do, maybe more important. A person could never know all the roadblocks they would encounter before beginning.

She crossed the yard to the big house to ask Sarah if she could come along.

The house was fragrant with the smell of something sweet and spicy. Some kind of cookies, Reg thought. Not as strong as gingerbread, but very pleasant. She wouldn't mind trying one of them.

"Sarah?" Reg called from the kitchen, not wanting to go wandering through the house looking for her. "Yoo-hoo?"

The kitchen was cozy and cheery, warm light reflecting off of the copper cookware. It was a few minutes before she heard Sarah's footsteps on the stairs, and then she was coming into the kitchen.

"Oh, Reg, I thought I heard something. How are you?"

"Good. I, um… I wondered if you would be able to help out with a little project."

"That sounds intriguing." Sarah put the teakettle on to boil. "What sort of a project?"

"Well, it has to do with the… current situation. The werewolf-warlock… unrest. I'm sure you probably feel the same way about it."

"What way, dear?"

"Well, I want to do something to help. Something to stop it. So that it is safe for everyone to come and go without worrying about the violence."

"Of course," Sarah agreed. "We all want that."

Reg was encouraged. "Theodore has discovered something called the Oathstone. Have you ever heard of it?"

Even though Theodore had said that he had only found mention of it in very old books, it was entirely possible that Sarah was familiar with it and Reg didn't need to get into all the details. Maybe Sarah even knew more about it than Theodore had been able to glean. She was the one who had several hundred years of experience in the area and might have run into it before.

Sarah busied herself getting the tea things together and putting some cookies out on a plate.

"The Oathstone… no, I don't think I've ever heard of such a thing. Are you sure he didn't just make it up?"

"No, I asked him, and he said it was true, that he'd found it in some old books. He hadn't just made it up."

"But you can't trust what he says. If he makes things up, he can make things up to cover up what he's made up."

Reg shook her head, frowning. "I don't think it's something he just made up. He knew a lot of details about it. There was even a verse."

Sarah set the plate of cookies down on the table and rolled her eyes. "Of course there was."

Reg giggled. "He does like his verses." She sat down at the table to help herself to a cookie while they waited for the water to boil. It was still warm from the oven and was soft and chewy. Reg closed her eyes and savored it for a moment.

"You should verify this information with independent sources," Sarah asserted.

"He said it was in Sma's library and in Corvin's. I can't really look it up—I don't have access to Sma's library aside from what is in Theodore's head. And I don't know whether Corvin would let me look at anything in his library. He was kind of... uh... not happy with me for letting Theodore read his books in the first place."

"Well, you can understand that it was his research, not yours." Sarah picked up the teakettle as it started to whistle and poured the boiling water into each of their cups. Reg gave her teabag a stir and watched it, seeing the little eddies of color spreading out from the bag.

"I know, but we had to do it to find out how to reverse the petrifaction spell."

Sarah nodded thoughtfully while nibbling on one of the cookies. "Of course. It was the only thing to do, but I can see Corvin's side. And you're right. I don't think he will let you look through his library to find the backup information about this Oathstone. What is it, exactly? According to Theodore?"

"It is an artifact created by an ancient matriarch werewolf and a powerful warlock when they united their clans years ago. It has powers to unite the warlocks and the werewolves, and to heal curses too. I'm hoping it will be able to reverse the curse on Corvin. Wouldn't that be the best? To stop the fighting between the wolves and the humans and be able to reverse the damage that October did? That would be really good."

"Sounds too good to be true," Sarah dismissed. "Theodore probably made it up."

"He didn't just make it up," Reg insisted, frustrated. She stirred several spoonfuls of sugar into her tea.

"There's no way you can know that."

"I know Theodore, and he told me he didn't make it up."

"Does he actually know the difference?"

"Yes!"

Reg hoped he did. She made a motion, sweeping this part of the conversation away. "The question is… if I go to find this Oathstone, would you come with me? You're so good at this kind of quest."

"No, I don't think so."

Reg sputtered. She had not expected to be told no. "Sarah!"

Sarah looked amused. "I'm not required to go on a quest just because you ask, Reg. And why should I go on a quest to find a mythical stone that probably doesn't even exist, that was made up by your homunculus?"

"He didn't make it up."

"I'm sorry, Reg. I don't have the time to spend on something that is not going to get us anywhere. I have other plans, and there is no point in even attempting it."

"But you helped with the Tears of Poseidon and Zephyr Pearl."

"We knew that they existed, where they were, and the challenges we were likely to face in retrieving them. That is very different from something that is supposed to be… where?"

"In… the forest."

"What forest?"

Reg made a wide motion. "Out in… the werewolf territory."

"Oh, and you think it is a good idea to go into the werewolf territory looking for an artifact that probably doesn't even exist?"

"I think… it would be worth trying. And if I had people with me who could help…"

"Yes, you don't want to go about something like this alone. But I'm afraid you can count me out."

"There's… no way that you would help?"

"I can't think of one, no. I'm sorry, Reg; I know that isn't what you wanted to hear. But I do have a life of my own, outside of trying to recover ancient artifacts."

CHAPTER NINETEEN

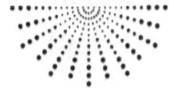

*S*arah had never rejected a request from Reg before, so Reg felt a little crushed that she had just turned her down flat. She thought about Theodore and his description of the stone and its origins, and she couldn't believe that it was something he had just made up himself. Especially when she had already asked him and he had referenced his sources. She knew he could make mistakes and just come up with something out of thin air when he couldn't answer based on known facts. But he'd assured her he was not just "hallucinating."

The next person on her ask list was Corvin, and she already doubted whether he would agree to go with her. Since he hadn't even been out of the house since his attack, as far as she knew, he seemed less likely to agree to help her with a quest. Even though it was something that might help him to regain his powers. If she told him about that part, he would surely want to do everything he could to help.

She drove to Corvin's house and sat at the curb for a few minutes considering the matter. She wasn't sure of the best way to approach him to get a positive result. If there even was any way to get the answer she wanted. But he owed her, didn't he? It wasn't the first time she had saved his life. And she had been visiting him ever since his attack to make sure that he was okay, to bring him a little present, and to try to help keep his spirits up, day in and day out. She had done more for him than anyone, even his own coven. How many of them had visited to see how he was doing or to bring him a bottle of Jack or other "get well soon" gift?

How about John, his own son? Had he been there to visit Corvin? As far as Reg knew, he had not. Granted, Corvin had not raised John and had not even known of his existence until recently. But still, a son should show his father some kind of respect, shouldn't he? Especially when he wanted to go up the ranks of the coven and eventually take Corvin's place.

Reg couldn't sit still any longer, so she was finished stewing. She got out of the car and went to the door. As usual, it took some time to get Corvin to the door. Reg could have just manipulated the lock and let herself in, but that would not likely endear her to Corvin when she was asking him a favor.

"Reg." Corvin checked behind her to ensure no one else was with her, then opened the door wider to let her in.

He led the way to the living room, where they usually sat, and Reg hesitated, wanting to go to the study this time.

"What?" Corvin asked irritably.

"How about your study? Aren't you about ready for a change of pace?"

"I use my study other times. I entertain in the living room."

"I'd like to see your study again. The living room is…"

"What?" Corvin sniffed the air, checking whether it needed airing out. "There isn't anything wrong with it."

But he looked around guiltily at a number of glasses and bottles that had not been properly taken care of. Unlike Sarah's welcoming, fragrant kitchen, Corvin's living room smelled mustily of books, stale whiskey, and sweat.

Reg cleared her throat and didn't back down on the request to use the study and, eventually, Corvin nodded and motioned for her to go ahead of him into the room.

Reg looked around at the large volumes on the shelves and relaxed. Of course Theodore hadn't made up everything about the

Oathstone. There were so many books there, he had picked it up from one of them. Maybe Corvin even knew which one and was familiar with the story. She settled herself into the chair nearest to Corvin's desk. He leaned his elbows on the table and looked at her.

"So what is this about, Reg?"

"Well, I wanted to see how you were doing…"

"I'm doing the same as I have been doing since the attack. Healing physically, but it isn't the injury that is slowing me down. As you well know. Nothing has changed, Reg. And nothing is likely to change in the near future."

Reg nodded. She knew all of that, of course. She had been hoping he would be in better spirits but hadn't expected him to be.

How would she feel if she lost all her gifts?

She knew what that was like. She had once had them stripped from her by none other than Corvin. Now, he was finding out what that was like, too. Although his case was different because he still had the gifts, he just couldn't use them. And was tortured if he tried to use them. Even though Reg had once had no idea that she had any powers, she now knew about them and how often she relied upon them. If she experienced pain every time she used them… she didn't know how long she could have stood it. She thought maybe Corvin was getting used to life without powers, but perhaps he hadn't adjusted. Maybe he was just barely holding on.

He needed the curse to be removed if he were going to survive. He looked older than Reg had ever seen him before. And he would be older every time she saw him,

She met his eyes. "What if there was a way to reverse the curse?"

CHAPTER TWENTY

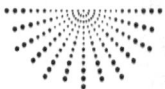

*H*e stared at her. "Don't tease, Reg. If there was a way to reverse the curse, I would have found it by now. Do you think I haven't looked at every possible counterspell, charm, herb, and enchantment? I have been driving myself crazy looking for a solution, but we both know there probably isn't any. Unless October was to choose to reverse it, and I'm not sure if he even could. He wanted a way to stop me permanently, and that is what he has done."

"What about the Oathstone?"

Corvin shook his head. "The Oathstone? I don't remember hearing anything of an Oathstone."

"Theodore said that it was mentioned in one of your books."

She knew she was taking a risk by mentioning Theodore and his intrusion into the library. But she needed to reach Corvin. She needed him to understand that she wasn't being stupid or naive; she really knew what she was talking about and could do something for him.

"My library." His voice was hard and flinty. "I think I know everything that is in my library."

"This may only have been one mention. And there was a mention of it in Sma Firea's books, too, so it wasn't just that isolated book. Being in two different places is good. It is more likely to be true."

"Except that your homunculus hallucinates. There is no mention of an Oathstone in my library."

"There is. Theodore saw it. He said he didn't just make it up; he saw it in your library."

"He doesn't know when he is telling the truth and when he is 'mistaken,' Reg. I'm not saying he is lying to you, I'm telling you he doesn't know the difference between the truth and confabulation. It just comes out of his mouth and it must be true."

"You just don't remember it. You can't remember everything in all those books."

"I have been studying those books for years. Centuries. There is no Oathstone. I have been spending all my time, night and day, going over my library. If there was a stone that reverses curses, don't you think that would have jumped out at me?"

"That wasn't its main purpose. It was called something else. It was the... Eid-stone or something like that. It was to enforce peace between the warlocks and the werewolves. But it was also supposed to be able to break curses."

"The Eidsstein?" Corvin's brow wrinkled. "That's very obscure... I don't remember any mention of it being used to cure curses."

"Well, maybe that was the part Theodore found in Sma's records. But you remember that it was mentioned in yours? You remember hearing of it before?"

"I've heard of it, but there is nothing in my records about it. Not by that name, anyway. There are sometimes mentions of relics that have long since passed away, and old myths and legends that are long-dead. Nothing that I can use."

"Theodore says we can find the Oathstone, and we can use it to reverse your curse, and to bring the werewolves and warlocks together in peace. Isn't that what we all want?"

"I'm not sure that's what everyone wants. I couldn't care less whether the wolves and warlocks are ever reconciled. In fact, I hope they are not. But to reverse my curse, yes, of course. You know that is what I want."

"Yeah." Reg blew out her breath. "So will you join me on a quest to recover it? And then we can use it to fix you up?"

"On a quest."

"Yeah. To go get it…" Reg trailed off.

Corvin was already shaking his head. He spread his arms to indicate his surroundings. The house that had become his prison. "What part of this don't you understand, Reg? I'm not leaving here. Not until I am back to normal."

"Why not? Just because you've lost the use of your powers… you would be just like the regular people. No one would know you were any different from them. And besides, we're not going to the city or something. We're going into the forest. There wouldn't be anyone there who would know the difference."

"You think all I care about is what people think? That they would know I lost my powers?"

"Well, no. There could be a lot of reasons you don't want to go out in public, but I think you need to get over it and realize that it isn't all about whether you can use your powers. A lot of people don't even *have* powers, and they get around all right. You can come along on the quest, and then when we find the Oathstone, we'll be able to heal you."

"Why would I come on a quest?"

"To help get the Oathstone!"

"What don't you understand about me not being able to use my powers? I can't help with a quest."

"You could come along. You could help in other ways. You could help us figure out what to do about any challenges or road-blocks. You can still help physically. And if I need more power, you've been asking me to take your excess powers."

"So you want to bring me along as your personal battery pack."

"Well… no, not like that. I didn't mean that."

"Who else is going on this quest?"

"I'm still getting everybody together."

"So, no one?"

"Theodore for sure. He's the one who knows the location of the Oathstone."

To say that she knew exactly where it was would be a fib, but Theodore did know *approximately* where it was. It wouldn't take them long to find it. Then she could use Corvin's advice of the best approach, how it might be guarded or booby-trapped, and how it could be used. And he was the leader of the coven, so he was the one who would need to reconcile with Aleph and the wolf pack, despite his assertion that he didn't care if they ever reconciled.

"That's one more reason I'm not coming along."

"Why are you and Sarah so prejudiced against homunculi?" Reg demanded in frustration. Then she held up her hands. "Never mind, I know. You think he shouldn't exist, and he lies all the time."

"Not all the time, just enough that you can never be sure whether he is telling the truth."

"So you don't believe him. You just go by what you know. And you help bring that knowledge to the quest. You can help to keep him on track. Make sure we know what is one hundred percent true and what is questionable."

"You and Theodore, and who else?"

"I haven't asked everyone yet."

"Sarah? You live on the same property. You must have asked her."

"Sarah… is busy with other things."

"She told you no."

"Yes," Reg sighed.

"It's a 'no' for me too."

"Come on," Reg wheedled. "I didn't think you would be too afraid to come."

"I'm not afraid to come. I want nothing to do with the homunculus. And I have no intention of brokering peace between the werewolves and the warlocks. I thought you got that message when I didn't attend the town hall."

"But I can't do this on my own."

"I'm sure you have other people you can ask."

"You and Sarah won't help? Seriously?"

They were the two people she relied on the most. She couldn't believe that they both refused to be involved.

"No, Reg. And maybe that should tell you something about the foolishness of this quest. I doubt that your Oathstone exists or that it will do what you expect it to. You're going to run headlong into trouble and get nothing out of it."

"You said that the Eid-whatever exists."

"I have heard of the Eidsstein. That's all. Does it *still* exist? Probably not. If it does, will you be able to find and retrieve it? Doubtful. If you do, will it do what you hope it will?" He shook his head. "I doubt that too."

CHAPTER TWENTY-ONE

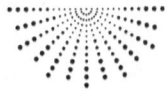

*R*eg was getting a little worried about her quest. She really didn't want to go into werewolf land alone, with only a homunculus for protection or company. Theodore was great when she needed information, but she wasn't sure that he would be able to provide all the support she would need when she went into the werewolf territory in hopes of finding the Oathstone. He had protected Sma, preventing anyone from passing onto her land who did not have the passwords required. But she wasn't sure what he would have done to stop them if they had not been able to give the keywords that had allowed them access.

What about Marta Jessup? She was a law enforcement officer, so that was always helpful if they happened to be confronted about what they were doing there. But Marta didn't have any magic to speak of, and Reg was worried that she would think it was trespassing or some other infraction and would not want to be involved. There was no point in telling law enforcement ahead of time what she was going to do. Easier to get forgiveness than permission. And she hoped not to have to seek forgiveness, either. What they didn't know wouldn't hurt them. She was full of bits of wisdom.

Damon Knight had always been a reliable protector but, lately, he had seemed distant and unapproachable. Reg couldn't shake the feeling that ever since their encounter with the cabal, something had shifted between them. She wondered if he were preoccupied with a new romantic interest, leaving her behind in his thoughts. Perhaps there had been some incident at the cat sanctuary that had caused him to withdraw. Or maybe it was just her imagination running wild, and there was nothing between them. But she hesitated to call him out of the blue to take on this new quest.

Davyn, then. She couldn't think of anyone else she would rather have on her side during such a venture. He had been with her when they had retrieved the Tears of Poseidon and Zephyr Pearl. He hadn't had much to do in those cases but had been there for support. He was her mentor and knew more about firecasting than anyone in the world. Or at least in Black Sands. And he was the current guardian of Ember, the young firedrake who had hatched in her garden. And it was time to see Ember again, even if Davyn decided he didn't want anything to do with the quest.

She was surprised at being able to drive all the way up to the house without catching even a glimpse of the dragon. Normally, he dive-bombed the car and landed in front of her once she turned off the main highway. And he was always there by the time she reached the house. Reg got out of the car and knocked on the door. Davyn arrived at the door within a few seconds.

"Reg!" he looked surprised. "Good to see you. We didn't have an appointment today?"

She was probably lucky to have found him at home. He did have a day job that took him into town. Was it a weekend? She couldn't remember what day it was. But it was starting to get dark. Maybe he was already home from work.

"No, I just wanted to ask you about something." Reg looked around. "Where's Ember?"

"Off exploring. I haven't seen him for a couple of days."

"Oh, wow." Reg had known that the day would come when he would begin to fly farther afield, and maybe find a cave or another place of his own. Maybe there were other dragons out there, and he would be able to find a mate or at least a friend. He had already moved his hoard of treasure out of Davyn's cellar as it had gotten harder and harder for him to fit down the stairs. Even getting into the house had proven to be a challenge lately.

"I guess our little dragon is growing up," she said, trying to sound upbeat about it. Was that how parents felt as their children gained independence? It had been different for Reg. Aging out of foster care, there hadn't really been anywhere else to go but on her own. She hadn't had someone she could rely on for food and shelter anymore. She'd heard of kids whose foster families had let them stay after they turned eighteen, maybe working a job to pay rent to cover for the income the family lost when they aged out. Maybe even going on to university, some of them.

That had never been in the cards for Reg. No one had ever wanted to keep her for that long.

Davyn motioned for Reg to come in. "Yes, it's been a little weird not to have him hanging around here, lighting fires, stealing trinkets, curling up on the floor to sleep right where I'll trip over him." He laughed. "It seems like he's been here forever... and it has gone so fast; I can't believe he's old enough to make his way out into the world."

"Well, most hatchlings don't even have one person to take care of them, let alone two. Especially firecasters. But I wish... he didn't even say goodbye."

"I'm sure he'll probably be back another time or two. I don't think he's gone for good. But we can't hold him back."

"No." Reg's eyes were burning. She shook her head. It was ridiculous to feel bad that he was growing up. She wanted him to grow up and to be independent. She didn't need to be trying to guide and mentor a dragon for the rest of her life. It was good for him to move on into an adult dragon life.

Davyn went into the kitchen to get them each a cup of coffee, and then he and Reg settled down on the couch. Reg sipped the strong, fragrant coffee. She could never get hers to taste like Davyn's. He just had the knack for it. And the fancy machine and the right imported beans.

"Mmm. This is good. Like it always is."

Davyn nodded. "So, to what do I owe the pleasure of your visit?"

Reg took another long sip, putting off telling him. Trying to figure out how to best introduce the topic.

"Things have been... pretty bad in town lately."

"Between the coven and the wolf pack? I hear about it, but I have been lucky not to experience anything myself. One of the benefits of living somewhere a little more isolated. I hope you haven't experienced any violence...?"

"Not personally, no... but I have seen a few things. And talked to Zora." Reg shook her head. "The way that she and her cubs have been treated... what makes a grown man harass a little kid? And not just verbally, but grab him and bully him, throw him around. People are sick." She clenched her fists tightly, then forced herself to release them.

Davyn shook his head. "Who did that? If it was someone from the coven, I will expel him. We are bound by peace and respect for others. That kind of behavior cannot be tolerated."

"I didn't know them. Maybe some uninitiated members."

"There have been strangers from out of town looking for trouble. People hear about the troubles between the pack and the coven and want to get involved."

"Why would they want that?"

"Some people actively seek chaos and conflict. They get a thrill out of violence. I would hope that no one in the coven is like that. But... people change." He sighed, shaking his head. "It's baffling how anyone can distort our core values of peace and harmony into malice and cruelty."

Reg shook her head. Of course she had seen that kind of violence before. But she had hoped not to find it in the coven. If it were being perpetuated by anyone in the coven, she would bet it was John. Could he be calling in reinforcements? Trying to get a real war going?

"Was Zora okay?" Davyn asked. "And her cubs?"

"They're... it's been pretty hard on them. I worry about them getting PTSD or something. I know it doesn't seem like a big deal, but for kids, especially when they are just developing… they're already dealing with the challenges of transformation that they shouldn't have to yet."

Davyn nodded seriously. He didn't try to talk her out of her opinion or say that he thought they would be just fine and everything would turn out all right.

"It's a hard world," he acknowledged. "I wish I could say there was an easy fix, but I'm not sure how to get around the current state of affairs… we can't change the fact that the wolves attacked Corvin without provocation. There have been tensions between the two groups since the wolves were released from Jake's lab and didn't go back to where they came from and settled here instead. Even though this is their ancestral land… people feel like they are interlopers. And I'm sure they have their own resentments about the humans. Being imprisoned by them in the first place. Acting like they are the apex species in the state and the wolves are not even worth mentioning."

"If there was a way to improve things, maybe to even sign a peace accord and fix it all up… would you do it?"

CHAPTER TWENTY-TWO

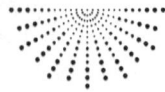

*O*f course. I—" Davyn met Reg's eyes, and his brows went up. "What are you up to? If there was a way to fix things...?"

"Maybe there is. Have you ever heard of the Oathstone?"

"No, I can't say I have. What is it?"

"It was created by an old werewolf and warlock to heal the rift between their people. I don't know all the details but, you know, they swore oaths to each other and everything, so that's why it's called the Oathstone. It was used to keep the peace between them. And it is supposed to be able to reverse curses too, so..."

"That seems like a lot to expect from one article. How did you find out about it?"

"There was information on it in Corvin's library."

"Corvin came up with this?" Davyn seemed impressed by this. "Well, that's encouraging. He thought that it might actually work?"

Reg tried to figure out how to tell Davyn that she was sure it would work, at least sure enough that they should go get it and find out, without telling him that Corvin didn't have any confidence in the venture.

"Oh," Davyn read her face. "Corvin *doesn't* think it will work."

"He isn't even sure if it still exists," Reg admitted. "But how will we find out if we don't look?"

"How solid are your sources?"

"I… don't know."

"You don't know?" Davyn's eyes were piercing. "Why not?"

"I haven't… read any of the information myself. I'm not really a *reader*, you know…"

"So this came to you secondhand, through rumors and—oh, through Theodore."

Reg nodded. "Yeah. That doesn't mean it is bad information, though. Theodore is really good at reading and figuring stuff out. He's the one who knew about the elementals and figured out how to reverse the petrifying spell. He is really smart."

"Yes, I know. The problem is that he's not reliable."

"But what information about an artifact that's hundreds of years old is reliable? We believe a lot of stuff that is just rumors or traditions passed down for years. It could be true. We won't know it's true unless we find it."

He sipped his coffee, staring off into space. "So that's why you came here. You want to go after the Oathstone and see if it can do what Theodore says it can."

"What's the harm in trying? If we can't find it or it doesn't work, then it doesn't. What have we lost?"

"I don't know. A lot of things could happen. You remember that our attempts to retrieve the other artifacts were not exactly… uneventful. The same is true of some of the other undertakings we have attempted. It isn't without risk. I assume there will be some sort of magical protections surrounding this Oathstone. They are rarely left out in the open where you can just pick them up and put them in your pocket."

Reg rubbed the back of her calf, which was still healing from the encounter with the ocean guardian and Sarah's misguided attempt to treat the injury. It had been a couple of weeks, and she was beginning to wonder if it would ever fully heal. At least she hadn't had to go to the hospital with wolfsbane poisoning from Sarah's poultice.

"But we have to try," she said. "Don't you think? If we think it might help and then just don't do anything, what good does that do? If we can stop people from getting hurt, especially innocent people, then I think we should. I don't want Fenris or any of the other cubs getting hurt. I want them to stay here and to be able to grow up in a nice place. Without being harassed and bullied."

"I can't argue with that," Davyn sighed. "Have you been able to find anyone else to help you?"

Reg shrugged. "Just Theodore. Sarah and Corvin both turned me down flat."

"Because of the homunculus."

"Yes. They are so prejudiced against him. It isn't like he's been wrong or done anything to harm them, so I don't understand why they are convinced he will. He's really useful. And if he has found the one thing that will help to reconcile the two sides to each other... I want to see if it will work."

"We don't know for sure that it will. You might be taking a risk for nothing."

"But I'll be doing something. I hate just sitting around waiting for something bad to happen. Especially when there might be a solution."

"Where do you think the stone is?"

"Not here. In the woods. Theodore thinks he has enough clues to pinpoint it. We might have to do some looking around."

"We can put our heads together. I'm sure we can come up with several effective methods of finding such a powerful artifact."

Reg's heart leaped. "So you'll come? You agree?"

"I agree that this opportunity is too important to ignore. If we have the chance to end this unrest before things get any bloodier... I think we should."

"Thank goodness!" Reg blew out her breath. "I thought everybody was going to turn me down. How soon can we start? I don't know if you have a bunch of stuff scheduled. Work, and all that."

"I have the next two days. I'll have to move a couple of things, but it won't be bad. I don't know how much longer it might take than that. We can re-evaluate if it appears that it will go on for longer. Maybe regroup and try again when we have a better chance at success."

"So, tomorrow?"

Davyn nodded. "Do you have anyone else you want to talk to about it? Or will we be the initial recon team, and then we can gather together others when we know what skills will be needed to recover it?"

"Yeah, that sounds good. Maybe if we know for sure that it exists and just need more help, Corvin or Sarah would help. But maybe we won't even need them."

"Hopefully, we'll be able just to get in and get out quickly, like you did with the Tears of Poseidon."

Except that hadn't exactly been an easy job. Reg had almost not made it. She had been injured and had barely escaped at the last minute.

"Yeah. Maybe it will be as easy as getting the Tears of Poseidon."

Davyn gave her a wry smile, realizing his mistake. He shrugged. "All we can do is our best. I know you're not an early riser, but let's get as much of a head start as we can tomorrow morning. We want to get as much as possible done in the light of day. Midnight is great for seances, but not so great for searching the woods."

"Okay. I'll make sure I get myself up early."

"As soon as you get here tomorrow, we'll go."

Reg sighed with relief. "Great. Thank you so much!"

He patted her on the shoulder. "We wouldn't want you going by yourself! I think these things should always be done in pairs, at least. More if possible. You never know whose gifts might be the ones most needed. I'm sorry that Sarah and Corvin didn't come through."

Reg nodded, but she was less concerned about it now. She'd had two people to start with, even if Davyn didn't consider Theodore a real person. And now she had three. Davyn was experienced and would be able to help her out and make suggestions. They would be agile, ready to make quick changes on the fly. They didn't need a big company.

"I'll see you tomorrow, then."

CHAPTER TWENTY-THREE

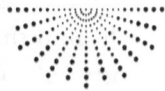

*R*eg had not left Corvin's house without first taking some of his power from him, as she had done each time she had seen him recently. As she had discovered, the overflow of energy not only made her more productive, but it kept her from being able to sleep for at least a day, possibly more. So she didn't need to worry about waking up in good time to go on the quest with Davyn, since she wouldn't actually go to sleep. She had the evening and early night hours to see her clients, and then a few hours to prepare for her quest, and then she could head over to Davyn's nice and early, maybe even beating *him* out of bed.

He would be shocked when she showed up that early.

Full of nervous energy, she cleaned, went through the fridge to get rid of anything she didn't want, and flipped through shows on the TV, looking for something to distract her. Starlight yowled crossly at her for not going to sleep again and paced around the cottage as if he wasn't sure what to do.

Dawn started to streak the sky with color, orange and pink, and Reg got into her car and drove back to Davyn's house. She had everything she would need in her backpack.

She didn't usually get to enjoy the sunrise in the morning. She was sometimes awake when the sun started to come up, but she was headed to bed rather than getting up and didn't stick around to watch the colors change and the sun make its way above the horizon. It was pretty, and she could see why some people like to get up early in the morning. It wasn't that she was philosophically opposed to waking up early. Her body chose for her. She just couldn't get up that early in the morning, no matter when she went to sleep or what strategies she employed. Other than just staying up all night.

The car crunched over the gravel as she stopped in front of Davyn's house. Davyn came out onto the porch with his morning cup of coffee and wide eyes, satisfyingly surprised to see her there so early. Julian followed him out and smiled a greeting at Reg.

She would never understand what Davyn saw in him as a romantic partner. Julian was diametrically opposite Davyn; she didn't even know how they could stand being around each other. Davyn was a stable, kind, naturally good person. A great mentor for Reg. He never lost his temper with her and was happy to explain things to her and to show her what to do over and over until she got it. Julian was a loose cannon, a bully by nature, superior and snotty in everything he said to her. He was, she knew, damaged by all that had happened to him in his childhood. She had seen the brokenness of his mind and, despite her hate for him, had to admire how he managed to act so "normal" most of the time.

"I'm here!" she told Davyn, shouldering her backpack. "Are we taking your car? The ATVs?"

"I think we'll take Julian's truck. It will hold everything we need and is nearly as good as the ATVs in getting around off-road. With the ATVs, we would have to split off into pairs."

"Pairs?"

It was just Davyn and Reg until they needed to call on Theodore. They could just take one ATV unless he had a bunch of equipment that he wanted to take as well.

Davyn nodded. He took a sip of his coffee. "You, Theodore, me, and Julian."

CHAPTER TWENTY-FOUR

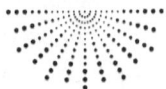

*J*ulian?" Reg repeated stupidly, and looked at him.

The birds in the trees were silenced. The voices in her head stopped. The whole world seemed to be waiting for the response.

"Julian." Davyn looked at Reg, back to Julian, and then at Reg again. "You're okay with Julian coming along, aren't you? When I said we could come yesterday..."

"I... I didn't realize you meant Julian, too," Reg said faintly. She tried to think of an objection other than the truth that she didn't want Julian along and hated even being near him. She always tried to be polite to Julian because of Davyn and never said anything negative about him unless couched in the most careful of terms. "I... are you sure he is the best person to come along? I just mean... he must have to be on call for work, and he works hard. He needs the time off when he can get it."

"I appreciate your concern, Reg," Julian said in a smarmy voice. "But I think I am the best person for the job, all things considered. The well-being of the wolves is very important to me personally and my job. They are an endangered species and have only just been reintroduced to Florida. We do not want to lose this new community. Especially when they are already breeding."

"I thought you were the one who was all for driving them out of Black Sands."

"Out of Black Sands, yes, but not out of Florida. And not with violence. I recommended sanctions, not violence. I don't want any of them hurt. Or any of the warlocks either," he added as an afterthought.

"I don't know. I'm used to working with Davyn, but I don't know anything about your... skill set. I don't know if our first job together should be something as important as this."

Julian shook his head. His blond hair ruffled in the morning breeze and he fixed his cold, pale eyes on Reg.

"Let's put it this way, Reg," he said in a calm, measured voice with plenty of tension behind it. "There isn't a thing you could do in this world that would keep me away from this quest. I need to be there. I am going to be there. So you might as well get over your reservations about it now."

They all stood there looking at each other for what felt like a very long time. Reg accepted that if Julian wanted to be involved, he would be involved. He had the full force of magical law enforcement behind him. While in general, the magical communities were self-governing and not hierarchal, a few authorities enforced laws for the well-being of vulnerable populations or in special circumstances.

And Julian's branch, the Endangered Species Division, just happened to be one of those agencies.

"So," Davyn said eventually. "Let's hop in the truck and get on our way. Reg, do you know specifically where we want to go, or do you need to summon your... companion."

Reg nodded. "Yeah, I know approximately where to go, but he knows a lot more details than I do. He can guide us where we need to go."

She could summon Theodore with just her intention now, or a few muttered words if she needed him immediately. But she fell back to the method she had initially learned to call him, not sure how well she could concentrate with Julian watching her. She stooped down to scoop up a handful of gravel and dust and tossed it in front of her.

"From soil and stone, by magic spin,
　　Theodore reform, our work begin."

Reg watched the small dust devil form in front of her, resolving into the figure of her homunculus, resplendent in his Spider-Man T-shirt and red-rimmed sunglasses.

Davyn chuckled. "It seems he's had an upgrade."

"Sma didn't take very good care of him," Reg snapped. "She never gave him any clothes other than when she created him. He's had those dirty, tattered clothes forever."

Julian was looking at Theodore with fascination. "This is the homunculus you were talking about."

Davyn nodded. "Yes, this is Theodore. Theodore, this is Julian Sabat. He and I are both going to be helping Reg with her quest. Trying to recover the Oathstone to use it to strike an accord between the warlocks and the werewolves."

Theodore looked at Reg.

"Bound by craft and ancient lore,
　　In service, I arise once more—"

"I know, I know. You don't have to do the verse," Reg told him. He'd been better about it lately, but she hadn't summoned him formally for a while, and maybe he thought he needed to respond formally.

Theodore stared at Reg. She felt like there was something else he expected her to do or say, but she wasn't sure what it was. Maybe there was a special quest kick-off speech or ritual he was expecting her to perform.

"We're going to do it now," Reg told him. She felt a little guilty that she hadn't asked his permission beforehand. Maybe he had other plans. She'd told him he could do other things when he wasn't working for her. "Is that... okay?"

He gave a little bow. "I serve at your pleasure."

"Everybody is impressed at the information you managed to gather about the Oathstone. We're really hoping that it will do what the rumors say."

"I hope the Oathstone is the solution to your problem."

"We do too," Reg agreed. "How close do you think you can get us to it? Can you give Davyn driving directions on the way? Be his navigator?"

Theodore looked Davyn over. They had met before, but Theodore seemed to be evaluating him for the first time.

"Better than the *other* warlock," he decided.

Julian decided to be offended. "He doesn't even know me! How can he say that?"

"He doesn't mean you," Reg told him. "He means Corvin. He didn't want to have to go on a quest with Corvin."

Theodore nodded his agreement. "And we are not," he said with evident satisfaction.

"Oh." Julian was appeased by this. "I'm a warlock, too," he told Theodore. "I am an investigator for the Endangered Species Division."

Theodore clicked. "You must be very proud," he returned.

Julian frowned, unsure whether Theodore was being sarcastic or sincere. Reg wasn't sure herself. Theodore didn't normally joke or use sarcasm, but the response was so apt she had to wonder whether it was something he had seen on TV.

Davyn motioned again for the truck, and they all made their way over to it. Reg positioned Theodore beside Davyn and climbed into the front seat beside him. She did not want to sit with Julian in the back of the cab. So Julian sat in the second row by himself but didn't seem to object to the arrangements.

Reg said nothing, letting Davyn and Theodore work out the route. Davyn frowned as he drove and they drew closer. "This is in the werewolves' territory?"

"Well, that makes sense," Julian offered.

Davyn ignored him, looking at Theodore and waiting for his answer.

"Yes," Theodore agreed, "In the werewolves' ancestral land."

Davyn shook his head and pressed his lips together in a thin line. Reg knew he was worried about what would happen when they got there. She was a little queasy thinking about it.

But no one had said that she couldn't go onto the werewolf land. It covered a large area, from what Reg could tell, and she had never been reprimanded for getting close to it or driving onto it to talk to them. There were no marked borders or check stops or anything to stop them from exploring on their own.

"Do you think it is a problem?" she asked Davyn.

"I think it is a problem," Davyn confirmed. "I am a warlock, and so is Julian and, right now, there is a war going on between the werewolves and the warlocks. It isn't exactly the situation I was imagining."

"But I'm a friend of the pack, and you are with me," Reg assured them. "I don't think they'll do anything if you are with me."

"I'm not as confident."

"Well… if we're stopped or you're not comfortable with it when we get there, we can reconsider."

Davyn grunted and fell silent. Reg hoped they would get close to the Oathstone and there would be no group of wolves there to guard it or tell them to go back. She really wanted to be able to do something to resolve the situation.

They all needed things to be resolved and go back to normal.

CHAPTER TWENTY-FIVE

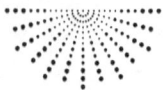

*T*here was not much conversation on the way to the werewolf territory. Davyn kept his mouth closed—that long, thin, disapproving line. Reg supposed that if he had known all the details before agreeing to help, he would have turned her down, too. Everybody wanted the werewolf-warlock conflict to be resolved, but no one wanted to do what it took to bring both sides to the table again.

Theodore didn't seem to notice how the mood had shifted and gave Davyn directions, straining to sit up tall enough to look out the window and see the surrounding landscape. He hadn't told Reg how he was going to find the Oathstone, but she assumed he had a bunch of obscure clues he had managed to decipher. He didn't seem to need anyone else's help.

Julian sat in the bench seat behind them, occasionally leaning over the front seat to make a comment or point out something he thought they all might be interested in.

They were not.

"Isn't this exciting?" he asked Reg. "Aren't you thrilled to be a part of this historic event? The quest for the Eidsstein?"

Part of this historic event? He made it sound like he was in charge of the quest rather than Reg. He was only there because she had allowed him to come along on *her* quest. She wasn't excited to be a part of his.

"You've heard about it before?" she asked, deciding to focus instead on his use of the Oathstone's other name.

"Well…" Julian got a little pink, "I looked it up after Davyn told me about it. Tried to do a little research to see what I could find about it."

"It's not on the internet," Reg told him. "I already tried that."

"No. The legend is much too old, much too obscure for that. But I have access to other primary documents through my work. Of course, we keep lots of archives about endangered species. Some that you may never see or hear of, but that we hope to find in the wild someday. Scientists are always discovering creatures that they once thought were extinct. You don't know how tightly animals hold on to their existence. How they can fight tooth and nail—fang and claw—to survive as a species. It really is quite amazing."

"You have a library?" Theodore asked, looking at Julian with interest for the first time.

"We have a great library. Very extensive. Documents you won't find anywhere else in the world."

"Can I go there? Reg said I could go to the library after we find the Oathstone."

"Well, this is a different library, one that Reg doesn't have any access to. Nobody has access to it except for those who work there, like me."

"I could work there," Theodore suggested.

"They would never hire a homunculus."

"You could take me there. Tell them that I am your son."

Reg supposed they might be able to pull it off. Theodore's coloring was different; he was darker than Julian, with dark hair and shining black eyes. But genetics was a funny thing. And there was always adoption. People couldn't tell just by looking at two people and whether they were legally related or not.

Julian chuckled. "Maybe I could."

"If we find the Oathstone, you will take me there."

Julian looked at Reg, shaking his head. "You've got quite the little negotiator there."

"You can take him if you want to. As a reward."

Julian shrugged. "I don't know if they would allow it."

"You have online access," Davyn pointed out. "You don't need to take him anywhere. You just log on for him."

"Uh... yeah, I guess I could do that."

"So you will do it?" Theodore demanded. "You must let me read this library."

"The whole thing? Slow down, buddy. I couldn't let you on for that long."

"I'm a very fast reader," Theodore assured him.

"The library is very extensive."

"I could read it."

Julian shrugged. "We'll see," he said indulgently, and Reg figured he thought that Theodore would forget about it, like a child, if he agreed and then distracted him with something else.

But Theodore would not be so quick to forget. Once he got an idea in his head, he didn't just forget about it.

"Turn up here," Theodore instructed suddenly, pointing to a turn that was coming up too fast, making Davyn slam on the brakes so that he would be able to make the turn. "The Crossroads of the Brotherhood," he said portentously.

Reg couldn't see any sign that would prove Theodore right or wrong. She couldn't see any landmarks that would have told Theodore this was the right intersection. All she saw were road and trees and more trees.

"You're sure this is the right place?" Davyn asked. The car was bumping over roots and rocks, like driving over a washboard. There wasn't much of a road. Reg could see where one had once existed, but it had become very overgrown, and whatever track had once been marked there was almost completely faded.

"This is the way," Theodore assured him.

In another minute, there was nowhere else to go. Large trees towered over them on every side. Reg had no idea where the road had gone. Had it always been a dead end, or had nature taken over and erased every sign of it?

"We get out here," Theodore announced. He bounced on the truck seat, waiting for Reg and Davyn to get out so he could disembark.

"Here?" Reg demanded. She hoped that the Oathstone was nearby. She didn't fancy hiking through the dense forest for miles looking for it. It could take days to get through the thick woods, and they only had two days. And she had hoped not to have to camp overnight, though she had known that it was a possibility. No one would want to go home and come back after fighting their way through the forest and start all over again the next day.

Reg silently climbed down from the truck and retrieved her backpack from the bed of the truck. She had an overwhelming urge to open it up and check the contents, worried that she did not have everything she would need for the quest or for an overnight stay.

She had packed food as well as a sleeping bag that compressed into a little tiny ball. She always worried about food. That she wouldn't have it when she needed it. It would run out or be spoiled, and she would go hungry. But she was only going to be gone for two days; she wouldn't starve to death even if they did stay overnight. And it was Florida. There were probably fruit trees around there somewhere. Or something else edible.

And if there were not, Reg could provide food for herself. Harrison had taught her as a child how to call food to her to prevent her from starving to death when he was not there to look out for her.

"This is it?" Julian asked, looking around at the dense woods. The morning heat was setting in. "We're going in from here?"

"Where did *your* research say it was?" Reg asked.

Julian scowled. "I didn't have a lot of time for my research. I found mentions of the Oathstone, but nothing that indicated exactly *where* it was. Does he know?" He nodded to Theodore. "Does he know *exactly* where it is?"

Reg was irritated by his asking about Theodore instead of addressing him directly. If he was used to talking to nearly extinct creatures, hadn't he learned how to talk to them? To get the stories direct from the horse's mouth?

"This is the right place," Theodore said calmly. He looked up at the sky and then pointed. "East of the Crossroads."

CHAPTER TWENTY-SIX

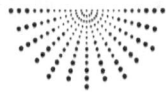

*R*eg had to accept that Theodore knew where he was going. He was the only one of them who did. If, as Corvin and Sarah had warned, he was just making it all up and had no idea where to look, they would have a long hike in a beautiful setting. Good exercise.

Davyn and Julian grabbed their daypacks as well. Theirs were smaller than Reg's. She would be the slowest one in the company. They would have to follow her pace.

Theodore led the way, and Reg focused on keeping a steady pace despite all the obstacles. Nothing seemed to slow Theodore down. His body seemed to be fluid, just flowing through the rocks and undergrowth that Reg and the others had to navigate over and around. He could go like that all day. He wouldn't get tired. He didn't need rest or sustenance. But the rest of them did. The ground was carpeted with vibrant green ferns, their fronds unfurling in delicate spirals. Ancient cypress trees stood sentinel, their gnarled knees draped with Spanish moss in ghostly tendrils.

Sunlight filtered through the dense canopy overhead, casting dappled patterns on the ground where bright yellow and lavender wildflowers added splashes of color to the lush greenery. A few iridescent dragonflies darted here and there, a sign that there was water nearby.

As they trudged on, Reg couldn't help but marvel at how alive the woods felt, the rustle of leaves overhead mingling with bird songs and the distant tap of a woodpecker. A bead of sweat trickled down her back as she pressed forward.

Reg saw a flash of movement in the trees and turned her head to look. It was there, and then it was gone. An animal, probably. But by the time she got her eyes focused, it had disappeared. Maybe a deer.

"What was that?" Davyn asked. "Did you see something?"

"I thought I did. I don't know."

"I thought I did too."

They were more vigilant after that, heads turning back and forth on a swivel. Eyes alert. Reg shaded her eyes from the sun. She should have brought a hat with a visor. She had sunglasses, but the forest was shadowy and dim, with little sunlight making it through the thick canopy of trees to reach them on the ground.

"There it is again!" Reg pointed, and everyone tried to make out what it was before it disappeared again. A dark shadow, low to the ground. Not a deer; it was shorter than that but still a good size. An animal? A panther like she had run into in the Everglades? Another animal like a lynx or a fox?

Or a wolf?

As soon as Reg thought it, she reached out to the mind of the wolf.

Who is there?

What are you doing here? The response came back. The voice and personality were feminine. Familiar.

Very familiar.

Zora?

Who are you looking for? If you wanted to see someone from the pack, why didn't you come to us?

Reg held up her hands to the others to make sure they stopped and understood she was communicating with the wolf and didn't do anything to distract her or threaten her friend.

We are not here to talk to you, Reg informed Zora, reluctant to explain why they were there. *We are… hiking.*

A snort of derision from Zora. She approached them, a slow lope through the woods. Like Theodore, she almost seemed liquid, flowing around the rocks and trees.

Two warlocks and a psychic out for a hike in the woods? Zora challenged. *And whatever that is?*

A homunculus.

She stopped a few yards away and shifted from her wolf form to human, allowing her to converse more easily with all of them at the same time, without the need for Reg's telepathy.

"What are you doing here?" Zora repeated. "Why did you come here?"

"We are… looking for an artifact that was left here a long time ago. We hope… that it will help unite the wolves with the warlocks."

"Unite them?" Zora's tone was heavy with disbelief. "*Unite* them?"

"Yes, that's what we are hoping. To put an end to the friction between the two clans. We don't want the cubs to have to deal with bullying and violence when they go into town. We don't want there to be any more curses or attacks. We want to live together in harmony like we were before. Or at least, peacefully coexisting."

"You will never unite the warlocks and the wolves," Zora disagreed. "They do not want to come to an accord. If they do not want to agree, they will not. Eventually, it will turn into a full-blown war. One that will not end until all wolves are dead or gone."

Fear clutched at Reg's chest. She shook her head. "No. We can't let that happen. We won't let that happen."

"It is inevitable."

"We have been here before," Theodore said. "This is not the first time the wolves and the warlocks have fought over the same thing. Vargrena and Drakskald forged the Oathstone. They swore to each other's clans. They brought peace to both of their tribes."

Zora's eyes flickered. "The Oathstone?" she repeated. "That is a fairy tale. Told to cubs at bedtime."

"It was real," Theodore insisted. "It *is* real. And it is here. We can use it to bring peace about once again."

"It is a dream," Zora said. "A hopeful dream that someone made up years ago."

"Will you help us find it?" Theodore demanded.

Reg caught her breath. The most she could hope for was that Zora would not stop them, but would let them go on in their foolish quest for a stone that did not exist. After all, what harm would it do to search for something that could never be found?

She would never have dared to ask Zora to join them.

Zora turned to Theodore, lifting her chin slightly as though she were catching his scent on the breeze. She looked at Reg, tilting her head slightly to the side.

"Help you find it?"

Reg nodded and repeated the invitation. "We need all the help we can get. If you want to come along to see what we find and help us out... I would love to have you along."

"You will not find the Oathstone."

"Maybe not," Reg agreed. "Maybe it is just a fairy tale. But it wouldn't hurt to come along with us, would it?"

"I am supposed to be watching for trouble. Guarding the perimeter."

"Then you should probably come with us to make sure we don't get into any trouble. If you just let us through and don't come with us, who knows what trouble we could get into."

"Humans are like puppies," Zora agreed dryly. "Always getting into everything. They can never be trusted to behave themselves."

"Yes," Reg agreed. "And some of us get into more trouble than others."

"It is no wonder you get along so well with Fenris. He is so independent. Never wants to listen to wiser heads."

"Come with us. Theodore knows the way. Or most of the way."

"I don't know." Zora touched her temple. "Let me think."

Reg could tell she was doing more than just thinking about the situation. She was communicating with other wolves about what she should do. She blocked her thoughts from Reg, so Reg could not tell exactly what she was asking them, but she was not about to leave her post guarding the werewolf lands to chase some fairy tale. She wasn't an impulsive human, but a wise, thoughtful wolf.

Reg was glad to take a break from the trudge through the woods. Even though it was relatively flat land and they had just barely started, it was much more arduous than Reg had expected. She hoped they wouldn't be walking for hours. She wouldn't be able to move the next day, let alone find some treasure and outwit whatever measures were guarding it.

Zora lowered her hand. "Okay. I will come with you and keep an eye on you. One of the others will take my place here."

They started on their way again. Zora was slower in human form than her wolf form, no longer skimming through the forest as though she were as insubstantial as Theodore; but she still walked faster than Reg, even in flowing skirts. Reg had even dressed for the occasion, leaving her long, colorful skirts at the cottage and sporting khakis. She didn't wear shorts even though it was very warm, figuring there would be bugs, saw grass, poison ivy, and other hazards she hadn't thought of. Best to protect her tender human skin, especially the injury to her calf that was still healing.

Zora must have really good shoes, because she was really moving.

CHAPTER TWENTY-SEVEN

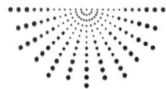

*T*heodore, is it much farther?" Reg called for another break and drank half a bottle of water. She was beginning to think everyone in the company could move faster than she could. And were in better shape than she was. Davyn was a desk jockey. Something to do with insurance claims. How could he be in better shape than she was?

"We are almost there," Theodore told Reg. Of course, he wasn't sweating or out of breath. He didn't actually have a body of flesh and blood. He didn't have to sweat or breathe or eat or drink. He couldn't twist his ankle or hurt himself in any of the other creative ways Reg seemed to manage every two minutes. Ruan had once told her she sounded like a buffalo crashing through the bush. She didn't think she was *that* bad, but hiking was definitely not one of her strengths.

"How much longer will it take to get there?"

She knew Theodore wasn't a GPS, but she needed some kind of assurance that they would get there sooner or later. Preferably sooner.

"It depends how many times we stop," Theodore said. He didn't mean it in a rude way and gave no indication that he was impatient with her constant need for breaks. He just meant he didn't have all the information he needed to calculate it.

"We'll get there today?" Reg demanded. She wiped her arm across her sweaty brow. She was regretting that she had packed so much into her backpack. She had wanted to be prepared, but now she was just overburdened.

"Are we going to continue to walk?" Theodore returned.

"Yes. If we keep going at the same pace we have been, will we get there today?"

"I haven't been there before. I am following clues and signposts, not a map with a scale."

"So you don't know how far it is?"

"No."

"You said we are almost there!"

"Yes," Theodore agreed. "We are almost there. I am looking for the last signpost on my list."

"The last one?"

"Yes."

"Then we will get there today."

"It depends how far we have to go to get to it."

Reg growled in frustration.

"I'm sure we'll get there soon," Davyn assured her. "If this is the last step, we are probably almost there. All that Theodore is trying to tell you is that the distance between two clues could be two meters or two hundred miles. But I don't think it's two hundred miles," he hastened to add. "That was just an example. So far, the signposts have been fairly close together, so I don't think you have to worry."

"You know how far apart the signposts have been?"

"I've been watching Theodore and paying attention to what he is looking for and how long it takes to get there."

Reg had been doing little more than watching where she put her feet down, trying not to trip, step in a hole or puddle, or make a fool of herself. She had been paying little attention to what Theodore was doing as he led her through the woods. A good thing she wasn't Hansel or Gretel, wandering off and getting lost in the woods because she had no idea where she was. Getting gobbled up by a wicked witch.

She took a few more gulps of water. "So you think we'll be there soon?"

"I think we're most of the way there. One more signpost should mean that we're within half a mile. But that's no guarantee, just a guess."

"Another half mile." Reg sighed and picked up her backpack. "Okay. I can do that. Let's go find it."

Theodore looked happy to be on his way again. He didn't have to carry anything or get tired. He could keep going all day and didn't understand her need for breaks or why she was getting so tired, hot, and cranky.

Davyn gave Reg a pat on the back as she walked by him. Her shirt stuck to her skin, pasted in place by her sweat. Davyn's hand did not linger on her back and she understood why. Ugh.

"This is so much fun," Reg told him. "Why didn't you just tell me no? Why did I think I could just walk in here and find the Oathstone after hundreds of years? If the werewolves don't even know it is here, how do I think I can find it?"

"You have a good guide. Hopefully, he'll be able to take us there. I'm hoping it won't be too hard to find once Theodore gets us into the right vicinity."

Reg had been resisting the idea that Theodore could not identify *exactly* where the Oathstone was. She pictured him walking her up to a clearing, and they would find the Oathstone in the center of it. But in her experience with quests, getting into the right area would only be the first step. There would be a series of challenges to pass once they got there. Would Reg be up to them? Would they be physical challenges? Mental? Magical? Did she have the right people in her company to complete the challenges?

Reg passed everyone else until she was the first person behind Theodore. She knew she would lag behind them all before too long. She needed to start in a position of strength. And she *would* succeed. They *would* find the Oathstone. They *would* successfully meet all the challenges. They *would* bring the Oathstone back, and they *would* be able to end the conflict between the warlocks and the wolves. That was, after all, what the stone was for.

They would succeed.

Maybe.

Either that, or fail miserably.

Maybe everyone else was right, and the Oathstone was only a fairy tale. It had never existed or it had been broken, deactivated, or lost. Or maybe they would all be killed trying to retrieve it.

Reg had fallen to the rear of the group again, and walked smack into Davyn when he stopped in front of her. Reg yelped and fell back, rubbing her nose.

"Sorry, ow! I didn't know you were going to stop."

Davyn turned to her, his face serious. "Sorry, Reg, I should have warned you." His hand was on her shoulder, steadying her as if worried she might fall. She wasn't *that* thrown by his stopping.

Reg pressed her finger to the bridge of her nose. It wasn't broken. She hadn't run into him that hard. But she'd broken it in the past and the jarring blow made the old injury pulse in pain.

"What's going on?" She looked past Davyn to see why they had stopped. The others were all stopped, Theodore and Zora looking ahead, Julian looking back at Davyn and Reg.

"Let's go see," Davyn said. He and Reg continued forward a few more feet to see what everyone else was looking at. Julian's arm snaked around Davyn's waist to hold him close, as though he thought Davyn might stray.

Reg saw that they were at the top of a ridge. The ground had been gently sloping upward for the last portion of their hike. Just enough that Reg knew she was working harder, her breath coming in tired puffs.

Now they all looked down the other side, which was far steeper. Reg wasn't sure if they had stopped just to survey the land and to find the easiest way down, or if the others had seen something important that she hadn't. Theodore knew what landform or signpost he was looking for but hadn't shared it with Reg.

"What is it?" Reg asked.

Although it was steep, it didn't seem like it would be too hard to navigate their way down. Harder to get up again, but maybe they wouldn't need to. There might be another way out. Or it might not be until the next day, when she had recovered some of her energy.

"The Lake of Whispers," Theodore announced.

Reg looked down the slope. She saw the grass and short brush just below the ridge they stood on, forest to the right, another ridge on the other side of the bowl, and a wash of rocks and scrubby, hardy little bushes to the left. What she did not see was any water.

"Lake? What lake?"

Theodore gestured at the hollowed-out valley below. "That lake."

"I think it used to be a lake, Reg," Davyn explained. "Now it is dry. Climate change, or just the way landforms continuously change over hundreds of years. Maybe a beaver dammed the flow of the spring that used to feed this lake, and there is a new pond on the other side," he motioned to the ridge on the far edge, across from them.

Reg tried to envision it. She could see how it might have looked. The wash of stones might have once been the shore or floor of the lake. The bowl shape of the valley had once been full of water. The Lake of Whispers.

"Okay. So we found the Lake of Whispers. Good thing you guys are smart enough to recognize this as a dry lake, so we don't keep looking for something that isn't there. Where do we go from here?"

"This is where we stop," Theodore said, looking down into the valley. "This is the place."

"This is where we find the Oathstone? Really?" Despite her fatigue, hope rose in Reg's heart, and she had a burst of new energy. This was it. She had hiked as far as she needed to. She had made it. Just a careful walk down the slope into the lake, and they would find the Oathstone... where? On an island in the middle? Was there a shrine or temple somewhere close by? Or an X marking the spot where it was buried?

Theodore nodded. He looked at them, then started moving

down the other side of the ridge. Reg let the others go ahead of her and watched their various attempts to navigate down the steeper land. Julian seemed to have found the easiest route, so she followed him, alternating between watching her feet to make sure she didn't slip or trip, and watching him to see which way he was going and whether he was having any problems.

They had to change direction as they got towards the bottom, and Theodore headed toward the wash of smooth stones at the edge of the lake. He looked out over what was now a field of rocks, his expression unreadable.

"Where do we go now?" Reg prompted.

He pointed at the rocks. Reg couldn't see an altar or shrine or anything special. His eyes were probably better than hers. He knew what he was looking for.

"What? Where?"

"I don't know."

"What do you mean, you don't know?" Reg demanded. She looked at the others in the company, wondering whether she were missing something obvious that everyone else saw. But they just all looked back at her with frowns or blank expressions.

"It is here," Theodore told her. "But I don't know how to find it amongst all the other stones."

Reg looked at the field of stones with mounting horror. It was one thing to be looking for a temple, shrine, or special marking to indicate the location of the important artifact. Finding one specific stone among hundreds or perhaps thousands of stones was quite another.

If the Oathstone was there, it was no wonder no one had managed to find it. Even if they looked every day for a hundred days, they might not be able to find it.

Reg and her company had one day.

CHAPTER TWENTY-EIGHT

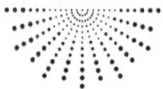

For a while, they all just stood around, looking at the lake stones. They didn't speak. No one swore. Reg walked to the edge of the wash of stones and picked up a few of them, checking to see what she had to work with.

There were stones ranging from pebbles to large rocks that she would not be able to move. Most fell into the range of fist-sized to watermelon-sized. They were mostly smooth and roughly round in shape. No special markings or coloring. Nothing that immediately spoke to her as being magical or significant.

Reg dropped the ones she had picked up.

"Okay." She sighed. "So how was the Oathstone described in the stories? What exactly are we looking for?"

Theodore gazed out over the field of rocks. "Small enough to fit into the hand of a man. Larger than the paw of a wolf."

About the size of a baseball, Reg guessed. Maybe a little smaller. That eliminated the largest and smallest rocks, but still left hundreds to be considered.

"Anything else? Color? Type of rock? Special properties?"

"There are runes carved into it," Theodore advised. "I assume they were deep enough to still be visible today. Nothing about the color or type of rock. I guess just… like all of these."

Runes. Well, that was something, anyway. But if it only had runes on one side, it might be face down. They would still have to pick them all up to see if they had markings.

They all looked at the huge area that was covered by rocks. There was no way they could pick up every one of them and see whether they had runes carved on them. And no guarantee that the runes had been carved deeply enough to have survived however many years it had been since they were made. If it had been in the lake, worn by the movement of the water and the sand, the runes might have been erased over time.

"You can do a find," Theodore suggested to Reg.

Reg remembered he had asked her about that before. She was good at finding things. It had long been a talent. When a foster father had lost a watch and Reg found it in the possessions of one of the other foster kids in the house, when elderly clients were missing precious possessions, when Reg had been scatterbrained and forgotten where she had put something down or hidden it somewhere safe… she was very talented in finding them. She had used this gift when looking for the fairy Calliopia, when Sarah's emerald had been stolen, and other times since then.

But it wasn't like magic on TV, when she just waved her hands or a magic wand around and whatever she was looking for glowed or tinkled or appeared in front of her. She still had to search, and just let herself be pulled to the object she sought. Like when she stared at a word search puzzle, and her eyes were drawn to one spot before she knew why, and a word was cleverly hidden there so well that her conscious mind would never have been able to find it. Still, her subconscious mind immediately identified the pattern of letters.

"Yes, of course," she assured him, more confidently than she felt. Of course she could find the Oathstone among the hundreds or thousands of stones there just by focusing her consciousness on her desire. It would be a cinch.

She knew she would be lucky to be able to use her powers to find it. More than likely, she would be blocked from finding it by some counterspell. Whoever had hidden it would not have wanted just anybody to come in and use their powers to find it.

Theodore nodded and waited. Everyone looked at her, waiting for her to do her thing.

"Uh… this is a little awkward," Reg said, her cheeks heating. "I'm going to need a little space and time to prepare. This isn't a magic trick, you know."

They all looked away from her, pretending they hadn't been paying any attention to her. And that was just as awkward as when they had all been staring at her.

"Why doesn't everyone pick a side to start searching?" Reg suggested. "There's no point in us all just standing around like idiots. It will take time for me to find it, even with a find spell."

Davyn took charge. "Yes, let's organize a search. There are four of us in addition to Reg. Let's each take a side of the rock field and start working from the edge toward the center."

Reg ignored them as they organized themselves, and each of them started to search for the Oathstone. It was a massive job. Davyn had told them to work from the edges to the center, but Reg couldn't see how they could even search one edge thoroughly. But Davyn was getting everyone out of the way, which was what she had needed. She walked toward the rock field aimlessly. She unfocused her eyes and wandered along the edge, not even looking at the rocks, just feeling with her heart, letting her consciousness flow out over the rock field, thinking of the runes and how the rock would look and how it would feel in her hand.

She tried to picture it as clearly as possible and was suddenly filled with heat and light. The Oathstone resolved in her mind's eye. She could see it as clearly as if she held it in her hand. The size, shape, and texture of it. The shape of the runes. She didn't know what they meant, but she could see them clearly. They had not been worn away by the passage of time.

Reg tried to control her breathing and to stay focused on the stone. She turned slowly, reaching out with all her senses, waiting for the stone to tug at her and pull her over to it.

But she couldn't locate it amongst all the rocks. She didn't feel pulled in any particular direction.

She kept concentrating on the bright, detailed picture in her mind. She tried to enlarge it, to see the rocks and terrain around it. There were many other rocks around it, all the same general size, shape, and color. There was nothing to differentiate them other than the runes and the power she felt from the stone.

She looked out over the field and tried to identify the area she was looking at in her mind to fit them together like a puzzle. Here was the Oathstone, and here was where it fit into the great wash of lake stones.

But it didn't work. Reg shook her head, frustrated, trying to clear out any cobwebs, any shred of doubt or hesitance that was holding her back. She *needed* to find the Oathstone. It was their only hope. The only way to end the tensions between the warlocks and the werewolves. She tried to pull the stone to her. If it didn't want her to come to it, maybe she could pull it to herself. She didn't need to see the spot where it was nestled among the other rocks. *She could hold it in her hand. She could feel it in her hand.*

But it wasn't there. It didn't appear when she called it to her.

Reg sat down. She was hot and tired. She had done a lot that day and had not slept the night before. Chances were, she needed some rest, some food and water, and then she would have the strength to complete her task. She slid off her backpack and opened it. She cracked open a bottle of water and took a few swigs. She had crackers, granola bars, and other ready-to-eat snacks, including Fenris's favorite pepperoni sticks. She sat there eating, watching the others work their way around the dry lake, beginning their impossible task.

After a few minutes of resting, eating, and rehydrating, she was definitely feeling better. Stronger, more focused, more like herself. She called to the stone again, but it did not come to her. She pictured it once more,

It was just as clear as it had been the first time. Very detailed, as if she held it in her hand. She could see where it lay with the other stones. But she could not tell where it was in the great wash of rocks.

"Come on," Reg complained to herself. "It isn't even that hard.

If you can see it, you can find it. Just zoom out a bit more. See the landmarks around it."

When that didn't work, she tried again, "Which side is it closest to? Which big rock is it closest to?"

But anything she did to try to nail down the exact location failed.

It wasn't Reg. There were obviously counterspells protecting it, preventing it from being found through those means.

After a while, Davyn approached Reg. She was sitting slumped over, staring out over the tumbled mass of rocks, trying to imagine just how many there were and how long it would take to thoroughly search each one to find the Oathstone. She knew it was impossible. A manual search would only turn up the Oathstone if it wanted to be found. She knew she should be searching with the others, but she also knew there was no point in it.

"No luck, Reg?" Davyn asked gently.

"I can see it... but I can't find it. I can't call it. I don't know what else to do."

"You think it *is* here?" Davyn asked, looking out over the rocks.

"Yes, it's here. But if it doesn't want to be found... Or someone else didn't want it to be found..."

Davyn nodded. "Makes it kind of hard, huh? Okay, I'm going to call the others in. The sun is setting, and you'll be surprised at how quickly it will get dark out here. Not like in the town where there are always lights."

"Okay," Reg agreed. There was certainly no point in looking for the rock in the dark.

"We'll sleep on it. Maybe one of us will have a good idea in the morning when we are fresh. Right now, everyone is tired and frustrated."

Reg nodded her agreement and didn't say anything. What else was there to say? She didn't know where the stone was. She didn't know how to get it. The others didn't know how to get it. Their quest would be a failure.

CHAPTER TWENTY-NINE

*W*hen everyone gathered together and broke out their snacks, there was a festive atmosphere. It was strained at first, Davyn pushing for everyone to change their attitudes and enjoy their time together. Reg didn't want to be there with Julian. Davyn didn't want to be with Theodore. Zora probably wanted to be at home with her cubs, not supervising a group of helpless humans searching for a rock.

But the snacks were good. Davyn let Reg start a campfire, and it immediately boosted her mood. She loved playing with fire and had always enjoyed a good campfire, even before she knew anything about being a firecaster. She put her powers to use calling a package of extra-large marshmallows to her, and everyone was occupied for a while finding the perfect long, straight stick and trimming off the bark so they could be used for toasting sticks. Theodore had never experienced a campfire or roasted marshmallows. He took off his sunglasses as it got darker. In the dimness of the fire, he didn't look as inhuman. His eyes were dark hollows, but it wasn't obvious that they were so different from everyone else's.

With an apology, Zora shifted into her wolf shape. Reg knew it was her preferred form. It probably took effort for her to hold her human form, and Reg imagined that releasing it and returning to her wolf form was like slipping into a comfy pair of jammies at the end of the day, putting all the stresses and expectations aside, putting off everything uncomfortable and just letting herself be herself. She sprawled beside the fire, apparently enjoying its heat, appearing just as Reg thought the earliest domesticated dogs must have looked. Wolflike, enjoying the warmth and the companionship of the campfire.

"You can hear them," Julian commented.

Reg cocked her head and listened. At first, she only heard crickets and the sound of the wind rustling the trees. But then she caught snatches of wolf howls in the distance. The wolves were too far away for Reg to read their thoughts. The wild sound sent a shiver through her.

Zora raised her head and listened, but did not jump up to join them.

There was no conversation as they listened to the wolves howling back and forth. Reg wondered whether they were on the hunt.

They seemed to be drawing closer. Zora gathered herself and sat up, sitting on her haunches and sniffing the wind, her ears pointed alertly toward the howling voices.

The wolves were getting close enough for Reg to sense brief snippets of thoughts. She swallowed and looked at Zora, worried. Davyn frowned.

"What's going on, Reg?"

"It's… I don't know. It's like… they're fighting."

Davyn and Julian tensed, sitting up and looking toward the howls as they drew closer.

"Fighting warlocks?" Julian asked, his voice cracking.

"No." Reg held her fingers to her temples, trying to separate the voices and understand what was happening. "Fighting each other."

Zora's head turned in Reg's direction. *No!*

Reg nodded. "Can't you hear them?"

Something is going on… I hear the warning howls… but I can't tell what it is.

It hadn't occurred to Reg before that she did not necessarily hear the same things from the wolves telepathically as they heard from each other, either in their howls or in their minds. They had never sat down and discussed werewolf communication. She had just assumed that they heard the same thing she did.

"Why would they be fighting?" she asked Zora.

Zora was sniffing the air, trying to gather what she could from the wind. *There has been... talk lately about whether Aleph is the right wolf for the job. With all the unrest and the problems between the wolves and the warlocks, It has been suggested that... He might not be the best alpha under these circumstances.*

They want to make someone else alpha?

Zora gave a brief nod.

There is talk that he is too traditional. That a younger, more worldly wolf would know better how to handle the friction and participate in the talks, smooth things over and come to some kind of peace treaty.

Reg shook her head in bewilderment. She had never considered that there was any internal strife within the wolf pack. They had always seemed to be of one accord when she heard from them, and she had always believed that whatever Aleph said would go. He had always seemed confident and authoritative to Reg.

"What is it, Reg?" Davyn asked. They couldn't, of course, hear Zora's thoughts.

"It's a coup," Reg said. "Pack politics... some of the wolves don't think that Aleph should be alpha."

Davyn's face looked pale even in the rosy light of the fire. "They're going to take him down?"

Reg listened for a moment. "I guess they're trying to. I don't know whether they will be successful. He still has wolves on his side." She shook her head. "I don't know how anyone else could do a better job of leading the pack or negotiating with the warlocks. At the town hall meeting... he seemed confident, acted like he knew what he was doing."

"But he hasn't been able to resolve things. Maybe they think that another alpha would be able to. Things have been getting pretty tense."

"More than tense," Reg declared, thinking of how Fenris had been bullied. The warlocks had clearly been in the wrong. Yet they would undoubtedly turn the tables and say that the wild young werewolf had attacked them unprovoked, and he had the injury to prove it. Fenris had not sustained any physical injury during the confrontation. "Things are getting really bad."

"The wolves undoubtedly know that. They know that some of the warlocks will do everything possible to drive them out. They will want to strike back. Aleph is a cautious old wolf. He would counsel against physical violence against the warlocks. The younger, less-experienced wolves…"

Zora's head snapped to the side. She quickly sniffed the air and rose to her feet, her muscles tense.

Reg saw another wolf loping toward them. A long, liquid stride that ate up the distance. From the time she could see him approaching from the trees to the moment he reached the fire was mere seconds.

"Aleph." Reg stood as well, and the others followed her example. Reg didn't know whether it was good etiquette for her to be towering above him, but it seemed more respectful to be on her feet than sitting on the ground. "Is everything okay? We could hear… I could hear…"

CHAPTER THIRTY

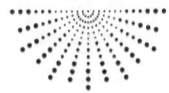

A leph looked them over. Despite all that Reg had heard, he did not seem to be in any great hurry. Reg had worried when he appeared so suddenly that he was running away from a pursuer, but no one else burst out of the trees behind him and he did not seem to be out of breath.

Zora has passed on word of your quest.

Reg nodded.

Aleph looked down the slope at the long pale wash of rocks. *If you are looking for a stone, this is a good place for it,* he observed.

Reg was impressed that he could joke around when everything was in an uproar. His position as the leader of the pack was in jeopardy, and he had stopped to find out what they were doing and to tease her about it.

"There are a lot of rocks here," she admitted. "But you know that I am looking for a special one. The Oathstone."

A fairy tale for young cubs. I outgrew the need for such bedtime stories long ago.

"It does exist," Reg told him.

His yellow eyes glittered in the firelight. *Long-ago uttered oaths have little to do with us today. Whatever oaths the warlocks and wolves once made have now been broken, and we are once again at war. Perhaps we are incompatible. Wolves and humans are too unlike each other to live so closely together in harmony.*

"You can't blame the entire race for what a few have done," Reg argued.

Reg, Zora reproved.

"You don't want to be judged by what October did, do you?" Reg pointed out. "Just because he attacked Corvin, that doesn't mean that all wolves will attack humans unprovoked. That was just one wolf. He might have thought that he was preventing harm, but he knew better than to ask you to join him."

It was more than just one wolf, Aleph said. *But you are right. If he had come to me I would have said no. Not just for myself but for all the pack. What he did, whatever his reasons, did far more harm than good.*

"I think we can still unwind it. Maybe we can't reverse all the harm that has been done, but I think that we can reverse the curse on Corvin and reconcile the wolves and the warlocks."

Aleph's head swayed back and forth. *You have been misled by children's fairy tales. It is foolishness. What happens now, happens.*

He looked back the way he had come. *I don't have much longer. Fare thee well. Get out of this place tomorrow. Do not stay.*

He loped back off into the trees and disappeared from sight.

Reg looked at the others.

"What did he say?" Davyn asked.

Reg hesitated, thinking about how to express it. She didn't want them to leave before they were finished their quest. Maybe they couldn't find the Oathstone in a day. But they had to try. Things were getting desperate.

"He didn't believe that the Oathstone would be any help. But he doesn't know for sure. He can't see the future."

"Is he okay? You said they were fighting, but he looked okay."

Reg looked at Zora, whose senses were much sharper than hers, and who was more familiar with the wolf culture and Aleph himself.

Thick fur can cover many wounds, Zora told her. *He was matted and breathing quickly. The other wolves are not far behind him.* Her nose pointed in the direction of the howls and yelps in the distance. They seemed far away to Reg, but she knew they were closer than they sounded.

She relayed the information to Davyn. "We need to find the Oathstone. We can end this."

"I don't know if there is any hope of it," Davyn warned. "Either that we will find the artifact or that it will make any difference to this situation."

"I know you don't believe in it. But I've seen it. I know it is here."

"But can you find it?"

Reg pressed her lips together. She sat back down by the fire again. "I'm not giving up."

"And neither are we. But the chances that we will be able to find it are… very slim."

Reg couldn't think that she had gotten all the way there and wouldn't be able to find it. She had seen it for a reason. It wasn't just an obscure story; the wolves still told it to their children. She had seen it. That was a sign to her that they would find it. She couldn't believe that she would see it so clearly and not be able to find it.

Tomorrow.

They had one day. They had to make the most of it. Aleph's leadership hung by a thread. Corvin was doing nothing to lead the coven. Both organizations needed the help of the magical artifact. The guidance of their ancestors. It was just the thing to bring them together and help them to make a pact that would bring peace back to Black Sands.

Julian checked the time. He and Theodore had been very quiet during the discussion. "If we're going to get an early start in the morning, we should probably hit the hay soon."

Reg gazed at Julian. "Do you believe in the Oathstone?"

He knew of the stories, but did he believe it existed or offered them any hope? Julian didn't answer for a few seconds. "I didn't come to see you fail," he said eventually.

So he did believe her. And not like Davyn, who acknowledged that the Oathstone might exist but didn't think she had any chance finding it or making it work for her. Julian expected her to succeed in her quest. To find the Oathstone, use it to cure Corvin, and broker peace between the two factions. Julian thought she could do it, even if no one else did.

Her old nemesis.

She looked at him with suspicion. Did he really believe her or was he just saying that? She waited for the other shoe to drop. He thought that she would succeed, but then he would throw the book at her for removing an ancient artifact from a protected werewolf sanctuary? She would succeed and he would take all the credit? How many different ways could he use her success to puff himself up or to hurt her? That would be the Julian she knew. The schemer who always had a way to make himself out to be superior to her. Who always had a new way to hurt her or keep her down. It was like he thought any success on her part was a personal affront or challenge to his reputation.

"When I succeed, what are you going to do?"

"What am I going to do?" Julian shrugged, smiling innocently. "I will applaud you. We will all be in your debt if you manage to bring an end to this conflict."

"But...?"

"But nothing. Can't you just take a compliment, Reg? I don't give a lot of them, you know."

No, he didn't.

"Julian's right, we should start getting ready for bed," Davyn agreed. "I know you're a night owl, Reg, but you were up early this morning, so maybe you'll be able to go to sleep early tonight, and wake up tomorrow morning."

Reg faked a yawn and agreed. She didn't know whether she would be able to sleep at all. Despite all the work and the hiking, she was still feeling the boost of energy she had gotten from Corvin. She was anxious, worrying about how they were going to find the Oathstone in the morning. Everybody but Julian believed she would fail. How could she find something that had been lost for centuries in two days? Theodore had been a help, of course. He had brought her to the right place. But his studies could only get them so far.

Reg thought about Theodore's hunger for reading. He could read thousands of pages in a day. And he didn't need sleep. Did he need light?

"Theodore, let's go for a walk," she suggested.

Theodore looked at her. She had caught him in the middle of shoving three roasted marshmallows into his mouth at once. His eyes were huge as he looked at her in alarm. Maybe he thought he was in trouble.

"I just want to talk to you," Reg told him. "Finish what's in your mouth. I didn't mean to interrupt you. Do you like the marshmallows?"

She didn't know whether he would have the ability to appreciate them or not. She had never seen him eat before. She didn't know if he actually had a digestive tract or taste buds. He was, after all, created through alchemy rather than having been conceived and grown through the usual means.

Theodore chewed, his cheeks puffing out because his mouth was so full. Reg waited until he swallowed several times and was able to speak again.

"Yes, they are very good," Theodore acknowledged.

"Have you eaten other foods?"

He shook his head. "I do not require feeding."

"But you liked it?"

Theodore looked down at his roasting stick, still smeared with marshmallow residue.

"It was very sticky."

"And soft and sweet."

"Very tasty," Theodore obliged. Did he mean it, or was he just saying what he thought she wanted to hear?

"Let's go for that walk."

Theodore nodded. He stood up and followed her. They walked

a good distance away from the rest of the company, so that they would not be overheard.

"You did a very good job finding out about the Oathstone," she told him. "That was really good research and I think it could really be the solution to our problems."

"The Oathstone is very powerful," Theodore agreed.

"But we're going to have a hard time finding it. There are so many rocks to look at in such a large area. Doing a find or a call didn't help."

"But you know it is here."

"Yes. I saw it. Saw what it looks like, but not where it is. It could still be anywhere out there." She motioned to the vast wash of stones.

"Humans are very slow searchers," Theodore acknowledged.

"Yes. I was just thinking that. How quick you are in reading and other tasks. How fast would you be at looking at all of those stones? Or all the ones that were the right size."

Theodore clicked, calculating. "Probably not in a day," he admitted, knowing her parameters. "Maybe… three. If that was all I was doing."

Reg sighed. It was not as quick as she had been hoping but, if he was that quick at processing all the rocks, then there was at least a chance that he would find the Oathstone the first day. And with Reg and the others looking as well, maybe they had a chance. Better than a one in three chance, which sounded pretty good.

"And if we have to leave you here, you can keep looking until you find it, and then come back to me and let me know?"

"Yes."

"And if anyone bothered you or tried to stop you, you could just disappear until they gave up."

"Yes," Theodore agreed again. "That is what you want me to do?"

"You don't need any sleep, so you could start right now."

"You are going to sleep with the others?"

"Well… I don't know about that. I'll wait until the others are asleep, and then maybe I'll come help you look for it. I brought a flashlight. It's not the most efficient way to search, but you never know, I might find something."

Theodore seemed to be cheered by the thought she was going to help him, not just leave him to do the job all alone for three days.

"Then we will do it together."

CHAPTER THIRTY-ONE

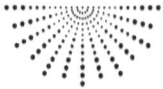

*W*hen the others started to wake up in the morning, Reg's fingers were already bruised and sore from searching for the Oathstone. Her back was killing her from bending over searching all night by the light of her flashlight. The battery had failed eventually, but then it started to get light out as the sun peeked over the horizon so she was able to just keep going.

She was grumpy and no further ahead than she had been when she had started. She didn't know how many stones Theodore had turned over. She hadn't counted how many she had searched through either. And it wasn't until the night was halfway through that she realized they had not done anything to mark the rocks they had already looked at. How could they know whether anyone was looking at the same ones again?

But she didn't have an answer to that, so she just kept going. She watched Theodore moving from time to time, his hands a blur as he moved from one stone to the next. He was much faster than she could ever hope to be, even in daylight. But she had nagging doubts. Was he looking at them carefully enough? Would he be able to see it in the darkness? What if he missed it?

"How can you be up already?" Davyn demanded when Reg returned to the place they had all laid their sleeping bags out the night before. The fire had gone out, but the embers were still warm. It would not be hard to get the fire going again, even if they were not firecasters. Not that they needed it. None of them was going to make a hearty pancake breakfast. They would each eat cold rations and get started on the work as quickly as possible.

Unless Reg surprised them all with breakfast from one of her favorite restaurants in town. She might at least have to get herself some good coffee.

Reg scowled at Davyn. "I've been helping Theodore."

They all knew she had given Theodore the assignment to search through the night. To search for twenty-four hours a day until he found it or someone forced him to stop.

"But you are never up this early in the morning, and you were up early yesterday too. Did you sleep at all?"

Reg looked for a way to suggest that she had gone to sleep and gotten all the rest that she needed without actually lying about it, but couldn't come up with anything. She shrugged. "Sleep is overrated."

"I've never heard you say that before. You're usually pretty determined to get your sleep."

"Well, I wasn't tired. It was more important to try to find the Oathstone."

Davyn looked across the rock bed at Theodore, who was still searching. It was obvious that they had not succeeded or, instead of scowling at him, Reg would be showing him their find.

"I don't know if there is much hope of us ever finding it, even if it is here."

"It is."

"I believe that it could be... but finding it is an impossible task. Even if you were to go through all of these rocks one at a time, you could miss it. And I don't see how any of us can do that, even Theodore. He still has limitations on how much he can do in a day."

"He can stay here to work on it after we are gone."

"I suppose he can." Davyn considered this for a moment and

didn't offer any opinion on whether that was a good idea or had any chance of being successful.

Reg was getting tired of being told that what she was trying to do was impossible. Or foolish. Or that even if it were found, the Oathstone would be of no help to them.

"You need a break," Davyn divined. "And maybe something to eat or drink."

"I'm really craving a caffeine hit," Reg admitted.

"Well, I've got some instant. If you want to get the fire going, I can brew some up."

She suspected he was suggesting that she light the fire, hoping it would put her in a better mood.

"I don't really want instant," Reg said. "I could get something good."

"I don't think anyone delivers out here."

"I could call it or send you home to make some."

"I thought you wanted to get an energy boost, not expend it."

"I want good coffee more."

Davyn rolled his eyes. "Well, I'm still going to make camp coffee for everyone. If you want something fancier, go ahead and get it. I want to keep everyone focused here. It probably takes the least amount of energy for you just to call one drink, not be transporting people all over the place."

Reg nodded. She sat down on her sleeping bag by the fire. Zora was awake and transformed into her human form to be able to talk to everyone and prepare for the day.

"There was no more trouble in the night?" she asked.

Reg shook her head. "Everything was quiet. All the wolf howls had died down by the time everyone went to sleep, and I didn't hear anything after that."

"Aleph didn't come back?"

Reg shook her head. "Did you expect him to?"

"I thought he might," Zora said. She smoothed her skirt thoughtfully.

"You don't think that means... anything happened?" Reg asked tentatively.

"It would be foolish to speculate. There is no one close at the moment, or I would ask. We will have to wait until we get closer to the pack or someone comes here."

"I hope nothing happened." Reg felt guilty. Here she was worrying about coffee and her bruised fingers, and how they were going to find the artifact, and Aleph had been fighting for his life. Or at least for his position in the pack. Had he succeeded or failed?

"I, too," Zora agreed.

"Where are the cubs? Will they be safe?"

"They are with my sister. She would not have been involved in any fighting; she is heavy with pup and would not leave my cubs."

Even though Zora claimed not to be worried, she still looked concerned.

There could always be collateral damage. Even if her sister and the cubs had tried to avoid the fighting, innocent bystanders could be hurt or injured during a conflict.

"I'm sure they're fine," Reg assured her.

Zora nodded, but she didn't agree or disagree.

Davyn reignited the fire when Reg didn't do it, and quietly made the coffee. It didn't smell half bad. A campfire always made everything taste better. Maybe she would try Davyn's coffee after all. It wasn't like she hadn't lived for years on instant coffee. When had she become such a coffee snob?

CHAPTER THIRTY-TWO

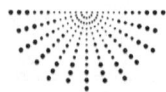

*J*ulian stirred as the smell of coffee drifted over to him. Sleeping, he looked young and innocent, his face almost angelic. It was hard to believe he was the same damaged bully Reg knew him to be.

Davyn handed Zora a mug of coffee and raised his brows at Reg. She nodded and took the mug he offered her. He sat down beside Julian and nudged him gently until he tensed and sat up, rubbing his eyes.

"What time is it? Did anyone find anything?" he demanded. "What's the news?"

"No news," Davyn told him. "We haven't found anything yet or heard from anyone."

Reg reached out to Theodore, inviting him to return to the fire while they figured out how to approach the problem. He disappeared from the rock field and rematerialized beside her.

"Coffee?" Davyn offered.

Theodore nodded without reservation. Davyn gave him a mug and he put it to his lips. After a couple of swallows, he spat and wiped his mouth with the back of his hand. "It is vile!" he objected.

Reg supposed that answered the question of whether he could

really taste or was just pretending to enjoy the marshmallows the night before.

"It's an acquired taste," she told Theodore with a laugh.

"Why would anyone want to acquire it?"

Everyone chuckled at that.

"Theodore and I have been looking throughout the night with no luck," Reg informed everyone. "There is no sign of it yet. No magical field protecting it, no rocks with runes. No kind of signpost."

She looked at Theodore for his confirmation of these facts.

Theodore nodded. "I have looked at many stones. It may take longer than I estimated to examine them all."

"How long?" Reg asked.

He shook his head. "Longer... maybe twice as long... maybe three times." He looked back at the wash of rocks. "It may be deeper in certain portions."

"You can't possibly look at every stone," Julian said.

"Theodore can," Reg insisted.

Julian shook his head dismissively. "It's not possible."

Reg sipped her coffee and put down the mug to rub her temples, hoping the caffeine would give her the boost she needed to address the others' doubts. She appreciated that they had all come to help her on her quest, even if they didn't believe that she would be able to accomplish what she had set out to do.

"Theodore... I need to know more about the story of the Oath-stone. Or maybe Zora can help." She looked from one to the other. "We need to be smart about this. If it was meant to be used, there must be a way to find it. There has to be something in the legend that tells us what to do."

"What makes you think it was meant to be found?" Julian challenged. "It seems to me that it has just been lost in time. No one had any use for it and it was discarded, whether they knew what it was or not. By that time, they had probably forgotten."

"No," Reg shook her head. "When I try to find it, there is a counterspell at work. It has been protected. Whoever put that spell on it knew what it was and knew that someone would be looking for it or would need to use it again in the future."

Julian's mouth twisted into a frown as he considered this. The lines across Davyn's forehead deepened. Zora sipped her coffee, considering. Though she had told Reg that it was just a fairy tale, she had not argued against the existence of the Oathstone since Reg had said she had seen it and that she knew it was there somewhere. She had looked diligently like the others but had not offered any suggestions.

"You said it was a story told to cubs," Reg said. "What are the details of the story? Does it say anything about how they hid or protected it? Or how to find it if it was needed in the future? They must have known that the peace between the warlocks and werewolves wouldn't last forever and that it would be needed again."

Zora nodded slowly. "It has been a long time since I heard the old legend. We have forgotten a lot of the traditional stories." She closed her eyes, concentrating.

"Vargrena, the she-wolf, and Drakskald, a powerful warlock made a pact. They created the Oathstone and endowed it with great powers. Powers to heal physical ailments as well as to mend the rift between the pack and the warlocks. Without it, the two sides could never have reconciled." She shrugged. "I don't know if that is true. That they could not have reconciled without the Oathstone. That was probably added later."

"This is what I learned, too," Theodore agreed, nodding. "It was a pact between the wolves and the warlocks. That is what I told you."

"Yes, you did," Reg agreed, not wanting him to think she didn't believe him. "And it was your research that got us here. We could not have made it without you. Especially discerning all the sign-posts to get here. That was amazing work. And we know that this is the place we are supposed to be. I saw it in my mind. But it is protected. We just need to figure out how and what we have to do to find it."

Reg looked at Zora. "There weren't any other parts to the

legend? About how they hid it? How people will need to be able to access it in the future?"

She shook her head. Reg bit her lip, looking out over the huge wash of rocks, wondering how they were going to find it. The "brute force" method of looking at every single rock was so labor intensive that it could not have been what the creators of the stone had planned. It was one thing for Theodore to take a week or two to look at every rock at his high speed, night and day. For a normal person, such a search might take years and never be resolved. There had to be another way.

"A she-wolf and a warlock." Reg looked at Zora and then at Davyn. "Did the two of you try looking together?"

Davyn raised his brows and looked at Zora. "We were looking at the field at the same time."

"But not together," Reg said slowly. "Could you... hold hands or something, and just walk over there? See if you see or feel anything different?"

Davyn rose to his feet. "I'm willing to try it." He extended a hand to Zora. "Would it bother you?"

She shrugged and took his hand. "No, of course not. Let us see."

They walked over to the edge of the rocks. Reg thought both of them were a little awkward, barely knowing each other but expected to act as if they were together. Reg stood up as well and followed at a distance. She didn't want to crowd them or hover, but she was curious whether the experiment would have any noticeable effect. Theodore walked with her, leaving Julian behind by the fire, nursing his mug of coffee. He probably didn't like Davyn holding Zora's hand. But he had wanted to be there.

Davyn was saying something to Zora, but Reg couldn't hear what it was. They walked along the edge of the formation and then ventured out into it, picking their way carefully across the rocks, which was difficult while holding hands.

Reg was bursting to ask them questions. But they would tell her when they knew something. She just had to wait.

Waiting was for suckers. She hated waiting.

"Davyn?" she called, "Anything?"

"Maybe," Davyn answered over his shoulder, immediately turning away from her again.

Reg hurried forward. Maybe what? Why didn't he say more than that?

"Maybe? Maybe you feel something? Is something different? Maybe?"

"Yeah. We're just going to go over there…"

"Is there something over there?" Reg climbed over the rocks, trying to catch up to them. There was no way they were leaving her behind on her own quest. She wanted to see the Oathstone the moment they found it. Or the moment they found anything that led to it.

She slipped a few times trying to catch up to them. Zora was a lot more sure-footed in a skirt than Reg was in pants.

"Did you see something?" She asked Davyn, puffing a little as she reached them. "Feel something?"

"We just both thought we should look over there." He pointed to a place in the rock bed that was a little more shadowed, scooped out to form a little hollow. It was right at the edge of the field, on the far side from the campfire.

"Is that it?" Reg asked eagerly.

"Reg, you're as bad as a little kid asking if we are there yet. We don't know. Not until we get there and have a look."

Reg wanted to run on ahead. Or transport herself across the rocks to the other side so she wouldn't have to wait and wouldn't have to trip over all those rocks. The last thing she needed was to fall on her face.

But as they got closer to the edge of the rock formation, something moved in the trees on the other side, slinking in the shadows.

CHAPTER THIRTY-THREE

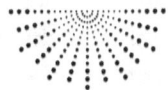

avyn!" Reg warned sharply.

Davyn looked around quickly, hearing the alarm in Reg's voice.

"In the woods," Reg told him. "There's something in the woods right across from you."

He focused on the shape in the shadows and pulled Zora slightly closer to him protectively.

"It is a wolf," Zora said, shaking her head. "It's okay."

They stopped, not going any farther. Reg's heart was pounding in her throat. The wolf—for wolf it was—came slowly out of the shadows of the woods, revealing itself.

Long flowing fur, iron gray, muzzle grizzled with white specks. Reg thought it was probably the oldest wolf she had ever seen. Not part of the pack, not one of the wolves she had helped to rescue, or, as far as she knew, one that had joined the pack since then. He was completely a stranger to her.

"Stop there," the wolf growled, though Davyn and Zora had already stopped moving. "Identify yourselves."

"I am Zora, daughter of Eryk and Gerwyna," Zora answered and proceeded to recite a more detailed pedigree. She then looked at Davyn.

"I am Davyn Smithy. A humble smithy," Davyn said with a brief bow.

"A smithy," the wolf sneered, not sounding like he believed it. "You cast fire?"

Davyn nodded. "I do."

The wolf paced back and forth along the edge of the stones. "I am Ulfrikarr, the guardian. Why have you come?"

"We look for the Oathstone," Zora said in a soft voice. "There is a conflict between the pack and the warlock coven. Things are getting worse instead of better despite our best efforts. We hope that the Oathstone could be used to help broker peace between our peoples."

"What conflict?" the old wolf demanded. "What has happened?"

Zora hung her head and didn't answer. Davyn waited for a moment before saying anything. Eventually, he spoke up. "A wolf attacked one of the members of the coven during our spring equinox ritual. He—and several others—attacked without provocation and cursed Corvin very grievously. There has been retaliation from some of the warlocks. A few incidents, each escalating, resulting in injuries. There is… some kind of infighting among the wolves too, even though those who attacked the warlocks have made themselves scarce."

"This is true?" Ulfrikarr asked Zora.

She nodded her agreement and did not attempt to give him any more details or an excuse for October's attack or the infighting among the werewolves.

"And who told you of the Oathstone?"

Zora and Davyn looked at each other. "I heard about it from the cradle," Zora said, "But I did not think of it as being real or the solution we needed. Our friend…" Zora looked over her shoulder at Reg, who had stopped at what she hoped was a respectful distance and was waiting to be invited forward before she got any closer. "Our friend Reg was the one who found out about the Oathstone and wanted to come look for it. She is a friend of the wolves as well as of the warlocks."

"A human friend of the wolves?"

"She rescued me and my pups from terrible abuse and moon madness. She saved the whole pack. She is a good friend to me and my cubs and has been concerned about us during these troubles."

"How did you know it was here?" Ulfrikarr demanded, deigning to speak to Reg directly. She took a few steps forward to be closer to him when she answered.

"I had help from my... from Theodore," Reg said, indicating the homunculus. He had his sunglasses on so that Reg hoped Ulfrikarr wouldn't ask additional questions like what was she doing with a homunculus that she hadn't created herself. She was starting to get tired of that particular question.

The old wolf continued to pace back and forth along what would once have been the shore of the large lake. Reg waited. Would he approve them and tell them they had made it to the next level? Would they be rejected as unworthy? What would it mean if he gave them the Oathstone? What would it mean if he turned them away? Would it be their last chance to impress him either way?

"It has been a very long time since anyone was interested in the Oathstone. I thought it had passed from all memory."

"It is still spoken of in story," Zora said, "though I did not think it was anything more than legend."

"And there are a few records," Reg contributed. "A few books that tell the old story. Theodore was able to piece it together and to bring us here. And then... I guessed that if a warlock and a wolf were working together... maybe they had a better chance of finding it than any of us working alone."

"Your efforts of last night were not very profitable," observed Ulfrikarr.

Reg's cheeks warmed. "You were there watching? You knew I was looking for it?"

"Not many people come here anymore. I was curious to see who you were."

"So... can we have the Oathstone? To restore Corvin and to negotiate peace between the two factions?"

"You must first promise me something."

CHAPTER THIRTY-FOUR

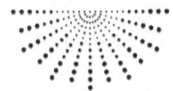

*R*eg swallowed. She looked at Davyn and Zora and saw the same anxiety in their faces that she felt. She did not know what was going to be required of her. The hunt for the Oathstone had not required any feats of courage or strength. Not yet, anyway. Only dogged persistence in the face of everyone telling her it couldn't be done and wouldn't matter if it could.

"I don't fight dragons," she told the old wolf jokingly.

Ulfrikarr just stared at her. Davyn gave Reg a disapproving look.

"I like dragons," Reg clarified. "I have a—we have—well, I don't know what you're going to ask, but I just had my coffee. I'm not quite one hundred percent yet."

"Reg," Davyn said in a low, tight voice. "Shut up."

Reg couldn't help giggling. She was so tense, it just bubbled out of her. She didn't mean to laugh.

"Well, Reg Rawlins, wolf friend, dragon friend, Vargfrid, I do not require more of you. But from Zora, daughter of Eryk and Gerwyna, I call on you to carry on the tradition of the story. Our cubs will forget if we do not tell them the old tales. They may be old and musty, not as entertaining as their new toys, but they have much to teach."

Zora nodded quickly. "Yes. Of course. I will teach the old tales. I am sorry I did not believe it myself, to begin with."

"And you, Davyn Smithy," It occurred to Reg for the first time that the wolf was speaking aloud to all of them so that Davyn could understand as well as Reg and Zora. Cool trick. "We do not trust warlocks easily. I will require your oath to do no harm to any wolf. If you do, you will be cursed and will lose everything."

Davyn nodded. "Of course. I have never harmed a wolf. I helped with the rescue and have not participated in any of the harassment of the wolves in town."

"What of the wolf who attacked your friend?"

"October?" Davyn shook his head. "He is gone. I did not retaliate, and I do not intend to." He paused. "Corvin is my brother in the coven, but he is not my friend. I have at times helped him, or he me, but we are not friends."

"If you do not keep your oath and raise your hand against any wolf, you will be cursed. And this is a curse that the Oathstone will not be able to heal."

Davyn nodded. "I understand. I will not harm any wolf."

Ulfrikarr stopped pacing, sat on his haunches, and scrutinized them for a long moment.

"Warlocks and wolves can live together in peace," he assured them. "But it is difficult. The Oathstone can be a great advantage, but it cannot function alone."

They all nodded. Of course the stone could not do everything by itself. They would still be needed to help with the mediation or negotiation; it would take some time and effort for everyone to get on the same page. It wasn't magic.

Well, it was magic, but not like on TV. In real life, magic took effort and time. It wasn't an instant solution to every problem.

"You may retrieve the Oathstone," Ulfrikarr said with a nod. He lowered his head and lay down, still watching them, but his body finally at rest. Reg wondered how many years it had been since he had last rested.

Davyn and Zora looked at each other, then proceeded toward

the little hollowed-out area they had been aiming for when Ulfrikarr had first appeared.

Reg stayed where she was, though she wanted to rush ahead and get the first peek at the stone that would solve all their problems. As long as they put the work into it.

Davyn lowered himself onto one knee like a football player praying. Zora transformed back to her wolf shape. They both stayed in tableau like that for a few seconds. Then Davyn picked up a rock about the size of a baseball. He held it out toward Zora, who touched it with her snout. Davyn rose back to his feet and walked toward Reg.

"Would you like to see what all the fuss was about?"

Reg nodded eagerly. "Yes!"

The stone was the same in coloring as the rest of the rocks in the dried-up lakebed. Gray with a little rusty brown. Round, like a stone that had been in the river for a long time, all the rough edges worn away.

With their long, straight lines, the runes still looked freshly carved. Reg's concern that they might have been worn away until they were invisible was unfounded.

"Do you know what the runes mean?" Reg asked, touching one of them. She expected the stone to be warm or to give her a bit of an electrical buzz when she touched it, but she didn't feel anything. Just a rock. Apparently like any other rock, except for the runes. And the magic.

Davyn looked at the markings and shook his head in response.

They all crossed Whisper Lake back to the other side, where Julian watched with his coffee cupped between both hands.

"Was that Aleph?" he asked, nodding across to the spot where Ulfrikarr had been standing when Reg had last looked. But he was gone now.

"No!" He had seen Aleph the night before. Reg couldn't believe he would think they were both the same wolf. Their physical features were very different. Aleph was a wolf in the prime of his life, muscular and vital. Ulfrikarr was ancient, skinny despite the breadth of his shoulders, his coat almost uniformly gray with age. "His name was Ulfrikarr, and he was the guardian of the stone."

"You got it?" Julian asked Davyn with interest. Davyn sat down on his sleeping bag, next to Julian's, and held the stone so that Julian could see it. Julian reached out to take it, but Davyn pulled back and shook his head. "I can't give it to anyone else. I need to be very careful how it is handled. I need to protect it and keep it safe."

"I am not going to do anything to harm it."

"It's the principle," Davyn told him. "You know how important it is to follow the rules."

Julian had a curious relationship with rules, enforcing them strictly with everyone else but playing fast and loose himself, doing whatever he had to in order to get his own way.

"Fine," Julian agreed, pulling his hand back. "If you say so." He still looked like he might snatch it at any moment. "What did he say to you? The wolf?"

"A number of things. I will fill you in later." Davyn's eyes were bright and animated, though he still acted as slowly and methodically as ever, acting like this was something he did every day and not the exciting key to solving the warlock werewolf war. "Now that we have the stone in our hands, I think we must act as quickly as possible. We do not want anyone else to get hurt, wolf or human, simply because we were too slow to act."

Reg agreed. "It's time to get out of here. I'll put out the fire and we can all pack up our gear. Does anyone need anything else to eat? More coffee?" She felt energized, even though she'd only had one cup. The encounter with Ulfrikarr and the thrill of having the Oathstone in their hands had her amped up without the need for more caffeine. Who knew when she would need to sleep again.

They all worked together in silence, each focusing on their own gear. Reg also dealt with the fire. It was easy for a firecaster, who could quickly snuff out the flames and embers of a small fire. Of course, she would rather play with fire than extinguish it. That would happen another day. Theodore liked marshmallows. Maybe they would go camping again one day in the near future and Reg would help him to toast his marshmallows.

Rolling up the sleeping bag as tightly as it had been when she first bought it was impossible. They must use pixie workers or a vacuum machine that sucked out all the air to collapse it down to the smallest possible package. But Reg did her best and crammed everything else into her bag around it. She was the last one ready, but had not lagged much behind the others.

"Okay," Davyn looked at them. "Next step? Do we hike all the way back? Do we transport directly to the truck? Or to Corvin's house? The pack's dens?"

Reg hesitated to be the one to answer. She and Theodore were the only ones who were not wolves or warlocks. They should probably not be making the decisions for the ones who were.

"I fear to go back to the pack's dens," Zora, back in human shape, said finally, her tone tentative. "With the pack fighting within itself last night, I fear what I would find. I think we need to go elsewhere first, until we've had a chance to learn more of what happened with the pack."

Reg thought of the cubs, being cared for by Zora's sister. She couldn't imagine how hard it must be for Zora not to rush back to the cubs immediately to ensure they were okay. Zora had said that her sister would stay out of the way and not be near any fighting. Hopefully, that was true, and the other members of the pack, no matter how frustrated they were with the warlock unrest, had not done anything to endanger the pregnant wolf or Zora's cubs.

"Then we should probably talk to Corvin," Davyn suggested. He looked at Zora and Reg in particular to see what they thought of this.

"It all started with Corvin," Reg pointed out. "He is the one who is cursed and needs to be healed. Maybe once we do that, we'll be able to negotiate with both sides."

"Makes sense," Davyn agreed. "There's just one thing." He sounded very serious.

Reg nodded. "Yes…?"

"I just wanted to make sure that… you're okay with him being healed."

CHAPTER THIRTY-FIVE

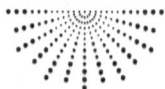

*R*eg had not even thought until then about the consequences of what she had set out to do. She knew that they had to do something about the warlock werewolf war, so that was what she had been most focused on. When she learned from Theodore that the Oathstone was also capable of reversing curses, she had known that they would have to try it on Corvin, to see if they could reverse his curse.

But she had not thought about what that would mean to her.

The past few weeks, it had been nice not to have to worry about Corvin ensorcelling her, pulling her in so that he could steal her gifts again. She hadn't had to be careful of his charms, because if he tried to use them, even instinctively without any intention, he was overcome by pain and could not go on.

It had allowed a tentative friendship to grow between them. There had always been a tug-of-war of attraction versus hostility between them. While Corvin had always been charming on the surface, Reg knew of the gaping maw that lurked beneath, just waiting for the chance to consume her. They had helped each other more than once, out of necessity, and they'd had a psychic bond that each had used for their own purposes. But they'd never really had a friendship. It was always something else.

Since Corvin had been cursed, that had changed. Despite his grumpiness, something more had developed between them.

And now, if they were going to heal Corvin, that fragile friendship would wither up and be crushed beneath the weight of Corvin's predatory nature. Once more, Reg would straddle the divide between enmity and entrancement.

She let out a long sigh and nodded, meeting Davyn's eye. "Yeah. That's going to suck. But it's the right thing to do. If we can reverse the curse, it will go a long way to healing the rift between the wolves and the warlocks. If we don't, that will always stand between them."

Davyn nodded his agreement. "I think it would be hard to reconcile if we could not reverse some of the harms that have been done, especially October's curse."

Reg steeled herself. "I don't think we can avoid it. So I'd better just grit my teeth and do it."

He patted her on the shoulder. "You're a better person than you think you are, Reg."

She thought it was an odd thing to say. It was true that she wasn't doing this for herself. Maybe it would have been different if she were just making the selfish decision, not thinking about what Corvin was suffering or the conflict between the werewolves and the warlocks. But with things as they were, she didn't really have a choice. She couldn't choose her own comfort over the lives of everyone in Black Sands.

"Let's go, then. Is everyone ready?"

She looked over the assembled company, a heavy weight in her stomach.

"Theodore… I don't think I had better take you to Corvin's house. You know how he feels about me letting you read his books."

Theodore's mouth turned down. "But he will see that I found the cure. Then he will forgive me."

"I don't know that he will. He didn't forgive us when we unpetrified him. He said he would rather have stayed petrified than for you to have read all his books. That's pretty harsh. I don't think he's going to be any better about this, even if it succeeds in reversing the curse. He's still going to be angry at me for letting you find out his secrets."

Theodore shook his head, not happy with this decision.

"I would take you if I thought he would show some gratitude," Reg said gently. "But I don't think he will. You and I will celebrate later, when everything is fixed. We'll have marshmallows or ice cream or whatever you choose. Okay?"

Theodore swirled away in a small cyclone of dust. He was there, and then he dissolved and was gone. Reg sighed. She would have to make it up to him the best she could later. She shook her head at Davyn.

"Tell me again how homunculi don't really have will or feelings of their own."

Davyn looked grim and didn't argue the point. Reg took a deep breath. She pictured the remainder of their small company on Corvin's doorstep, all ready to go in and reverse the curse using the Oathstone. She breathed in the smell of the trees in his front yard, felt the roughness of the flagstones under her shoes, and felt the light kiss of the wind on her skin.

She opened her eyes, and they were all there.

Davyn let out his breath. "Wow, Reg. You are getting really good at that. And you don't even look like it took any energy."

Reg could feel a flagging in her energy level, but there was no point in telling them how much it had taken out of her. She would be fine. "Well, let's do this."

She rang the doorbell and knocked on Corvin's door. She hoped he wouldn't take too long. She wanted to get his healing out of the way so they could work on bridging the rift between the wolves and the warlocks. That was a big part of their mission.

She didn't have to knock a second time. Corvin opened the door. He looked at them and scowled. "What's this? An intervention?"

Davyn laughed shortly. "We hope to make right the damage that has been done," he told Corvin. "Invite us in."

Corvin's eyes went to each of them in turn, and lingered on Zora.

"Aren't you…?"

"Come on, Corvin," Reg said impatiently. "Don't you want to do this? You've been trying for weeks."

There were dark bags under his eyes, testifying that he still was not sleeping. He got occasional snatches of sleep here and there, especially after a session of Reg taking some of his power. He didn't look particularly hopeful that they would have the solution.

But Reg didn't want to give him the opportunity to exclude Zora from their company. She had worked hard and sacrificed her time and being with her cubs to help him. Whether she was a wolf or not, it was right that she should be allowed in to help.

"Just invite us in."

Corvin shrugged as if it didn't really matter anyway. He stepped back in the doorway to let them in.

"I don't know what this is all about, but be my guests. Join me in my humble abode."

He led them into the living room. When Reg visited him, he usually tried to clean a few of the surfaces of their fast-food wrappers and empty bottles. But this time, he left them all on display, as if challenging them to say anything about how he was living.

"We have come with the Oathstone," Reg announced.

CHAPTER THIRTY-SIX

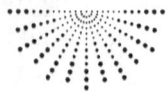

he Oathstone?" Corvin repeated. "Are you telling me
that it actually exists?"

Davyn had wrapped the stone up in a black cloth, and he took
it out now and unwrapped it, displaying it to Corvin.

"It does. We were able to find it and retrieve it, passing the
guardian. And now... we have been told that it has the power to
heal curses, and we would like to try. We would like to see if it will
reverse the curse that October placed on you."

Corvin looked interested, but cautious. His dark eyes glinted,
showing some life despite how exhausted and depressed he was.

"You think there is any chance it will work?" he asked. "I do
not think that is the primary purpose of this artifact."

"No, it is not," Davyn agreed. "But if there is a chance... I
would not want to withhold that opportunity from you."

"The Oathstone..." Corvin shook his head. "I didn't think it
still existed, if it ever did. I thought it was just a story."

"You're not the only one," Reg said. She seemed to be hearing
that line a lot.

"So how does this work?" Corvin asked, leaning forward to get
a better look at the stone that nestled in the black cloth in Davyn's
hands.

Davyn looked at Zora hopefully, and then back at Corvin. "We do not know a lot about it yet, but it appears that a warlock and wolf must work together to produce any results. I suggest... Zora and I hold it. State an intention and call on the stone and the ancients who created it for healing."

Corvin nodded. "Sounds fine."

Reg looked around. "Maybe... we should cleanse the space first," she suggested. She wasn't feeling any power from the Oath-stone and hoped it was just because they had not yet prepared the space for the ritual.

"What are you saying?" Corvin growled. "You have no right to judge me."

Reg rolled her eyes and didn't bother trying to argue reasons with him. She stood up and started to gather the garbage and empties. "Do you have sage? We can smudge before beginning."

She knew he had a variety of herbs and magical ingredients in his kitchen. He undoubtedly had plenty of sage.

Corvin muttered something under his breath and also stood up. He helped to gather the garbage and took it out of the room, disposing of it in the overflowing kitchen garbage. Reg wasn't sure how it had gotten so much worse in the last two days. She made no comment about it. Corvin fetched a sprig of sage from his cupboard stores and placed it on a silver salver.

They returned to the living room. It looked much tidier already. Corvin handed the salver to Reg and reached into his pocket to retrieve a lighter, but Reg used her own fire, singeing the sage and then waving the salver to each of the four compass points.

She immediately felt like it had been the right thing to do. The room felt better; it was not so dark and depressing. But she still could not feel any particular aura of power from the Oathstone, which worried her. If it was as powerful an object as they expected, then she should have been able to feel it.

"Okay." She nodded to Davyn and Zora.

"This isn't going to work," Julian said abruptly.

Reg tensed. She turned and looked at him, sitting to the side with his hands steepled in front of his face, looking all scholarly and thoughtful. She fumbled for something to say, tongue-tied at his intrusion. She should have left him out at Whisper Lake and not brought him to Corvin's house with everyone else. Then, by the time he managed to make it back to town, they would be finished and long gone. Why had she bothered to bring him with everyone else?

Why had Davyn invited him along on the quest in the first place? Reg had invited Davyn. He knew how she felt about Julian and must have known that she wouldn't welcome him along. She was quite proud of herself for managing to stay civil to him throughout the entire quest for the Oathstone, despite the negative and irritating things he was always saying. But now she felt like slapping him.

"Julian," Davyn said in a quiet, reproving tone.

Julian shook his head. "Do you really think it will have any effect?" he asked. "Even if it is the Oathstone and the Oathstone did have powers, and they did not wear off over the past, I don't know, two or three hundred years, its value was never in reversing curses. That was probably just something added by people who told the tale. Make it more interesting and exciting for the little kids who still believe in that kind of thing."

"We all realize it might not work. But that doesn't mean we don't try," Davyn asserted. "Let's just see what happens instead of being... *negative*. Okay?"

Julian shrugged and shook his head. "It's not going to work."

"Shut up, Sabat," Corvin snapped.

Julian gave him a smirk. He liked making trouble. He liked getting people worked up. And he particularly liked seeing powerful people upset or powerless. A bully always enjoyed watching someone else's distress.

But Julian closed his mouth and quit saying it wouldn't work, so they went on, getting ready for the ritual.

Davyn and Zora stood before Corvin, who remained seated in his favorite chair. Davyn removed the Oathstone from the cloth, and he and Zora held it between them, resting it on their fingertips.

Davyn took a deep breath. "We take this stone in our hands in peace, with single purpose. I, Davyn Smithy, member of the ancient warlock coven of Black Sands, and Zora, wolf daughter of Eryk and Gerwyna, join in the spirit of harmony and healing. We call on Vargrena and Drakskald, creators of the Oathstone. We invoke the power of the Oathstone for peace and a resolution between wolves and men. Corvin, harmed by a werewolf without provocation, must be healed from his curse to begin the healing of these communities. So mote it be."

Reg waited, still feeling nothing from the stone. No stirrings of magic in the room. There was no glow or flash, no reaction from Corvin. Davyn and Zora stood still, waiting.

Corvin shifted, the leather in his chair squeaking, and said nothing.

Davyn looked at Zora. "Perhaps you must be in your canid form?" he suggested tentatively, as though it might be rude to suggest such a thing.

For a few seconds, Zora did not react, and then she seemed to shrink, crouching down to the floor, her limbs twisting and reforming, fur rippling, until she was a wolf again, standing beside Davyn.

He knelt on one knee, as he had at the Whispering Lake, holding out the Oathstone in one hand. Zora raised a paw and laid it on top of the stone. Reg expected a reaction. She wanted it to start glowing, obviously activated by her wolf touch. But there was still no obvious magic.

Davyn recited a similar invocation again.

Reg reached out to Corvin, hoping for some sign that the ritual had made a difference. It didn't have to be dramatic. Some miraculous events were barely noticeable until a doctor did a blood test or looked at an X-ray and pronounced the patient cured.

Can you feel it? Reg wanted to know, prodding at the edges of Corvin's consciousness.

He convulsed, stiffening in pain, his face contorting. He grunted, stifling a cry, and held himself tense, waiting for the pain to pass.

Not healed. Not even a little bit. Reg clenched her fists, resisting swearing and complaining. If Corvin could be stoic and get through it without a fuss, she could too. It would be an insult for her to act like it was somehow an insult to *her* that the Oath-stone did not work.

"I told you so," Julian pointed out.

CHAPTER THIRTY-SEVEN

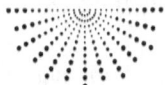

*J*ulian was lucky Reg didn't send him back to the dry lake for his insolence. She couldn't believe he would be so rude in the face of Corvin's disappointment.

Yes, it was true that he had been right. It was probably true that the Oathstone was not actually intended to reverse curses and that power might have been added in a fairy tale many years after the original events, when the details had already slipped from collective memory.

But it was still stupid and insensitive of Julian to say so.

Corvin straightened. "I will ask you to see yourselves out," he said with as much dignity as possible. "Good luck with your other endeavors. Perhaps you will still succeed in making peace between the factions."

Davyn wrapped the stone up again. He gave a little bow to Corvin and spoke quietly. "I am sorry it did not work as we had hoped."

"No matter. It was worth a try."

He leaned back in his chair and closed his eyes. "Come see me again, Reg."

"I will." Reg suspected that he wanted her to take more of his power to relieve the pain, but did not want to be obvious about it in front of everyone else. She skimmed off what power she could without anyone noticing, though a glance from Davyn suggested that he was aware of it.

Corvin nodded and bowed his head, chin touching his chest.

There was nothing else to do but to go.

They left their conversation for when they were out of Corvin's house.

"That was awkward," Julian declared, not bothering to lower his voice.

Reg glared at him, but he remained oblivious.

"We should get Julian back home," Davyn suggested, before Reg could think of the best way to slice and dice Julian and maybe feed him to her dragon. "In case he is needed for anything. Maybe you could get the truck, Julian, since I won't be able to get back there for a bit."

Julian looked from Davyn to Reg, and probably decided that no, he'd better not argue it unless he wanted to become dragon kibble. "All right," he said finally, "could you transport me back to the truck, Reg?"

Reg concentrated for a moment, picturing Julian in the driver's seat of the truck. She *really* wanted him to be someplace other than with her, so it was no surprise that he was gone when she opened her eyes again. Hopefully, she had sent him to the truck rather than the other side of the world, but she wouldn't be too upset either way.

"Thanks," Davyn said. He swallowed and held up his hands in a helpless gesture, unable to come up with something to say to her about Julian's behavior. Reg shrugged. Julian was Julian, and he wasn't going to change just because he was in a relationship with someone who was a decent human being.

"Next stop... I think should be the wolf pack." Davyn looked at Zora. "Do you agree?"

Reg knew she had sacrificed to go directly to Corvin without seeing her babies, so she was grateful to Davyn for suggesting they go to the pack before the coven.

Zora was once more in human form. Her eyes were moist. She nodded her agreement.

"Where will your sister be?" Reg asked.

Zora put her hand on Reg's arm and communicated the location to her directly rather than trying to describe it. Reg saw a picture in her mind of the scenery and location of Zora's sister's den and, in seconds, they were there. Zora let go of Reg's arm, instantly transforming back to wolf form and running across the grassy clearing to the rocky outcropping that the den was built into. There were no doors or windows and Reg did not feel comfortable following Zora in, even though the opening was certainly large enough.

There were growls, yips, and barks from inside. It sounded more like a fight than a family reunion, but Reg could feel the emotions of the little group and knew that all was well. The cubs came tumbling out of the den first, wrestling with each other and then gamboling around Reg's feet and bumping up against her leg. She reached down to let them smell her hand and to get a few ear scratches before they ran farther out into the field, running flat out. They had obviously been cooped up for too long, and Zora had released them to burn off some energy.

Zora came out of the den next, followed by her sister, a slightly smaller wolf, her body swollen with pups. She moved slowly and watched Reg and Davyn warily, not used to strangers near her den. With all the conflict between the wolves and the warlocks, it made sense that she would not feel safe around the practitioners, even if Zora told her they could be trusted.

"Everything is okay here?" Davyn asked, smiling as he watched the cubs playing.

Zora gave a nod.

"Do you want to come?" Davyn asked. "Or should we go on our own? You've done all you could be expected to do, helping us do so much when your only responsibility was to patrol the perimeter."

Zora looked toward the cubs and touched noses with her sister, and they conversed with each other privately. Eventually, Zora transformed back to her human shape.

"I will come," she said. "I want to see this to the end. We have put so much work into it; I want to see the results."

"Great." Davyn nodded. "Our next task, I guess, is to speak to the leadership. We need to get talks going between the wolves and the warlocks. Now that we have the Oathstone, they may actually be productive."

"They are not far from here. We will find out if they will hear us."

CHAPTER THIRTY-EIGHT

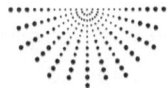

*Z*ora led the way through the forest at a quick clip. Reg feared that Zora's "not far" might be more than she could handle. Especially if she were going to run that fast. Reg was not used to running through the forest.

Luckily, she was not the only one. Davyn, too, was having a difficult time keeping up, so Zora was forced to slow down and wait for them, though she was obviously impatient.

It ended up taking half an hour to get to the council area Zora had in mind. Reg hoped that someone would be there to talk to them and they would not have to chase all over the county trying to find the people they needed to get the peace talks going again.

As they approached the clearing, Reg could see several dark forms lying on the ground. Her heart pounded in her throat and she picked up her pace, worried. Had all their work been in vain? Were the council members of the wolf pack already dead?

But at their approach, heads went up quickly, ears pricking forward, to see who was there. They were not dead or injured, just napping. Reg stopped and tried to catch her breath again. A little embarrassed and angry that she had been fooled, even if the wolves had not intended to trick her.

The wolves were all on their feet by the time Davyn and Reg

reached the edge of the clearing. They confronted Zora, snapping and growling in what clearly was not a friendly conversation. Reg fought off her anxiety over hearing their anger and trying to hear what they were actually saying. Though she could understand the wolves when they spoke to her one at a time in their minds, having them all speaking and interrupting each other was overwhelming. She focused on identifying which wolves were there.

Aleph was not.

Reg swallowed. She knew that there had been an attempted coup. If Aleph was no longer in the council circle, he had clearly been ousted. She didn't recognize all the wolves there. Most of the wolves had little to do with her, even when October had been there. There was not much mixing between the humans and the wolves even before relations had been blown all to heck by October's attack.

But there was one wolf in particular she did recognize. Even if she hadn't known the shape of his body and his mostly black coat, she would have known him by his consciousness alone.

Jake.

Jake had been part of the group that had overthrown Aleph. She could picture him causing problems—talking behind the alpha's back, sowing discord, pointing out the fact that he had not been successful in restoring relations between the pack and the coven. He was obviously not the wolf for the job.

Jake had wanted to be alpha and had thought it his rightful place ever since he had been turned. He had assumed he was the smartest, the strongest, and the best leader. It didn't matter that he had only been a wolf for two minutes. Of course he knew how the pack should be run. He was Jake.

The wolves spoke to Zora, talked among themselves and, eventually, turned their attention to Davyn and Reg. Reg felt out of place there. She was not a wolf nor a warlock. She wasn't the mediator between them. She wasn't the one who was holding the Oathstone. She didn't have any standing, and maybe she should have just stayed back at the den with Zora's sister and watched the cubs.

Eventually, Zora transformed into her human form. Jake

followed suit. He was looking at Reg, as she knew he would be, a smirk on his face. Proud of himself. He was, once again, top dog. Showing off his superior strength and intellect, coming up with a strategy to depose Aleph and take his place as Alpha.

What had he and John been discussing when Reg had seen them together at the bar? Reg was sure it had something to do with this. They had somehow collaborated or consulted with each other, figuring out how to take over the wolf pack. Reg looked around for Theodore to quiz him about what he had discovered about Jake and John before realizing he wasn't with her. She had sent him away, and it was not a good time to ask him about what he had found out anyway. Not in front of the wolves.

"Reg," Jake greeted, grinning at her, his body loose and relaxed. Looking closely, Reg could see a few minor injuries; cuts and bruises. Nothing that looked serious. "It's so nice of you to come here and be one of the first people to congratulate me on my achievement." He spoke aside to the other wolves who had not transformed. "You see, relations with the humans are not so bad. I still have my admirers." He barked with laughter.

There were growls from the other wolves. Reg didn't know whether they were laughter, agreement, or disapproval.

Reg swallowed back any angry reply. It didn't matter what Jake said or what he thought. He was not her boyfriend anymore. Even when he had been, it had been because of the spell he had woven to entangle her, not because she really liked him that much. He had bound her to him without her permission. Reg had loved him, but she had ended it, and she would never be taken in by him again.

"As Zora told you, we are here to help broker peace between the warlocks and the wolves. I'm sure you want to put an end to the trouble between the wolves and the warlocks in town as soon as you can."

Jake shrugged and didn't say whether he wanted to or not. Maybe he didn't. Maybe all he had wanted was to get in control of the wolf pack. But Reg believed that Jake was more ambitious than that. He didn't want just to be a figurehead, to have people think he was something because he was good enough to be the alpha wolf in the pack. He would want to show them he could achieve what Aleph could not. A peace treaty with the warlocks would be a good start. It would show the pack that he had value to them. That he could get things they needed.

"We have the Oathstone," Reg went on, expecting a reaction from Jake and the pack but not getting it. Here, she had found something amazing, an artifact that had been gone from their memories for years, a mythical artifact with great power, and they were acting like it was nothing. "It will help you to achieve peace with the warlocks. That is why it was forged," she told him, unsure whether he knew anything about the story behind it. He had grown up human. He probably knew nothing of werewolf bedtime stories.

"That's very nice," Jake said. "I take it you will want to be present for our discussion this afternoon."

"With the warlocks? Today?"

"Yes. You don't think we have given up on the talks, do you?"

"Well, I didn't know. I thought that with everything that happened with Aleph, you probably hadn't been able to start any peace talks yet. And with the Oathstone…"

"Yes, I understand; you brought your magical talking stone. I've seen how things like that work. You pass it around, give everybody a chance to talk. Eventually, after everyone has said their piece, you can start coming to an understanding on the things that you agree on. Weed through the things that you don't, make some concessions, some compromises…" He spread his hands apart. "Bing, bang, boom, you have a peace accord."

Reg stood there with her mouth open, not even sure where to start with that.

CHAPTER THIRTY-NINE

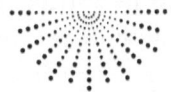

*R*eg was thrown off balance by the suggestion that Jake intended to continue the peace talks and believed he would be able to reach an accord. He wasn't excited by the prospect of using the Oathstone, but he didn't object to it.

"We should use all our resources," he agreed with a shrug. "If people believe in the power of the Oathstone, so much the better. They will be more open to coming to an accord. And if it actually has power…" He laughed. "Well, who am I to argue with that if it gets me what I want? But I believe that its power is simply of a talisman. A physical object that embodies the intentions of the holders. The hope of coming to an agreement, of reconciling the two factions. We all just want to live in peace. If both sides want that, what is holding us back?"

Reg was not a diviner like Damon, who could tell whenever someone was lying, but she knew Jake didn't believe in his own words. He had an ulterior motive. She didn't know what it was, since he was already installed as the Alpha of the pack, but Jake's desire was for power and admiration, not peace. It always had been. He was willing to trample over anyone in order to improve his position.

In the past, that had been Reg and the wolf pack. Aleph had

been one of his victims this time, but he wasn't the last, Reg was sure of that.

However, with Jake agreeing to continue the peace talks and to use the Oathstone, there wasn't anything to talk him into or any reason to challenge him about his plans or ulterior motives. If he had convinced the wolf pack to overthrow Aleph and install him as the alpha based on the argument that Aleph was not able to come to an accord with the warlocks but that Jake was, then the logical next step was for him to continue the peace talks and come to an agreement. That would show the pack that he had what it took to be their leader and was superior to Aleph.

The pack members had been resting before Reg, Davyn, and Zora had shown up, and that was what they planned to do as they awaited the appointed time for the peace talks. Considering the fact that they had spent much of the previous night in battle, that was perfectly logical. Reg had not slept the last two nights. No longer faced with the urgency of finding the Oathstone, healing Corvin, or convincing the warlocks and wolves to return to the negotiation table, she was not as wound up and started to feel a little drowsy herself.

She grazed on a buffet of fresh fish and meat and found a comfortable knoll a little way away from where the wolves were sleeping. She didn't trust the wolves entirely and was sure they felt the same way about a human sleeping with the pack. Zora was used to sleeping several times in a twenty-four-hour cycle, like the other wolves, so she didn't have any trouble curling up to go to sleep.

"I'll keep watch," Davyn offered. "You'll want to be fresh for the negotiations."

"What about you? You don't want to take a nap?" Reg asked.

"I slept last night. I'm more worried about you. I know you need your sleep and haven't been sleeping on your usual schedule. So get what you can now, if you're able to get in a nap. If you can't sleep..." He shrugged, "Just rest and relax. You need to get what you can."

Reg let out a sigh. As her body started to relax, letting go of the tension that had held her in its grip the last few days, the prospect of a nap sounded pretty good. Her eyelids were already getting heavy. It was before noon, when she was normally still in bed. She unrolled her sleeping bag and lay down on top of it.

* * *

Reg woke up to voices. Not loud and angry voices, no threats. The warlocks who were to participate in the talks were arriving. The wolves were waking up. Soon, the talks would resume. And this time, with the power of the Oathstone, they would be successful.

She sat up, rubbing her eyes, and looked around. Davyn was sitting nearby and nodded to her. He had the Oathstone in his lap, unwrapped and lying on top of the black cloth as he pondered it. Zora was no longer in the clearing.

"Are we ready?" Reg asked.

"Soon. They are just getting ready now. We will probably start in the next ten to thirty minutes."

Reg wished that she wasn't so far from her kitchen and the coffee maker. Or that she had one of her favorite fancy, sugary coffees from The Witches' Brew. She looked down and saw that she held a travel cup filled with a light brown coffee that smelled delightfully of caramel and cream. She raised it to her lips. It was still piping hot. While she did her best not to call objects to her that might belong to someone else, she had a particularly difficult time resisting the temptation to call food or drink when she needed it. Harrison, her immortal godfather, had taught her to call food to her as the starving child of a junkie. She would probably not have survived childhood if she had not picked up the skill quickly.

Davyn raised his brows and looked amused at the appearance of the cup of coffee.

"Do you want one?" Reg asked, a flush of warmth spreading over her cheeks.

"No, Thank you. I'm fine." He tapped his backpack. "I have all the provisions I need."

"Yeah… I do, too. But there's no fresh coffee in there."

They sat for a few minutes longer, Reg enjoying her coffee and waking up the rest of the way. Without saying anything, they both rose and walked back to the clearing where the wolf council had been sleeping and was now assembling with a few of the warlocks.

Reg looked over the warlocks who had come. Corvin was not among them, which should not have been a surprise. He would not want to appear before the warlocks in his coven helpless and power-less. She supposed that Davyn would stand in for him.

John had come, though, and with his chest puffed out, he appeared to be the main player among the other warlocks. Reg shuddered as he got close to her. As with Julian, she knew he was broken. His mind was twisted and warped by the domineering witch who had raised him. As far as Reg could tell, he had no ethics, and his only desire was to grow his power and eventually lead the coven, as Verity had told him was his right.

Despite John's mother being dead, Reg could still hear Verity's voice when she was close to John. He could never escape her constant whispers in his ear. He heard her comments and instruc-tions all day, which was enough to drive anyone crazy, if he wasn't already.

"Come to listen to the negotiations?" he asked Reg, leaning close to her. She smelled the scent of baking brownies, the pheromones he exuded when he was charming her. Reg raised a psychic shield against him, reflecting back the heat and any magic he tried to use against her.

"I brought the Oathstone," Reg told him, irritated that he thought she was just an observer here. Then she amended, because Davyn was the one who had brought the Oathstone with him, even if it had been Reg's quest in the first place. "I found it. Well, Davyn and Zora—we found it. We went searching for it. Theodore had the details of where to look... I organized the company and we went to find it."

John smiled. "Do you think I need some artifact to conduct these negotiations? I am... very persuasive. I know how to get people to see my point of view."

Reg was confused. "You? Davyn will be the one conducting the negotiations..."

"Why would he be? He's not the leader of the coven."

"Well, he's the previous leader, and he's been stepping in while Corvin has been… unable to."

"I have been elected as the leader of the coven."

"What?" Reg felt the blood drain from her face. She reached out for something to steady her, finding a tree and holding herself up. "What do you mean?"

There had been no word of an election in the coven, no campaigning that she was aware of. There was a whole process for electing a coven leader, and she hadn't heard of any preparations for a new election.

"We held an emergency election yesterday." His eyes were steady and his grin grew. "We could not continue to go on without a leader. No one knew where Davyn had gone off to. I am Corvin's son, so it was natural that I step into his place. Everyone agreed that I am a persuasive speaker and have what it takes to make these negotiations work. We couldn't keep floundering around as we were."

"What?" Reg couldn't believe it. She looked around for Davyn and saw him standing a few feet away, looking just as pinched and pale as she felt herself. "What? How could you do that?"

"Someone had to take the reins. I was the natural choice."

And his charms, though more effective on a woman, could still be used to influence the decisions of the men in the coven. With enough of a boost, it would probably be a simple matter to talk them all into voting for him to take over the leadership of the coven.

"Is that… is that legal?" she asked Davyn.

"There are no laws around the leadership of the coven," Davyn told her. "Just traditions. This is unusual, but if the coven agreed on it, then it is done. I never asked to take back over as the leader of the coven. I've just been trying to keep my hand in and keep things running smoothly until someone else could take over. We couldn't have the coven unrepresented while all this stuff was happening in town."

"And now I'm here," John said, smiling. "So you don't need to be. You can go home and get caught up on your gardening, or whatever it is you do." He looked at Reg. "And you don't have any standing here. You are neither a warlock nor a wolf. You don't claim to be a witch. So *you* can go home too."

"I found the Oathstone," Reg said stubbornly. "Without me, it wouldn't be here. I am going to supervise its use."

"I don't see the need for it," John dismissed. "It's too bad you don't have more faith in the abilities of the coven and the pack to reconcile and come to an agreement on these matters. Maybe if people had given us a better chance and more support, things would have been smoothed out by now."

"The Oathstone will help. That's what it is for. Its whole purpose is to reconcile the wolves and the warlocks."

Reg didn't want to think of how the Oathstone had failed to perform for Corvin. But they agreed that healing was probably not one of the properties of the stone. It was something that had been added to the legend later. But when Davyn and Zora used the Oathstone as they mediated the interactions between the wolves and the warlocks...

Davyn was pulling the Oathstone out of his pocket. He handed it to Reg, still wrapped up in the black cloth. "I don't know whether you will need that or not. It will be your responsibility." He looked at John. "I would like to stay to observe. I will stay out of the way and will not give my opinion on anything if you don't want me to."

John scowled at this. Verity's voice grew louder. She wanted John to get rid of Davyn. But John just smiled blandly and shrugged. "If the council does not object to observers, that is up to you. I will be able to manage the negotiations on my own just fine."

Davyn nodded and didn't argue. John looked at the wrapped stone in Reg's hands. Even though he had said more than once that they would not need it, he was still curious about it.

"Can I... see it?"

Reg hesitated. The guardian had given it to Davyn and Zora to use and protect, and Davyn had given it to her. If John didn't have any respect for it, then why not just shove it into one of her pockets and let him manage on his own?

But she desperately wanted the negotiations to succeed. She wanted the talks to be blessed with whatever power or good mojo they had. After all the searching for the Oathstone and her certainty that it would be the pivotal piece to the negotiations, she couldn't just walk away with it because she didn't want to work with John, didn't want him to be the leader of the coven, and didn't want to give him any advantages. He was the leader the coven had elected. They weren't going to get anywhere in the talks without him.

Sighing, she unwrapped the stone and showed it to him. John was disappointed with the small, plain rock. He shook his head.

"I thought it would be an emerald or other precious stone. This is just... a rock. Like any rock you can find on the riverbed."

"It has an inscription," Reg pointed out, showing him the runes.

John peered at them. "I can't say I'm impressed. Really, I don't think this has any powers at all." He hovered his hand over it for a moment as if feeling for warmth. Reg had seen Corvin do the same thing to evaluate an object imbued with powers. His kind could take the powers from an object, if they did not have a live person to draw from. Though Corvin had informed her that it was not as satisfying to draw power from an object. He much preferred live prey. The chase and the intimacy of it.

Reg pulled the stone back from John slightly, worried that if the stone did have any powers, John might just suck them right out without her realizing what he was doing. She could not feel any special warmth or see a glowing aura around the rock, but that didn't mean that powers didn't still lie dormant within it.

"I am not going to do anything to your rock, Reg," John told her with amusement.

As the group was organized and seats assigned, all participants sitting on the ground, the situation slowly dawned on Reg.

Both the wolf pack and the coven had been through an abrupt change in leadership the previous night. Jake and John were now the leaders of the two factions. Just days earlier, she had seen the two of them collaborating in the bar, heads together as they worked through some plan. Had they engineered this whole thing then? Was that why they had been meeting in the bar? Trying to work out how to get the negotiations back on track? Spitballing solutions or concessions?

Was everybody else just there as window dressing, and Jake and John already had everything worked out beforehand?

It seemed like a stretch, but the fact that they had both taken over the leadership of their factions in order to meet with each other today did not seem like a coincidence. It seemed to have been planned down to the last detail.

CHAPTER FORTY

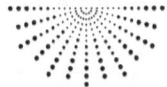

*R*eg braced herself as everyone quieted, getting ready for the talks to begin. She had a role to play here, whether or not they thought it would make any difference to the course of events. She had to assume from the fact that they had successfully retrieved the Oathstone that they were meant to use it.

The peace talks would have a better chance of success if they used it. Even if it were just because of the faith people put into it. Even if it were just because they passed it around to those who wanted to speak and everyone else was forced to listen and not interrupt. Even if it were just because of their respect for an old tradition, a story shared with cubs as they nursed at their mothers' sides.

No one else was going to make a big deal of it. Everyone was too focused on the changes in the leadership of the clans. So it was up to Reg. She stepped up front and center and uncovered the Oathstone with a flourish, making it the focus of the opening ceremonies.

"Brothers and sisters," she announced, "If you will all listen to me, I shall tell you the story of the creation of the Oathstone, Eidsstein, symbol of the great pact formed by Vargrena, an ancient werewolf matriarch renowned for her wisdom, and Drakskald, a powerful warlock whose mastery over magic was unmatched. In reconciling and swearing to not harm each other, the two great leaders drew the fates of their clans together and ensured that they could live together in peace and harmony. Until now."

She looked around the group. Everyone was quiet, paying close attention to her. Even Jake and John, who she had assumed would roll their eyes and disparage what she had to say, sat quietly, eyes on her, listening to the story.

"A rift has been formed between our two peoples. A rift that can be healed. You have before you two great leaders, Jake Bosco, alpha of the wolf pack, and John Saunders, serving as the leader of the warlock coven. Both have a great deal of skill, knowledge, and power to bring to bear in these talks."

John and Jake exchanged looks and nodded respectfully to each other. They looked toward their small audience of wolves and warlocks, preening, making sure everyone knew just how true Reg's words were. They were masterful, the right men for the job, brought together at this time in this place to do something great.

Reg pulled the Oathstone from the black cloth that concealed it. "Behold, the Oathstone."

Despite its rather ordinary appearance, there was a gasp at Reg's theatrics. The members of the audience whispered to each other.

"I talked this morning to Ulfrikarr, guardian of the Oathstone. He blesses its use at today's peace talks and guarantees that it will aid in coming to an agreement that will ensure the peace between our two peoples. Davyn and Zora, will you come forward?"

Davyn gave Reg a warning look, but she didn't back down. She knew what she wanted. Reluctantly, he rose from the audience and approached her. Zora, sitting on her haunches in the front of the audience rose to her feet and transformed back to her human shape to approach Reg.

Reg put the Oathstone into Davyn's hand and then drew Zora's slim white hand over the top so the Oathstone was clasped between them.

"Davyn and Zora have both made oaths today to acquire the

stone. Would you please take the stone to the leaders of the warlock coven and the wolf pack?"

With ceremony, Davyn and Zora carried the stone a few feet to where Jake and John sat. They were forced to stand again, and to receive the stone from Davyn and Zora. They held it between their hands, as Davyn and Zora had done, and then sat down again. John passed it to Jake.

"I call on Jake, leader of the wolf pack, to speak first," he declared.

Jake took the stone. He sat there looking down at it for a moment, as if the significance of what he was doing and the responsibility he bore was just now becoming real to him. He swallowed and nodded.

"Thank you, John. It is a great privilege to open up the talks today. I would like to begin with an apology from the wolf pack for the attack on Corvin and the rest of the coven at their spring solstice ritual. Such a thing ill befits our people. It was wrong, and I acknowledge that on behalf of the wolves. It was not an approved action, but the impulsive choice of a rogue wolf filled with anger and fear, who has since been banished from the pack. I apologize to you especially, as the son of the man most affected by that attack."

John nodded graciously. "I accept."

There were murmurs among the spectators.

The talks progressed. Reg couldn't always hear what was being said between John and Jake or the others on the council. Sometimes, they spoke for the audience to hear; other times, they whispered between themselves or wrote notes.

Reg saw immediately why John had let Jake speak first. Not just so that he could apologize for the werewolf attack, which she had to admit was a good start to the talks, but so that he could subtly dismiss anything Jake said. He used his charms on the other members of the council, fogging their brains, enticing them to make the decisions he suggested to them. Even Jake himself had difficulty staying on point and arguing anything that John said.

In the end, Reg wasn't sure that it was all bad. The problems between the warlocks and wolves were not really about who was

right and who was wrong. They were emotional. Hurts and grievances on both sides. Fear and anger that needed to be soothed away.
And John did soothe them away. His calm voice, the waves of
pheromones and flush of warmth, everything he did was designed
to make the werewolves and the other warlocks feel heard and
comforted.

She could see why those like Corvin and John had been denied
a place in coven leadership and other councils for so many years.
While it seemed like John was cooperating and treating everyone
with concern and respect, he was enticing them into the positions
he wanted them in. He was getting them right where he wanted
them.

Maybe the Oathstone helped things to progress more smoothly
than they would have otherwise. Reg couldn't be sure that it had
made any difference. She couldn't see or feel the magic, but that
didn't mean it wasn't there. The members of the council continued
to pass it around as they spoke, taking their turn and making sure
all opinions were voiced and no one was interrupted. It was very
different from the town council meeting that Reg had attended.
Maybe, as Jake had suggested, that was all the magic they needed,
and they would come to an accord if they just listened to each
other.

CHAPTER FORTY-ONE

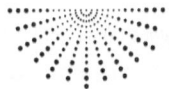

*W*hile there was a great deal of celebrating after the accord was signed between the two clans, Reg felt that the whole thing was anticlimactic. People being patient and reasonable seemed flat after all that had happened and her efforts to secure the Oathstone and get the two sides talking again.

But maybe she was just tired. She had not slept in days and, though she had skimmed a little energy when she had been at Corvin's house, she had not dared to take too much and make it obvious while the others were there. Davyn, in particular, was sure to notice what she was doing, and she didn't want to be seen as a predator like Corvin and John, sucking the powers from someone else.

She was ready for bed, and in the morning she would feel back to her normal self. She would be able to look at the accord as the positive resolution it was, rather than just a few words scribbled on a piece of paper that would not have any effect at all on the behavior of the warlocks and wolves when they ran into each other in town.

And she still didn't have the answer to Corvin's problem. He was still a voluntary shut-in, unable to use his powers or to live the way that he had become accustomed to. He was in almost constant pain despite his best efforts not to use any of his powers. It was an impossibility.

"It's been a long day for you," Sarah told Reg as she prepared to head to bed. "A quest takes a lot of effort, and you deserve a good long sleep. You should be proud of yourself for the way things worked out. The Oathstone really did seem to help things along."

"Maybe," Reg sighed. "I think they would have come to an accord without it."

"No, don't think that way. You were very helpful in all that you did. Finding the Oathstone, bringing the two sides together. You were instrumental in bringing these troubles to an end."

Sarah patted Reg on the shoulder and urged her to go to bed, heading to the door herself. "Morning will come soon enough!"

John had returned the Oathstone to Reg when the talks were over, smiling politely and saying that it had been instrumental when Reg was pretty sure it had done nothing. She set it on her dresser and looked at it for a moment, wondering at all the work that had gone into retrieving it. All for nothing.

There were fireworks outside as Reg changed and climbed into bed. Starlight was sitting on the windowsill watching them, and he did not approve. Cats did not understand the allure of fireworks. Despite the explosions, Reg's firecaster instincts were not triggered, and she felt useless rather than excited by them.

Time for bed. Time for a nice long sleep, and returning to her regular routines tomorrow.

* * *

It felt like her head had barely touched the pillow.

Sarah was shaking her. Reg tried to push her away. "You said you were going to bed," she protested. How the old woman could live on so little sleep, she didn't know. "Leave me alone."

"Reg. Reg, I need to talk to you."

"Later. Let me sleep for now."

"Reg, you have to know what's happened." Sarah's tone was distressed. "We thought everything was worked out, and it wasn't.

They were just waiting for the right time. It was an ambush, and it was terrible. They don't know yet how many were injured or killed."

Reg sat up, her eyes flying open. A head rush nearly made her pass right out, but she held herself steady and tried to see Sarah clearly through the bleariness of sleep and the dizziness of sitting up too fast.

"Injured? Killed? Who? What happened?"

Sarah sat on the edge of the bed. She was a mess. Her hair was straggly and her eyes dark hollows. She wiped away tears as she tried to explain the situation to Reg.

"The warlocks. They ambushed the wolves. Not in town, but out there," Sarah waved, "in the woods where they live. John never planned to honor the accord. He just wanted the wolves to let down their defenses. It was all in his evil plans. I knew that he could not be trusted! But I was misled just like everyone else by his rhetoric and his charms."

"They attacked the wolves? All of them? What about the women and children? The pregnant mothers? The cubs?" Reg's heart pounded in her chest. She prayed that nothing had happened to the cubs.

"I don't know anything for sure yet. The reports that are coming in all contradict each other. You know how things are when there is an accident or a catastrophe. You hear all kinds of things. People think the worst and just make things up."

"Yes, they do," Reg agreed, swallowing. Maybe the reports of the attack were exaggerated. Maybe it was just one or two disaffected warlocks. Men who did not like the accord that had been signed. Surely not John himself, when he was the one who had drafted it and approved every line.

"Have you talked to Davyn?" Reg asked. "Who was involved in this attack?"

"I don't know. I can't get through to Davyn. Does that mean he is part of this? Or that he was… that something happened to him to prevent him from interfering? I just don't know what to do, Reg."

Reg slid out of bed. She grabbed the Oathstone off of the dresser. "We need to go over there."

"Where? We can't go to the wolves' dens. They are still fighting out there. We would be in danger. They will assume that we are on the side of the warlocks."

"But we need to stop it."

"We can't, Reg. There is nothing we can do."

"We can," Reg insisted. She couldn't just stand by and wait for news when people she cared about might be hurt. She needed to know that Davyn was okay. And then she needed to get to Zora and the cubs and know they were okay. She didn't know how the warlocks could have been convinced to behave so dishonorably.

Except that she did. It was John's doing. He had ensorcelled them, had convinced them that it was the right thing to do and then had led them out there to ambush the wolves. He had gotten to them despite their best intentions. Who knew how much power he had amassed, how much he had saved up for just this situation, determined to gain control over the coven and to use it for his own purposes?

"Come on." Reg put her hand on Sarah's arm and concentrated on Davyn's house, where so often she had sat with him on the couch in front of the big fireplace to talk about firecasting and Ember and whatever other topics that came up. Not in a romantic way. A mentor and his student. Two friends. The parental units of a young dragon.

She was sure Davyn could have had nothing to do with the attack. It was impossible.

CHAPTER FORTY-TWO

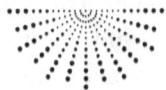

*R*eg and Sarah materialized in Davyn's living room. It took a moment for Reg to get her bearings, having been so abruptly woken up. Davyn was dressed, grabbing his cloak as he prepared to head out the door. Still in a silk dressing gown, Julian protested whatever Davyn planned to do.

"This is foolishness!" he insisted. "You swore not to raise a hand against the wolves."

"And I intend to keep that oath," Davyn snapped. "I'm going to help them, to stop whatever is happening. I'll talk to the warlocks and make them see sense. I don't understand how this could be happening."

"You need to stay out of it. What do you think is going to happen if you put yourself in the middle of that fight? It doesn't matter what you say or what your intentions are. They are going to see you as the enemy."

"I can't worry about that. I can only do what I can do, and that is not sitting at my desk refusing to get out there and put a stop to this. I know my role here."

"You are not the leader of the coven anymore. You don't have any authority over the members."

"It was never about authority. I might not be the elected leader of the coven right now, but I cannot let them continue to be governed by John and his whims. They have to see what he has done to them, how he is making things worse, not better. Did he really think that he could attack the wolves without consequences?"

"He's crazy," Reg said, jumping into the conversation without invitation. "I knew he was crazy. He has been ever since Verity died. Probably even before that. She broke him."

Davyn whirled around to look at Reg. He took in her state and Sarah's rumpled appearance and knew they had heard what was happening. "I'm glad of your help," he said briefly. "I don't know what I can do, but I have to do something." He shot a look of contempt at Julian. "I can't just stay here and let someone else fight the battle. I can't stand by while my coven does something so dishonorable, so reckless and… and wrong!"

"I know," Reg agreed.

"I tried to call you," Sarah told Davyn. "You didn't answer."

"Things have been a little disrupted here," Davyn explained unnecessarily, gesturing to a small, unrolled scroll on the sideboard. A message he had received by hand or carried by a bird? He pulled his phone out of his pocket to look at his missed calls or messages, and blood rushed to his face. He pressed the power button on the side of the phone and held it down.

"You turned off my phone?" he accused Julian. "Why would you do that?"

"Your phone? No, I shut off my phone." Julian scratched the back of his neck. "I don't want to get a call from my superiors telling me that I should be in the middle of that out there," he gestured toward the big window. "When everything is settled down, I will scout it out and inform the endangered creatures division of the extent of the casualties."

Davyn shook his phone at Julian. "This is my phone. You shut it off. Are you telling me that you're just going to stay here like a coward, not protect your precious endangered species, and just wait to see how many are hurt or killed?"

"There isn't anything I can do to stop it. And if you go out there… you're not going to be able to stop it either. What can one person do? Especially when you made a promise not to get involved."

"I didn't make a promise not to get involved. I promised not to raise my hand against a wolf."

"It's the same thing. Do you really think you can go out there and not be attacked?" Julian repeated. "You are going to get yourself killed!"

"Better than sitting around here doing nothing," Davyn told him. He took a step toward the door.

Reg closed her eyes. It was easier if she was touching them, but it was unnecessary. She took all of them to the wolf dens, including Julian in his silk dressing gown.

Chaos raged around them. Weak sunlight was starting to light the sky to the east. Reg wasn't sure what she had been expecting, but she was overwhelmed by the combat between the warlocks and the wolves; magical spells and curses seemed to buzz through the air around them.

The wolves howled and slavered and attacked wherever they could. They were clearly overwhelmed by the number of warlocks and fighting tooth and claw against superior magic.

Some of the wolves also had powers, but not all of them, and even those who did usually did not choose to develop them, preferring instead to live as wolves in their closed community. October's preference for living among the humans, performing a range of practical and magical services for them, was unusual.

Howls and shouts surrounded them. Davyn stepped forward to stop one of the warlocks Reg didn't know, shouting at him and using his flame to drive the furious warlock back.

Sarah went to one of the bloodied fallen wolves, crouching over him to see what she could do to help.

Julian stood there, clutching his dressing gown and looking around with wild eyes. Reg did not want to be like him, just standing there as if she weren't a part of this community. She had powers. She had to do whatever she could to help end the conflict.

She raised a psychic shield around herself and the nearest werewolf, putting a barrier between them and the curses and physical attacks.

A warlock with a huge barrel chest and bushy black beard pressed toward her, trying to break through the shield. He had a spear and, when curses did not penetrate the psychic barrier, he dove at them with the spear raised, aiming first for the wolf's chest and then, when his spear tip turned aside, he directed it toward Reg and tried to thrust it directly through her shield and into her heart.

The solidity of the psychic shield shattered the tip of the spear, and the warlock dropped the useless weapon to the side. With a wordless shout, he tried to attack Reg with his bare hands.

Reg sidestepped, unsure what else to do. She was not a fighter. She had been in fights. She'd rarely started them, but it had been impossible to get through childhood without them. Even as an adult, she had found herself in some sticky situations, sometimes with people on the street who thought she was infringing on their territory, had stolen something from them, or were just high on drugs or plagued by personal demons.

She would clearly be unable to best the big, burly warlock physically. He was at least three times her weight. She didn't know what paranormal abilities he might have, and she wasn't going to wait to find out.

In an instant, the warlock was gone. By the time he found his way home from the other side of the world, the battle would be long over.

Davyn was in trouble. Even though he was there to defend the wolves, they saw him as the enemy, as Julian had said they would. There wasn't time to explain to them what he was there for.

He held his hands up defensively as three wolves circled him, trying to identify his vulnerabilities and what powers and weapons they would have to contend with.

He tried to tell them he was no threat to them, but they were deaf to his pleas. He didn't use his fire against them and merely tried to hold them off, but Reg could see he was failing.

She dove at the wolves, screaming and scattering them with an attack from the rear that they had not anticipated. They whirled around once they were a few yards away, regrouping and evaluating Reg as a new threat.

Davyn might have promised not to raise his hand against any wolf, but Reg had not.

She called upon her fire and, in a minute, was ablaze. The wolves would not attack a being apparently being consumed by fire, but they returned to their attack on Davyn, circling around him so that they could attack from the rear. Davyn stood as a shield between the Reg and the wolves.

"Get out of the way," Reg warned him.

"Reg, I can—"

"Step to the side!" she shouted.

He obeyed, and Reg shot a fireball at the lead of the three wolves, forcing him to retreat.

She hoped that the others would follow the leader and decide to attack someone else instead, or even to retreat to their dens and protect their families from there rather than out in the open where they were more vulnerable.

There was a snarl, and a heavy weight hit Reg, knocking her over. Her arm burned with pain. She had thought that she was still protected by her shield, but she must have dropped it and made herself vulnerable when she had started manipulating fire.

Davyn had trained her to keep her concentration while playing with fire and had drilled her over and over again, but it was different in the heat of battle.

"Reg!"

"I'm okay," she told Davyn, but she could see the wolves gathering for another attack.

She searched for a reaction, some spell, some power she could use to protect Davyn and still be able to fight and protect herself.

Help me!

CHAPTER FORTY-THREE

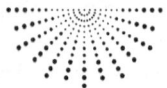

*a*t first, Reg didn't know where the answer had come from. It was not verbal. She did not see or hear his approach.

But she knew he was there, and he was on the warpath. No one was allowed to attack *his people*.

Even given the number of times she had seen him plummet out of the sky, it still always made her jump and give a little cry of alarm.

Every. Single. Time.

In the midst of the battle, it felt like the sky was falling. And not just falling, but blazing with fire.

The dragon hung, suspended in midair, just over Davyn's head. He bellowed with rage and let loose a blast of fire that put Davyn's and Reg's to shame.

For a moment, it seemed as if the battle had been suspended in time. Everyone froze. Their cries and the chaos of noise still rang in Reg's ears and she felt like she had been suddenly deafened.

Ember dropped the rest of the way to the ground and turned to attack the wolves who had been menacing Davyn.

"No," Reg told him. "Protect the wolves! We are here to drive off the other warlocks."

Ember turned baleful eyes on her, finding it hard to believe the warlocks were the aggressors. Reg formed a picture in her mind of John and the warlocks ambushing the wolves as they rested after the peace accord had been signed. She made it as detailed as she could, not having seen it herself.

With another roar, Ember looked around and identified the closest warlock.

A ripple of fear spread over the gathered company. The wisest of the warlocks immediately turned and ran, not waiting to find out what the dragon would do.

Those with egos bigger than their brains who somehow thought they could stand up to a dragon and come off as conquerors stayed to face Ember or to continue the fight against the wolves. Reg stood there breathing heavily from exertion and shook her head. Not the brightest bulbs in the drawer.

Ember's mouth closed around the torso of the nearest warlock, picking him up off the ground. He shook the man like a dog shakes a rat, eventually tossing him over the trees in the direction of the highway. He approached the next warlock, who brandished a staff and shot volleys of magical defense against Ember, staunchly believing he could overcome the dragon with his weak efforts. Ember plucked the staff out of the warlock's hands and held it in his claws, examining it.

He eventually put it into his mouth, crunched it like a large pretzel stick, and belched fire at its hapless owner, who stood fast for another two seconds, then turned tail and ran.

There wasn't much more for Ember to do. He chased after a few more warlocks, as playful as a cat full of kibble, then eventually trotted back to Reg. He saw Davyn, crouched down, and eyed him, shifting his head from side to side playfully.

Davyn chuckled and offered his hand to Ember, who accepted some jaw and ear scratches from him, purring away.

Julian crept out from behind a tree and stood near Davyn as if he had been fully aligned with Davyn right from the start and never left his side. He ignored Reg's glare.

CHAPTER FORTY-FOUR

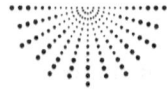

$\mathcal{A}$s amused as Reg was by Ember's delight over the encounter with the pesky warlocks, she wasn't smiling for long. She looked around the field of battle, her levity fading fast and the anxiety reasserting itself like a hole right through her middle. The sky was growing brighter, lighting everything around her dimly.

John's plan had been devastating to the werewolves. Waiting until the peace accord had been signed and the wolves were back in their dens with no reason to think that they were in any danger, he and the other warlocks had caught the wolves completely off guard. They had encountered much less resistance than they would have if they had attacked a day or two earlier. It had all been carefully calculated to cause as much damage as possible.

Reg was sickened by the amount of blood on the ground and on the discarded weapons. The troubles in Black Sands, the friction between the warlocks and werewolves, had been stressful and worrisome, but nothing like this. John had taken the war to a whole new level. He had planned to inflict maximum damage, and that was what he had done.

Reg and those who had been spared looked around, evaluating, trying to decide what to do first. Reg steeled herself and approached a werewolf who had fallen nearby, not sure whether she would find him dead or alive and grievously injured.

His wounds were severe, but he was still drawing pained, shuddering breaths. He had a mostly black coat that Reg recognized when she knelt beside him.

Jake.

Reg raised her hands. There was no doubt in her mind as there had been when she had considered healing Corvin. If she did not act immediately, Jake was as good as dead and even, after all that he had done to her, and done to the wolves before becoming one of them, it didn't even occur to her not to do everything she could for him.

She flooded Jake with healing heat. He was so severely injured that she didn't know whether there was any chance she could do anything but provide some relief from his pain. But as she warmed him with her healing fire, she saw the wounds closing. The bleeding slowed and stopped; the wounds began to crust over with dry scabs.

Werewolves were renowned for their rapid healing abilities. It seemed that Jake's natural regeneration, coupled with whatever enhancements he had developed during his experiments on the wolves had combined with Reg's own healing powers to transform fatal injuries into potentially survivable ones.

Jake groaned and writhed. He turned his head to look at her, his body still curled slightly to protect the soft belly, the vital internal organs. He transformed into his human form, which Reg thought a foolish and unnecessary use of the energy he needed to conserve if he were to survive his injuries.

"Reg."

She put her hand on his shoulder, trying to quiet him. He shouldn't be using up his energy trying to talk to her.

But Jake had never been one to listen to anyone, especially a mere woman, someone expected to serve him, not to counsel him.

"It was John," Jake ground out. He swore several times, stung by the betrayal. "He brought the warlocks. They ambushed us. Attacked us in our sleep. In the safety of our own dens. After we signed the accord." He grasped her hand and squeezed it. "Treachery! He and I had an agreement!"

"I know," Reg agreed softly, trying to keep him quiet and still. "Just rest, Jake. You're hurt. You need to be still. Give yourself time to heal." She looked out over the field of battle. "There are others who will need care as well."

"John promised—" Jake groaned, letting go of Reg's hand to clutch at his stomach, crying out. "The traitor. Perfidy!"

"I know," Reg told him.

He was quiet for a few minutes, breathing raggedly. Reg tried to push more heat into him, but his body could only do so much. He needed time and a safe, quiet environment. Reg brushed Jake's hair away from his eyes. "Just rest quietly."

In defiance of her instruction, he stared at her, his eyes blazing with hate and animosity. "Who were they?" he demanded.

Reg frowned. "The warlocks," she told him, wondering if he was already that far gone, so much so that he would forget what had happened, what he had just told her. "John and the warlocks."

"Who?" he repeated.

"John." Reg looked around, trying to reconstruct what she had seen from the moment she arrived. She didn't know all the warlocks in the coven, but she should recognize most of them, at least. Especially those who were more active in the coven. Wilf, who had sold Reg her car and others she had spoken to when Davyn had disappeared. When Corvin had been campaigning for election to the coven. There might be one or two that she didn't at least recognize. "Uh… I don't know. I didn't know all of them."

The same was true of the warlocks she had seen harassing the wolf in town. She hadn't recognized them.

She stared at Jake. "Who were they?" she echoed.

Sarah was circulating from one injured party to another, seeing if there were anything she could do. Davyn was doing the same thing, using his fire as Reg was, to provide strength and healing wherever he could. Sarah stopped to look at Jake and put her hand on Reg's shoulder, shaking her head.

She blinked at Reg. "You're bleeding."

"No, it's not my blood."

Sarah gripped Reg's arm gently and rotated, looking at it. Reg looked down at a deep gash that had already bled quite a bit.

"Oh... I didn't see that." She remembered getting hit and knew her arm was burning, but she hadn't been able to stop and look at it.

"Let me." Sarah held her in position as she murmured an incantation that relieved the burning pain and slowed the bleeding. "We'll need to get a dressing on this."

Reg nodded impatiently. If it wasn't actively bleeding, it could wait. "Sarah... did you know the warlocks you saw here?"

Sarah looked at her as if she had to travel a long distance to hear and understand what Reg had just said. She blinked, and her forehead wrinkled. "Did I...? I know the warlocks in the coven."

"Yes," Reg agreed. "You've known them for years. Who from the coven did you see here?"

Sarah thought about it some more, her eyes still far away and confused. She looked down at Jake's face and then around her again.

"They were strangers," she said with dawning comprehension. "Who were they?"

Davyn joined them. He looked down at Jake and, like Sarah, shook his head. "I'm sorry, Reg."

"You were the leader of the coven," Reg said. "Did you know the warlocks who were here? Did you see them before they ran away?"

Davyn inspected Reg's arm as well, looking over Sarah's handi-work, then added his own, pushing the warmth of his fire into her to help speed the healing. Reg felt energized and stronger, and the wound started to scab over.

"I was rather occupied with defending myself from multiple werewolves," Davyn told her.

"I know. But did you know them?"

Davyn said nothing, walking away from her. She thought his reaction rude until she saw his intent. He approached one of the fallen warlocks and, with an effort, rolled him onto his back. He looked down at the man's face.

"I... I don't know this man."

Generally, it was possible to tell the wolves and the warlocks apart even when in their human form. The wolves wore more natural clothing; wool, leather, and fur, in loose, flowing styles. The man on the ground appeared to be a warlock, dressed in modern style, synthetic blends, with a black cloak similar to the one Davyn wore. But his face was as unfamiliar to Reg as it was to Davyn.

They all looked at each other, trying to make sense of it. Jake groaned and gurgled. Reg put her hand on him and tried to press more healing heat into him, but there was only so much his body could receive. It still needed to do the work to heal itself. Even with his werewolf powers, he was struggling.

"There are others we need to help," Sarah said apologetically. "We will call for an ambulance." She cast another pitying look at Jake that told Reg she didn't believe he would make it.

She moved on to tend to the other injured wolves and warlocks. Reg was relieved to see some of the injured struggling to their feet. Sarah and Davyn circulated, helping whoever they could.

Reg saw Julian kneeling beside a werewolf, talking to him earnestly, and hoped he wasn't causing any trouble.

It was a while before an ambulance arrived, and the paramedics tried to triage the injuries, calling in additional ambulances from nearby towns. Reg reluctantly left them to look after Jake, rising creakily to her feet.

She looked around. The warlocks who were ambulatory had gotten as far as they could from the site. Ember was gone. Reg had forgotten about him, but Davyn must have told him to leave, or he had gone when he'd heard the approach of the ambulance.

A few werewolves were wandering around, some in human form and some in wolf form. The paramedics weren't paying any attention to them. Maybe they thought they were just dogs or refused to see them. Or maybe they were practitioners and knew exactly what was going on.

Reg didn't see Zora. Her stomach twisted with anxiety. Where was she? Zora was a soldier for the pack, not just a stay-at-home mom. Had she been one of the first wolves to respond to the attack? Reg worried that Zora was one of the bodies she could still see on the ground. She didn't know how many of them were injured and how many might be dead.

How many had the pack lost today?

Reg tried to orient herself to her surroundings, picturing the den she had previously taken Zora to. It was her sister's den, but did Zora live there too?

She followed her instincts, walking away from the field of the injured, watching for any landmarks, listening for any suspicious rustles in the trees. There might still be warlocks around if they had not all been able to get cleanly away. Or there could be frightened or injured wolves hiding in the trees who could mistake her for the enemy.

In a few minutes, she was there. She recognized the rock formations, the clumps of trees, and an old sabal palm she had seen the last time she had been there.

"Zora?" she called quietly. "Zora, it's Reg. Are you here?"

CHAPTER FORTY-FIVE

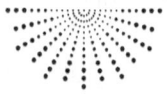

*S*tay away," a high voice warned.

"It's okay," Reg said. "It's Reg. I'm here to see if everyone is okay. The battle is over and the warlocks are gone."

"Go away."

Reg could hear movement—some yips and growls, the cubs moving around anxiously, getting in each others' way. It helped to calm her down. At least the cubs were okay.

"You know me, guys," she assured the cubs. "It's just Reg. No one is with me."

There was more movement within. Reg could hear someone coming toward her. She peeked in the entrance and, where she expected to see Zora's sister, she instead saw the gangly human form of one of the cubs, his clothes and hair in disarray. He crept toward her carefully, wary.

"Fenris," Reg said with relief when she could make out his face. "Are you okay? Is everyone all right?"

He had a bloody nose, and the blood had soaked into the front of his shirt. When he wiped at his nose with his hand, Reg could see that his knuckles were swollen and bruised. He had been fighting. Not a little tussle with his littermates, but a real fight.

"Did they come here?" she asked in horror. "The warlocks? Was one of them here?"

Fenris nodded. He was skittish, looking around like he expected the warlock to come back out of the trees behind her. It made Reg nervous, and she reached out with her senses, checking to see if there was anyone nearby. There could still be refugees in the woods, both attackers and victims.

She sensed someone coming toward them at a quick clip.

Who is there?

Stay away from my cubs or I will rip you to shreds!

Reg sighed with relief. She made a calming motion to Fenris. "Your mom is coming. Can you sense her?"

He looked at Reg with wide eyes, not believing her, then reached out to Zora himself, calling for her to come to him. Reg wanted to touch Fenris's shoulder, to comfort him, but he was skittish and the wolves did not generally like physical contact with humans, so she respected his space, just staying close by and trying to project calm, soothing thoughts as much as possible.

It was only a couple of minutes before Zora burst into the clearing in her wolf form. She transformed to human shape and hugged Fenris to her fiercely. She didn't engage with Reg immediately. She had other concerns.

"The others?" she demanded of Fenris, "Is everyone okay?"

He nodded. His eyes were shining with tears, but he didn't shed them. He stood straight-backed, as tall as his preadolescent frame would allow, his shoulders squared and chest thrust out. "I wouldn't let anyone hurt them."

Zora dug a white handkerchief out of the pocket of her long dress and wiped at the blood on Fenris's face. "You did well. What happened? They came here? Who was it?"

"I do not know. A warlock, but he was not big, and he did not get in. I would not let him hurt the others."

"You are a brave wolf. Even if he was not big, he was still bigger than you, and had magical gifts."

Fenris examined his bruised and swollen knuckles. "I hit him. They hurt now, but they didn't when it happened."

"No," Zora agreed. She looked at Reg, taking in her presence and her appearance for the first time. "When did you arrive?"

"Not long ago. Too late to protect everyone. Jake..." Reg's voice broke, and she changed the direction of her explanation. "I came with Davyn, as soon as we could. Davyn didn't know anything about the planned ambush. You have to know that. He would never have approved of something like that."

Zora nodded briefly. "I do not know him well, but I believe he was not involved. He has always behaved honorably toward the wolves in our negotiations. It was the other one. John."

Reg nodded. "Yes. And I'm not sure if anyone else in the coven was involved. Maybe a few of them. But most of the warlocks we saw were not from Black Sands. Davyn didn't recognize them."

"Not from Black Sands?" Zora looked puzzled. "That is very odd." But she nodded slowly. "There have been strangers in town lately. Many of the warlocks who have been involved in the problems in town are men that I did not know. I thought... it was just because we have not been here very long and I didn't know them yet. We don't have anything to do with most of the coven members. Most of the pack does not associate with humans and there are few like you and Davyn who are friends of the pack. So we don't have the opportunity to get to know most of them."

Reg wondered what was happening back in the clearing where most of the battle had occurred. She wanted to keep up on it, but didn't want to leave Zora and the cubs. It was far more peaceful at the den, and she didn't want to reimmerse herself in the aftermath of the conflict.

How many more would there be before they could put a stop to it? She had gone to bed thinking it was all over, that they had reached a peaceful settlement and everything would return to normal.

Now, she was faced with the revelation that John had never intended to keep the peace between the clans. He had done what he did only for show, to reassure everyone and to be able to catch the wolves off guard. It was a treacherous betrayal. She wouldn't have believed it of most of the warlocks she knew. Most of them were honorable, ethical, and devoted, and would never have tainted their souls with such an act.

She took a deep breath, trying to calm her still-racing heart. She was safe for now. Zora and Fenris and the rest of the cubs were all right. She thought of Theodore. He could let her know what was happening back in the clearing and perhaps also give her some intelligence on what was going on with John. She had, after all, tasked him with finding out his secrets, if he could. What had Theodore discovered?

Theodore stood before her. He looked down at the ground, perhaps sensing she was not pleased with him.

"Theodore. I'm glad you could come."

He cleared his throat. "I will always come when you call."

"Is that so? What is going on in the clearing back there? Have they figured out who was involved in the attack besides John?"

"John Saunders is the leader of the warlock coven. He was elected in an emergency election held two nights ago. He brought the warlocks here tonight."

"Who did he bring?"

Theodore clicked and cocked his head. "He is the leader of the warlocks. He brought the warlocks with him."

It was clear to her that he didn't know and was just guessing at the answers based on John's association with the warlock coven in Black Sands.

"Which of them?"

"The coven consists of John Saunders, Davyn Smithy, Corvin Hunter, Wilf—"

"Did he bring any of those people here tonight?"

"The former leader of the coven is Davyn Smithy. Corvin is also a former leader, but he only served for—"

"I know who they are. I want to know who was here tonight."

Theodore clicked a few times, trying to come up with another answer, then finally looked at her. "I do not know."

"What did you find out about John? I asked you to see what you could find out about him and what he and Jake were up to."

Theodore nodded his agreement, but didn't offer an answer. Reg caught herself putting her hands on her hips, unconsciously mirroring the various foster mothers who had confronted her about the truth throughout her childhood.

"Theodore. Tell me what you know about what John has been up to."

He cocked his head. "John and Jake have been meeting with each other in secret."

"To come to an accord? To work out what terms they could come to when they met in public?"

"No." Theodore's expression and voice were flat, but he seemed to have some regret as he shook his head. "They have been conspiring about becoming the leaders of their factions. The conflict between their clans has been helpful in their overthrowing the previous leaders."

"Show that the previous leader didn't have what it took to end the conflict. Stir the members up and incite a coup."

Theodore nodded his agreement. Zora was staring at him. "You knew this? How long? Why did you not tell us?"

Theodore glanced sideways at Reg. "A wolf is not my master. I have no fealty to you."

"You should have told me," Reg told him. "I could have told Zora and the coven what was going on. Why didn't you tell me? I asked you to find out what they were doing. I thought you were going to be James Bond and all that. Why didn't you report back what you found?"

Theodore vanished.

Reg stood there with her mouth open.

She had been warned. Sarah, Davyn, and Corvin had all warned her not to put her trust in the homunculus. They had said not to trust what he said, and that he might not have the loyalty to her that she thought he did.

He had never behaved that way before. She knew that he didn't always get the answers right and that his ability to answer truthfully was based on what information he had consumed. But she had not known him to actively resist doing what she had asked of him, or to disappear when she was talking to him.

She looked at Zora.

"You have a problem," Zora told her.

Reg stooped and picked up a handful of dirt. She tossed it in front of her and invoked Theodore formally.

"From soil and stone, by magic spin,
　　Theodore reform, our work begin."

The dirt swirled in front of her for a long time before Theodore finally took shape. Reg folded her arms across her chest.

"What else do you know that you haven't told me?" she asked. "About John and Jake."

He clicked a number of times, his head jerking. Reg didn't know if he were going to have a seizure or disappear again, or shut down like an overloaded computer.

"John had a plan to overcome the wolves once he was instated as the coven leader."

"The ambush."

Theodore nodded. "Yes."

"How did you know that? Obviously, that wasn't part of his discussions with Jake."

"No." Theodore didn't say anything at first, the silence drawing out long and uncomfortable between them. "He hired other warlocks. Warlocks from out of town."

"Mercenaries," Zora said.

Theodore glanced at her, then nodded his agreement. "Warlocks hired to cause problems in town and to participate in the ambush."

"Why didn't you come to me with this information?" Reg demanded.

He looked away. "You wanted to broker peace between the factions. You were interested in finding the Oathstone. I... didn't know you still wanted information about John Saunders."

"You knew I wanted peace and didn't think telling me that John was hiring mercenaries to cause trouble and ambush the wolves was relevant?"

"I didn't know about the ambush. They signed the peace treaty. I thought it was over and you had what you wanted."

So had Reg. So had everyone.

"You should have told me everything about the mercenaries."

Theodore kicked at the dirt and didn't answer.

CHAPTER FORTY-SIX

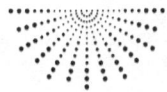

Still holding Fenris to her as she had been since her return, Zora gave him a squeeze and kissed the top of his head. "Where are the others? Everyone is okay?"

"In the den. I told them to stay there," Fenris said, his voice firm, demonstrating how he had given the orders and taken care of things while she had been gone.

"Come out, come out and see Mama," Zora called into the den, and the other cubs came tumbling out, eager to see her. In wolf form, they jumped at Zora on their hind legs, whining and rubbing their snouts against her as she scratched ears and greeted each one, checking that they had no injuries. Fenris was the only one who showed any sign of the attack.

One of the girl pups transformed, and Reg saw it was Adolpha. She tried not to make a big deal of the transformation. It was the first time one of the cubs had changed in front of her, and she didn't want any of them to be embarrassed to take whichever form they preferred or to change in front of her.

Adolpha clung to her mother on the opposite side from Fenris, nestled under her armpit, one arm gripping her waist.

"Mama, you should have seen Fenris," Adolpha said in her high, piping voice. "He told us all to stay in the den and he went into the tunnel as a biped. He wouldn't let them past him. He fought fiercely, refusing to let anyone past him."

Zora ruffled Adolpha's hair. "He was very brave. And very strong, to hold off a full-grown man bigger than himself." She stroked Fenris's shaggy hair. "He did well to protect his family."

Fenris's eyes shone. Not with tears this time, but pride at her praise. "I would not let anyone hurt the others."

"Where is your auntie?"

They all looked back toward the den. "She was not feeling well," Adolpha informed Zora. "She says the puppies come soon." Adolpha smiled, her eyes sparkling. "I can't wait for the puppies to be born! I am going to help her take care of them."

"You will be a very good helper. Go see if she needs anything. There is still much to be done."

Adolpha scampered back into the den. Zora scratched the other cubs' ears and jaws again, then straightened up. Reg could see her fatigue, but she made no sign she was ready to take a break from the chaos for a nap.

"Aleph!"

Reg had not been aware of the old alpha's approach. She turned and looked behind her at Aleph, immediately evaluating him.

She had feared that when Jake had taken over as alpha that Aleph might be dead, or at least badly injured. She had not asked at the peace talks, as inquiring after the past leader of the pack did not seem appropriate.

The old wolf did not have any visible injuries. He limped a little as he loped through the open area toward them, but he certainly didn't seem to be half-dead.

How fares your family? Aleph asked.

"They are fine. No injuries other than this one." Zora grasped Fenris's jaw to indicate his bloody nose. "He was a great strength and protected the others."

Aleph sniffed at Fenris's legs and let Fenris stroke his head and ears.

There is much to be done, he informed Zora. *We took many injuries. Jake's survival is doubtful and, if he does recover, he will be in the hospital for some time.*

Reg wondered how that would work, when Jake's preferred form was as a wolf. Would he be at the veterinary hospital? Did the doctors and nurses look the other way when one of their patients shifted into another form? It must be very complicated.

"I have news," Reg told Aleph. "About Jake and John."

He transformed into the man Reg had seen at the town council meeting, shaggy blond hair swept back over his shoulders and a wary expression. Experienced, careful, and slow to jump to conclusions. Reg gave a little nod of thanks, knowing he had changed to make communication easier for her.

"What news?"

"Jake and John were in cahoots. Using the werewolf-warlock tensions to make their people think that they needed a new leader, one who could resolve the situation peacefully or lead them into battle. They were intentionally agitating and making things worse so that they could get the votes."

"Our leadership process is not democratic," Aleph said dryly. "But it does help to have the pack behind you, to convince them that you are the better choice."

Reg nodded her understanding. "And the warlocks do vote on the next leader of the coven. John managed to convince them that he was the best choice to take over after his father."

"None of that changes anything. Though it was wrong of them to collaborate to take over their tribes, there is nothing to be done about it. They achieved the positions they set out to acquire. That takes determination, persuasion, and the ability to lead." He shrugged. "They achieved their goals. Jake got his day in the spotlight."

It had literally been only one day. Reg supposed he'd gotten more than his fifteen minutes of fame, but not much.

"That isn't all. John hired mercenaries to cause the trouble in town and to ambush the pack last night. It wasn't the warlock coven. It was hired guns."

Aleph scratched his jaw, thinking about this. "You are sure of this? It is a very important point."

Reg thought about her source. She believed that what Theodore had told her was true, particularly after observing that Davyn did not know the warlocks they had seen participate in the battle. She bowed her head.

"The facts will need to be checked," she admitted. "Will you talk to Davyn? We came to try to stop the fighting. He was still here the last I saw. He can tell you what he knows of the warlocks he saw here."

Aleph nodded his agreement. "You were not wise to come here in the midst of a battle with the humans," he pointed out. He indicated her arm. "You were injured?"

"It's okay. It's mostly healed." Reg looked at the slash mark again. It was good to have friends with healing skills. It looked as if it were a few weeks old rather than fresh. "What John and the hired warlocks did was… it cannot be forgiven. Signing a peace accord and then ambushing the wolves? I can't believe he would do that." She paused. "Except… I can believe almost anything of John. He is… not well in his mind."

"Humans have weak minds," Aleph allowed. "But for him to commit such atrocities… that cannot be blamed solely on a broken mind. That can be blamed only on evil."

Reg knew that it was true. She had tried to give John the benefit of the doubt because she knew how he had been raised and felt bad for him. She had hoped that once he was free of his mother and able to make his own choices that he would choose right. He would turn his life around and become a better person. The kind of person that his mother would never let him be.

But Verity had never left him, even when she died. She would not release her hold on him. Of course, John still had the choice whether to obey the voice in his ear or not. Reg had a similar problem, with the voice of her mother and siren sisters always talking— or shrieking—in her head. And all the other ghosts. It was never quiet inside Reg's head.

Aleph was watching her. "Don't feel sorry for him."

"I know I shouldn't. I just wish he'd lived out his own life and made better choices."

CHAPTER FORTY-SEVEN

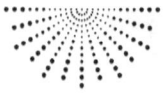

$\mathcal{W}$ ill you take over the leadership of the pack again?" Reg asked Aleph tentatively.

He looked at her. "What do you think?"

"I think Jake wasn't fit to lead it in the first place. I don't know how he and John managed to manipulate everyone so easily. I don't think he was ever qualified to be the alpha."

Aleph gave a brief nod, and Reg thought she had answered the question correctly. That made her stop and think about exactly what she had said. A plan started to form in her mind.

"Where is John?" Aleph asked. "Do you know where he lives?"

"Oh… uh, not really. I don't deal with him. But Davyn would know, and he was with the others in the clearing."

"Davyn was an honorable man. We did not have these problems when he was leading the coven. I have never seen these kinds of problems in all my years. Humans and wolves do not mix well, but this kind of violence," Aleph shook his head. "It has never been in all my memory. Not in the pack's memory. Perhaps not since Vargrena and Drakskald."

Reg touched the Oathstone, still in the pocket of her shorts where she had placed it before leaving the cottage.

"Maybe we will still get another chance to use the Oathstone."

"I fear it no longer bears any power."

"Maybe," Reg allowed, "or maybe we just didn't use it properly."

"We called on its power, and it failed us."

"Maybe we'll still get the chance to try it again," Reg repeated.

Aleph made a motion to sweep this comment away. "We need to go talk to Davyn. We need to take immediate action. Strike while the iron is hot."

Reg wondered if Aleph was joking about Davyn's family being traditional smithies when he mentioned 'striking while the iron is hot.' But he didn't smile or laugh and she didn't want to be the one to point it out. He might not appreciate the levity.

Before returning to their work, Reg reached out to Fenris and held her hands above his, and they both watched the bruising fade and the cuts scab over. Reg raised her hands to heal his nose as well, and Fenris objected, putting his hand over his nose. "Leave it," he protested. "I am a man!"

"And you will have plenty more opportunities to prove it. You will acquire plenty of other scars. No point in having a deviated septum, too."

He frowned at her worriedly. "What is that?"

"It makes you sound like this when you sleep," Reg told him, and demonstrated a resounding snore. "Now, do you really want to scare away all the wildlife in the area because you sound like a dragon while you sleep?"

Fenris shook his head.

"This won't make it perfect," Reg advised. "It will just help it to heal faster. You might still have a scar."

Fenris remained still while she exuded more healing warmth and did her best to heal his nose.

Then Reg and Aleph returned to the clearing. Still more of the bodies or injured had been cleaned away, but it was still a chaotic and bloody scene. Aleph looked around and approached Davyn, who was using his healing power where he could and looking tired.

"You need to eat and drink," Reg told him. "Replenish your energy."

"I know. You're one to talk. Have you stopped to take a break?"

"No, but you've done a lot more healing than I have."

"I saw you with Jake. You used a lot of energy trying to hold him together."

"Did you see when they took him away? Was he still..."

"He was still hanging on. I am not making any promises, though. He didn't look good."

"Then that is one less problem to worry about," Aleph said harshly. "We can look instead to the real problem. The warlocks."

Davyn was looking a little green. And it wasn't just because he was pale from all of the healing he was doing.

"You know that I am no longer the coven's leader," he said apologetically to Aleph. "What has been done here in the name of the coven is... despicable. That is not the way that honorable warlocks behave. It is not how the coven is run and never has been."

"Where is John?" Aleph cut across any apologies or explanation.

"I don't know. He may have gone home. Or he may have a special place where he meets with the imposters he has hired. Perhaps..." Davyn considered. "A sacred site like the Temple Orange Grove. Since that is where the wolves ambushed him, maybe he thinks it appropriate that he returns there after ambushing the wolves in return."

"This was nothing like the small, targeted attack of October's group," Aleph pointed out.

Reg moved her hands as if to wipe their arguments aside.

"No one should have ambushed anyone. Not at the beginning, and not in retaliation. That is not the way to reconcile and live in harmony."

Aleph and Davyn both agreed with this. They couldn't really argue the point.

"I will get a team together," Aleph said. "We do not have a lot of wolves left in fighting form, but we will go after John. He will not be expecting us to fight back so quickly. We can perhaps take him off guard and dispatch him so that he cannot do anything like this again."

Reg opened her mouth to object, then stopped herself. What *was* the appropriate way to deal with John? A slap on the wrist? Turn him over to the authorities? If they tried to explain to the human police that John had attacked the werewolves and used magic against them, they would be laughed out of town. Maybe they could understand some of what had happened today. But they were not equipped to deal with a warlock like John. Even if they tried to put him in jail as a murderer, he would just use his powers to escape and would go unpunished.

"John is very powerful," Davyn told Aleph. "He is like Hunter, a power eater. We have no way of knowing what gifts he currently has or how strong he is. From what I have seen of him lately... he has been building his power and is very strong. I don't know if there is a practitioner in Black Sands who is powerful enough to oppose him, wolf or human."

Aleph glared at Davyn, his eyes taking on a weird glow in the morning light. "You expect us to ignore this attack and not retaliate? To sit back, lick our wounds, and wait for him to attack again? When we have even fewer wolves to defend ourselves? If he wants us out of Florida, he has made a good start. He will either extinguish us single-handedly or force us to retreat and start somewhere else where there is less opposition. You humans say you want wolves in Florida again, but you clearly do not."

"You can't judge all humans by what John would do. No more than I can judge all wolves by Jake's behavior. I came here to protect the wolves, not to fight you. I came here as a friend."

Aleph had to concede it was the truth. Even faced with multiple attacking werewolves, Davyn had refused to raise his hand against them. He had kept his vow with Ulfrikarr.

"We will not be deterred from fighting John again," Aleph asserted. "As soon as possible. We must find out where he is and we must fight him."

"Corvin is the only warlock who could match John," Reg pointed out.

Davyn looked at her. "Yes," he admitted slowly. "That was once true. But because of the curse, he can no longer use his powers, no matter how strong they are."

"But he could if we healed him."

Davyn shook his head in disbelief. "We have already attempted that. We failed. I do not know the way to heal Corvin."

"The Oathstone. I still think that we can do it with the Oathstone."

"We already tried that."

"But I don't think we did it the right way."

Aleph looked back and forth at them. "You think you know the right way to use the Oathstone now? You think it still has powers?"

Reg hesitated. She had no way to know if it still had powers. She had certainly not found any. It was a rock. She didn't get the same feelings from it as from gems of power. Or the artifacts that she, Sarah, and Davyn had retrieved in order to unpetrify Corvin and set everything set to rights again. It didn't feel like anything other than a lake rock. There was nothing unique about it but the runes that had been engraved on it. She might have thought that it was just a replica or even a child's joke, except for the way it had been turned over to them by Ulfrikarr. If it had no power, why had he guarded it all those years? Why extract promises from Zora and Davyn before passing it on to them?

"I have not seen or felt its powers," she admitted. "Not even a bit of an aura. But I think that its powers must still lie dormant. They were not activated when we tried to use it."

"You mean when we tried to use it to heal Corvin, or during the peace talks?" Davyn asked.

"Both. I don't think it had anything to do with the peace treaty. I think that was all Jake's and John's plot to install themselves as the leaders and make themselves look good. And part of John's plot to put the wolves at ease and make them think they had what they had been looking for."

"I saw no sign that the stone had anything to do with them signing a peace treaty," Aleph agreed.

"Because it has not been activated." Reg tried to say it with as much conviction as she could, as if she were sure that what she said was the truth and all they had to do was follow her suggestions if they wanted to work things out between the wolves and the warlocks.

If they just used the Oathstone properly, it would all come together this time. She couldn't stand by and let the wolves and the warlocks keep attacking each other until one group or the other was wiped out.

CHAPTER FORTY-EIGHT

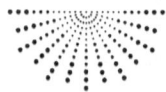

*C*orvin was, of course, not terribly excited to find Reg on his doorstep once again. When he saw Aleph there with her, he lowered his eyes and didn't complain about how hard-done-by he was that they kept coming to see him to ask him questions or favors.

"I heard from Sarah about the ambush," he told Aleph, and shook his head. "I want you to know I had nothing to do with it. I would never counsel John to do something like that. I thought he was... I thought he was better than that. I didn't raise the boy, you know. I didn't even know that he existed until last year. My son was presented to me as a full-grown man. I have little influence over him."

"I do not hold you responsible," Aleph growled. "Nothing like that ever happened before. Not while Davyn was the leader and not while you were."

"And I heard about Jake. I'm sorry."

Reg eyed him as they sat down in his living room. Sorry that Jake had overthrown Aleph? Sorry that he was injured? That he might not survive the day with his injuries?

Aleph made a huffing noise and didn't say what he thought of Corvin's sentiment.

"So…" Corvin looked at Reg, Davyn, and Aleph. "What are we all doing here?"

"Trying to heal you," Reg told him.

Corvin didn't laugh at her. He didn't act exasperated or complain that she should just leave him alone and quit trying. But he shook his head slowly, clearly not of the opinion that they could do anything to help him.

They had tried before. What would be different this time?

"How do you intend to do that?"

"With the Oathstone."

"You already tried that once. It has dried up, Reg. If it ever had any power, it has all been drained out now. I would have felt it if it had any power. You did your best. I know you wanted it to work, but sometimes… things just don't happen the way you hope."

"I think it did not work because we haven't yet activated the power of the Oathstone."

"You were given it by the guardian spirit. You had obtained it lawfully; if it had any power, then it should work."

"The Oathstone was created as part of the reconciliation between the warlocks and the werewolves in ancient times." Reg would be lying if she said she knew exactly when that had been. Ancient could be any time before last week, as far as she was concerned. "It was meant to be the bridge between the alpha wolf and the coven leader."

Corvin nodded. "Which is why we used Zora and Davyn before. A she-wolf and a warlock, just like in the beginning."

"But Zora and Davyn were not the leaders of the wolf pack and the coven."

Corvin considered this. He nodded slowly. "No. They were not. You think it can only be used by the leaders of the two communities."

"Yeah. That's what I'm thinking. If you want to heal the rift or sign a peace accord between two different factions, it doesn't make sense for it to be done by two people with no authority or binding power."

Corvin looked at Aleph, considering this, and slowly nodded his agreement.

"So, who is the leader of the wolf pack?" he asked.

Aleph had, of course, been deposed by Jake. But Jake was out of the picture now. Disabled, possibly killed.

"I have resumed my place as alpha," Aleph asserted.

Davyn looked at Corvin. "And who is the leader of the coven?"

"You elected John, did you not?"

Davyn shook his head. "Not me. I did not have a part in that vote. It was done while I was away. And without you, I assume, since you have not left this house."

Corvin made a motion that Reg assumed meant it did not matter who had voted and who had been absent, as long as John had been elected.

"He took leadership under false pretenses," Davyn pointed out, "He hired mercenaries to cause trouble in town and to participate in the ambush last night. The actual members of the coven would not participate in such a thing. But by hiring someone to stir things up, to cause complaints on both the sides of the wolves and the coven members, he managed to convince people that there was a problem where none actually existed—or at least, a problem that was not as large as it appeared—and that neither you nor I was able to manage it. He used all of these deceptions as well as his charms to manipulate the coven members into voting for him."

Reg would have expected Corvin to immediately accept what Davyn said and assert that his son had not been properly elected but, instead, he sat there thinking about it and saying nothing at first.

"Under the coven's traditions, is that enough to reject his leadership and say he was never properly elected? Or is it *caveat emptor*?" He looked at Reg, " 'Let the buyer beware.' The members of the coven knew what John was when they accepted him into the coven. They accepted that he might have influence over them. They still welcomed him into the coven."

It seemed odd at first that Corvin would use this argument against his own interests. If John was lawfully elected, then he was the leader of the coven and not Corvin, and he was the only one who could lawfully use the Oathstone.

But if he said that John's nature and his ability to charm the other members of the coven and influence them in their decisions invalidated anything that he did and was an unacceptable use of his powers, then he said the same for himself. Any decision the coven made under his leadership and influence could be challenged.

"I don't think this hinges on whether he used his charms and whether it was acceptable for him to use his inborn gifts to influence the coven," Davyn countered. "I think it hinges on his deception. His choice to hire mercenaries from outside the coven to deceive the townspeople and to increase the level of unrest. And to leverage the increasing concern over innocent people being injured to take over the leadership of the coven."

CHAPTER FORTY-NINE

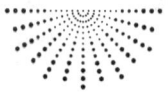

*C*orvin steepled his hands in front of his face, nodding. Reg realized that it was the first time since Corvin had been injured in October's attack that she had seen him without a drink in his hands. His hands were steady, and there was more color in his cheeks than there had been lately.

"Even if you accept that he was the properly elected leader of the coven," Davyn went on, "we as practitioners operate on one immutable rule. *An' it harm none.* John clearly broke that rule not only by hiring outside parties to harass the wolves and frighten the townspeople. Not only that, but he ambushed the wolves after a peace accord had been signed. I have seen what harm that caused on the battlefield, and that is probably only a fraction of the actual harm done, even to those who were not there."

"Are you expelling him from the coven?"

"I am not in a position to do that by myself. But for the sake of this discussion, John no longer qualifies as a member of the coven and, as such, cannot be the coven's leader. We cannot accept a leader who has shown such perfidy and caused such harm."

Davyn's eyes went to Reg.

"The coven is not a hierarchal structure. It is a brotherhood, a fellowship. Our leaders are not commanders of armies. They are servants to the coven and its members. Leaders by example, mentors, teachers. John has not served the coven but has caused it harm by his actions. It will be a hundred years before people will trust the warlocks of our coven again. The taint of this act will remain with us."

Corvin straightened. "I accept your premise. John cannot be the leader of the coven. At this time, the coven is without a leader."

Reg's heart fell. They needed a leader to activate the Oathstone. Deciding there was no leader worked against their ability to bring peace to Black Sands by reconciling the wolves and the warlocks.

"No one has the power to confront John and to stop him from doing anything further except you," she pointed out. "We need to reverse October's curse so you can use your powers against him and ensure he is permanently banned from Black Sands and the coven."

"That is why you came to me?"

She had told him that they had come to heal him. Now, she revealed their motivation to do so.

Aleph shifted in his seat. Reg thought he would probably be much more comfortable pacing. He had the restless energy of an animal pacing its cage. Or children forced to sit quietly at their desks at school.

Despite the fact that giving Corvin back his power meant that she would again be vulnerable to his charms, and any practitioner in Black Sands would again be potential prey to his never-ending hunger, healing him was the only way to deal with John. No other practitioner in Black Sands had the power to confront him. They could try to confront him as a group, but they had no idea how much power he currently had or what gifts he held. He could use every gift he took from another until it was used up. Even in battle, he could suck the strength from them, just as Corvin had done when they had fought the Witch Doctor.

"In the rare cases where the leader of a coven has fallen," Davyn said, "the interim leadership of the coven has fallen upon the previous leader until a new one can be elected."

Corvin said nothing.

"Whether we accept that John was not elected because of his

deception and the unlawful use of his influence, or whether we say that his actions against the werewolves last night removed him from membership in the coven and his lawful leadership of the coven, the leadership of the coven falls back to you," Davyn summarized. "The details can be worked out with the coven later. They can decide whether you were never replaced as their leader or whether you took up the leadership again because of John's fall. But for now, you stand as the only lawful leader of the coven."

"Except that with me being powerless and unable to act as the leader of the coven, it would revert again… to you," Corvin suggested.

"Leadership does not require you to wield any powers. Only to serve the best interests of the coven."

Corvin frowned at that, a deep crease line between his brows. His whole life had been defined by power. His hunger for power, finding and seducing potential victims, surrounding himself with objects of power. It must have been strange to consider that anyone would want him to lead the coven when he could not wield his powers.

"And if I abdicate?"

Davyn sighed and shrugged. "Then I guess, as you say, I must step up and take the position. But consider…"

Corvin raised his brows questioningly.

"If I take the position as leader, and we manage to heal you and reverse the curse so that you are able to use your powers again, then you will have your powers but not the leadership of the coven. If you still want to lead the coven once your powers are restored, you cannot abdicate."

Reg opened her mouth to ask whether Davyn could pass the leadership on to Corvin or if it would go back to him if Davyn then resigned, but she had to assume that Davyn knew what he was talking about. Their situation was complex and unusual, not one they had ever dealt with before.

They couldn't wait for things to go through the ordinary channels. If they waited, nothing might remain of Black Sands or the pack to be saved. Or even of the coven. If the rest of the world thought that the coven was responsible for the attack on the wolves, they would probably be disbanded. They needed to stop John before he could do any more damage.

Corvin and Davyn sat staring at each other for a long time. Aleph stirred, growling in the back of his throat.

"Humans think too much."

"What is there to think about?" Reg agreed, speaking to Corvin. "If it doesn't work and we still can't reverse the curse, then you can give up, and Davyn can take over as the leader of the coven. If there is any coven left. By the time you decide, there might not be."

Corvin flicked her a glance of irritation.

Reg shrugged. "I'm just saying… are you going to sit around here until John makes his next move? You know he's not going to sit around for long. He'll wait until everyone thinks this is over, and then he'll strike again. Maybe it will be against the coven this time instead of the pack. If he wants absolute power, he must break down the existing structure and build what he wants. A coven that is ruled by power and fear. You can forget all your ethics about it being a brotherhood and led by example and service."

CHAPTER FIFTY

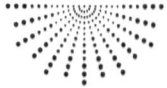

*C*orvin finally nodded.

"Okay," he conceded. "I am convinced that I am the true leader of the coven, even without the use of my powers. John was elected through deception or abdicated by violation of the coven's underlying principles and, in a time of emergency when there is no time for a new election, it falls to me to retake my position and lead the coven."

Reg refrained from rolling her eyes. She couldn't believe it had taken so much convincing to get Corvin to accept his position. She had thought that he would jump at the chance to acknowledge his leadership of the coven and attempt to reverse the werewolf curse to regain access to his powers. It was almost as if he were working against them in the restoration of his powers. Maybe he had finally come to terms with their loss and now wasn't sure what to do about the prospect of a second reversal.

"Then let's try this again," Reg encouraged. "If Aleph and Corvin hold the Oathstone, they should be able to reverse Corvin's curse. Then he can deal with John, and when John is gone..." Reg sighed as if coming to the finish line after a long race, "Then we can use it to restore peace between the wolf pack and the coven."

"Just what is your part in this?" Corvin asked Reg, shaking his head slightly in amusement. "You are not a wolf or a warlock. You don't even claim to be a witch. What do you get out of this?"

"It doesn't have anything to do with me. That's just the point. I'm not on either side. I was looking for a way to resolve the situation for both the wolves and the warlocks, not just one or the other. I was the one who found out about the Oathstone."

Through Theodore, of course. Reg tried not to think about the problem of Theodore for the time being. The information he had held back. The information he could still be holding back that would help her to negotiate peace between the two factions. She couldn't worry about that right now. She was sure she had what she needed to heal Corvin and to activate the Oathstone to facilitate an agreement between the warlocks and the wolves. She could deal with Theodore and his failure to provide all the information she needed later.

"I found out about the Oathstone and led the quest to retrieve it," she reiterated. "Not for my own benefit or for the benefit of just one of the sides, but for everyone. That's why I'm here. Because I want what everyone wants. A resolution that is not just one-sided. Real peace."

The glint in Corvin's eye told her she hadn't needed to explain anything. He had just been pushing her buttons. The scoundrel.

"Who has the Oathstone?" Corvin asked. "You?"

"Yes, me," Reg agreed. She had shoved it into her pocket before leaving the house in the middle of the night, and it was a good thing she had.

She drew it out now and unwrapped it from its black cloth. Corvin looked at it, shaking his head at its ordinariness. Aleph stood and drew closer to Corvin, ready to take his part in the ceremony.

Reg followed the pattern that she had when they had previously tried with Zora and Davyn. Smudging the room. Trying to put aside any other worries and grievances and focus on the curse placed on Corvin and the necessity of removing it. She knew there was little they could do about John if Corvin were not healed. It would be perilous for them to try banding together against him when he could draw from their powers instead of being subject to them.

Corvin held the stone in the palm of his hand. Aleph transformed into his wolf shape and stood on his hind legs, with one paw supporting him on the arm of Corvin's chair and the other resting on top of the stone, sandwiching it between them.

"I, Corvin Hunter, leader of the Black Sands warlock coven, do take this stone and call upon the spirits of Vargrena and Drakskald, its creators. We invoke the power of the Oathstone for the purpose of peace between the pack and the coven. For us to heal the damage and deal with the traitor John Saunders, I must regain the ability to use my powers. Restore that which was taken from me by October in a treacherous, unprovoked attack, and begin the healing of both families." He breathed, thinking. "So mote it be."

Aleph's part was unspoken, but Reg could feel his intention and see the glowing aura around him. She tried to feed more energy into it. Maybe it was wrong to inject her own power into the ritual, but so much depended upon the healing being successful. So many defenseless people had been harmed already, and more would be harmed if they did not. It could not hurt to add her own power to the spell.

The smell of the burnt sage hung in the air. At first, there did not appear to be any reaction. Nothing more than when they had previously tried to heal Corvin.

Then Reg could feel warmth exuding from Corvin's and Aleph's direction. Not startling, just a little flush of warmth, gradually growing. Reg didn't dare say anything or give any sign that she thought it was working. She waited, not moving, watching Corvin carefully.

He seemed to be changing before her eyes. His skin smoothing and getting rosier in color. His body relaxing instead of holding himself rigid. After a minute or two of silence, Corvin opened his eyes. They were so bright they seemed to be glowing.

Corvin's hand closed more tightly around the Oathstone. Aleph withdrew, landing on all fours in front of Corvin's chair.

Are you better? Reg asked Corvin in her mind.

The last time she had done so, he had convulsed with pain, and that had been her answer. This time, he looked at her with his bright eyes, all the wrinkles and lines on his face gone.

You don't know how good this feels.

She could feel his euphoria.

Like slipping into a warm pool at the end of a long, back-breaking day.

"It worked," Reg said aloud, knowing Davyn and Aleph could not hear the answers in Corvin's head.

I have been gone so long. Corvin took a deep breath and flexed his muscles. Reg smelled roses and quickly shielded herself from his charms. Of course he would lay it on thick now.

Now, after so much time fighting off his own nature, trying not to use his powers and getting her to siphon off excess energy, he was going to be hungry.

CHAPTER FIFTY-ONE

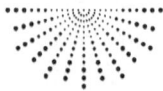

*C*orvin returned the Oathstone to Reg, though she thought he did so somewhat reluctantly, holding on to it for a fraction of a second longer than she expected, his eyes remaining on it as she wrapped it back up and put it in her pocket. Maybe not the most secure place to keep it, but she didn't have many options dressed as she was.

Now that Corvin knew that the Oathstone did have power—seeing as it had reversed the curse when nothing else had worked—he probably would have preferred to keep it in his possession. He did not like taking power from artifacts as much as he did from people, but he could do it as he needed to. In her own mind, Reg likened it to someone taking caffeine in pill form when they needed to stay awake to drive or to study, or taking it in the form of a delicious coffee concoction with all the sugar, whipped cream, chocolate, and flavor shots that she loved. A pill would do the job, but it wasn't nearly as enjoyable as the alternative.

"If you will excuse me for a few minutes." Corvin rose to his feet. "I… need to take care of a few things before we embark on our mission. I won't be long."

He walked out of the room. Reg listened to his fading footsteps and thought he had gone to his study. She heard a door click shut.

"What exactly do you think he needs to do to prepare himself?" she asked Davyn.

Aleph paced up and down the room in wolf form, clearly restless for them to be on their way.

"I would not like to guess," Davyn responded. "Maybe he just needs to brush his teeth and put on fresh clothes."

Reg laughed. She imagined instead that Corvin needed to replenish his power from whatever sources he had available. A whole bottle of caffeine pills. And perhaps he needed to look up a reference or two in his library as he decided what to do about John. Or to track his location through a phone app they shared.

She grew quickly impatient waiting for him. He had said he would not be long. She envisioned him locked in his sanctum, swallowing bottle after bottle of potion, transforming into Dr. Jekyll. Or was it Mr. Hyde? She could never remember which was which. And what exactly was Mr. Hyde? Was *Dr. Jekyll and Mr. Hyde* a werewolf fable? And would it be good or bad if Corvin transformed himself into some kind of a monster?

She considered joining Aleph in pacing back and forth across the room, but suspected he might not appreciate some else infringing on his space. She stood up anyway and made a slow circuit around the room, examining each painting, sculpture, and curiosity Corvin had on display.

She looked into the kitchen. It was no longer buried in discarded fast food boxes and wrappers. As with the alcohol, Corvin appeared to have cleaned up before their arrival. Had he anticipated their visit?

He'd said that Sarah had told him about the ambush, so he might have guessed that they would make another attempt at using the Oathstone or need his help or advice on dealing with John.

Finally, she heard the door click open again and, in a few seconds, Corvin joined them.

He looked like his old self. Maybe Davyn was right and he had just been changing his clothes and cleaning himself up. He looked smooth and sophisticated and ready to participate in a magical ritual or a wine tasting at a fancy restaurant, whichever happened to be required.

"Sorry to keep you," he apologized smoothly. "Shall we be on our way?"

Reg nodded. Davyn raised his brows. "Where, exactly, do you propose we go?"

"I have a few ideas. Reg, are you able to sense him?"

"Uh, I don't know him really well. I'm not sure about that..." Reg closed her eyes to focus and reached out her other senses. She had not been inside John's head like she had Corvin's, so it was not automatic. She pictured John, how she felt around him and, most importantly, that voice in his ear. She was accustomed to hearing Verity when she got close to John. Reg listened for that fiendish, noxious whisper. She would know it anywhere.

She opened her eyes after a few minutes. "Still in Black Sands," she said. "I can't tell where yet, but maybe once we're on the move, I'll be able to figure out the direction."

"We'll go in my car," Corvin announced, not bothering to ask anyone's opinion.

But it wasn't like they had arrived in someone else's vehicle. It was ride along with Corvin or use some other method of transportation.

Corvin led them out to the attached garage, large and well-appointed. His big black car sat there gleaming, waiting to be taken out after weeks of disuse.

Corvin indicated the front passenger seat. "Sit up front with me," he told Reg.

Reg was wary. She didn't trust him, but Davyn and Aleph were there and would ensure nothing untoward happened. Though he might be able to overcome them both after doing whatever he had done to top up his energy. He was practically buzzing with electricity.

"Come on," Corvin insisted when he saw her hesitation. "How will you give me directions unless you are beside me?"

Reg could give directions just as easily from the back seat, but he could also try to charm her whether she were in the front or back. Reg exchanged glances with Davyn, warning him to stay on his toes, then got into the front with a smiling Corvin.

"You know where he goes?" Reg asked, "Where he hangs out?"

"A few places."

"He's not going to just be waiting for us to come after him. He'll be in hiding. Somewhere he thinks the police or magical law enforcement or Davyn won't be able to find him."

Corvin nodded his agreement. They pulled out of the garage and onto the street, and Reg tried to orient herself to Verity's voice. She motioned to the right, tentative, and Corvin took the next right turn.

It wasn't easy to focus on the voice, and she couldn't always tell what direction it was coming from. It seemed to get more difficult the closer they got, but Corvin grew more confident of the turns.

"I know the place," he told Reg.

Reg sat back and just listened to the voice. Verity was not happy with John. Not that she ever was. Reg got the feeling that John had grown up with his mother criticizing his every move rather than complimenting him and encouraging him when he did something right. He had loved her and served her well, but she had probably never made him feel like he was good enough for her. Even after her death, he seemed to always be reaching, searching, trying to find a way to please her.

But Verity was not satisfied, even in death.

CHAPTER FIFTY-TWO

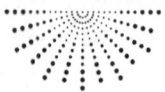

*T*hey pulled into a treed area. A park or preservation area. Corvin slowed and examined his surroundings, trying to make the correct turns, eventually stopping at a bench under a tree, which looked out over a cliff to the ocean below. The wind was brisk, and the tangy scent of the ocean was strong in the air. A tall, slim figure sat on the bench.

"He scattered her ashes here," Corvin told Reg.

What was left of them.

It made sense that it was a place John would come to sit and commune with his mother. A quiet, peaceful place where maybe he could feel good about himself and connect with her.

Or be tortured by her constant haranguing.

They all got out of the car quietly, not slamming the doors shut after them. Corvin naturally took the lead and approached John from the front.

"Hello, John."

"Corvin," John acknowledged.

John looked unsurprised to see him, despite the fact that Corvin had not been out of his house in weeks. Maybe Verity had warned him they were coming. Maybe he recognized the purr of the car's engine, even though he hadn't turned around to verify who was approaching. He had seemed oblivious to their approach, but maybe he'd been more aware than Reg had thought.

Corvin sat down on the bench beside John.

"Do you want to talk about it?"

After a few long seconds, John turned his eyes to Corvin, his brows wrinkled in a frown. "About what?"

"About what's going on in your head. Why you attacked the wolf pack. What you are planning to do next."

"You know why I did it."

"Tell me."

John stared out over the gray ocean. Ocean birds cried and mewed overhead, far in the distance. It was a lonely landscape, with not a boat or another person in sight.

"It is my birthright," John told him. "I was born to become a great warlock. The greatest warlock that this country has ever known. Others may try to hold me back, but I am going to achieve my destiny. One step at a time."

"There are ways to become great without all this... destruction."

"No," John disagreed. "Other people shirk this path because they let themselves get wrapped up in how everyone else feels. If you want to succeed, you have to keep your eye on the prize."

He stopped talking and just stared out over the water.

"You betrayed the coven," Corvin pointed out. "You acted dishonorably, attacking the wolves after the peace treaty was signed."

"That was necessary," John acknowledged.

Corvin looked at Reg. He swallowed, set his jaw, and, for a time, just sat there with John, letting him think about what he had done.

"What do you plan to do next?"

"You can't stop me," John told him.

"I'm your father. Aren't you interested in my view on the matter?"

John shook his head. "You were never there for my whole life. She told me about you. Told me how dishonorable you had been, how you had left her. How you kept your true nature from her so she did not know what to expect when I was born."

"Grace—Verity—is gone. It's time to start thinking for yourself. You can decide what you want to believe for yourself. She twisted the story. I didn't even know she was pregnant. I didn't leave you. She broke up with me. She twisted the story around to prejudice you. She told the story she wanted you to believe, not the truth."

"The truth is different things to different people."

"The truth is the truth," Corvin countered. "If a thing is true, it stays the same."

"Not always."

"John, I never left you. I welcomed you into my life when I found out about you. Why are you so intent on pushing me away? You need advice and counsel. You can't make all of these decisions on your own."

"There is no one else on this earth who knows what I have been through and what I need to do now."

"What are you going to do?" Corvin asked for the second time.

"I am the most powerful warlock in the country. One day, everyone will know who I am, and I will have power over all of them."

"All of them?"

"Yes." John turned to him. "You, Davyn, Reg, all of you."

He didn't mention Aleph; maybe he was not aware of him or thought he was just a stray dog.

"The entire country," he affirmed. "Maybe the entire world."

What an ego. John, ruler of the world? Why stop there? Why not the entire universe?

"Who would stop me?" John demanded. He looked at Reg, and she wondered whether he had read her thoughts. Who knew what powers he had. Telepathy was certainly a possibility.

"I will," Corvin said quietly.

John laughed. "You can do nothing. October took care of that. I don't know why no one else ever tried it. I congratulate him for his creative thinking and his success."

"You're behind the times," Corvin told him.

He put his arm around John, resting his arm across John's back and his palm on John's head. He ruffled John's hair like he was a little boy. They sat like that for a few moments without moving, John apparently content with the physical contact. Maybe even craving it. He'd lost his mother and knew little about this stranger who was his father.

John's hand went to his stomach like he'd been punched, and he looked at Corvin with alarm.

"No! No, you cannot do this!"

Corvin nodded sympathetically.

"How? How did you reverse the curse?" John wrapped both arms around his stomach. "Stop! You need to let go of me!"

"I used the Oathstone."

"It doesn't work!"

"Apparently, it does."

With great effort, John tore himself away from Corvin. He jumped up from the bench and turned to face them all, his back to the ocean, keeping them all in sight.

"You all came here to defeat me?" he demanded. "You don't have the right!"

Reg wasn't sure what rights they needed to have to face a murderer and do their best to ensure that he never killed again. As far as she was concerned, she had not only the right, but the responsibility to do whatever she could to stop John from hurting anyone else.

"What you've done is wrong, John," Corvin told him gently. "You can't keep this up. You can't just do whatever you like. There have to be limits. There are laws. Rules that you must follow to be a part of this society."

"Those rules do not apply to people like me!" John snapped. "I am not constrained by them."

"You're wrong. Verity is wrong. The rules have to apply to everyone, or society falls apart."

"Yes," John agreed. "The rules are to keep everyone on the same level, to make them all equal." His eyes constantly moved, checking one of them, then the other, making sure they did not try to attack him. "I do not *want* an equal society. I supersede it. I am one of those rare individuals who is meant to lead. I am superior to you, to all of you. This is my destiny."

Reg exchanged a wide-eyed grimace with Davyn when John was not looking in their direction. This was not going to be easy. Strong and crazy was a dangerous mix. But none of them had come here thinking it would be easy. Corvin was the only one who had a chance of matching and exceeding the powers that John held. The others would help where they could, but none of them had gone into it thinking that they could beat John single-handedly.

"You must really miss Verity," Reg tried to engage John in conversation. She tried to find the right emotional note to connect with him. "I know you can still hear her, but maybe that just makes it harder not to have her physically with you."

"Do you think I've forgotten whose fault that is?" John demanded. "I haven't forgotten how you took her from me. I won't ever forget that."

That had *not* been Reg's fault. Ember had just been doing what came naturally to him, protecting a family member from being hurt. It hadn't been Reg's choice or intention to incinerate Verity. Sometimes, these things just happened.

"I'm sorry for what happened," she tried to soothe John's anger and the fear that lay behind it. John was just like any boy who had lost his mother. Afraid and alone. "I know it must be so hard. I lost my mother at an early age. I really missed her for a long time. Even though she hadn't been the best mom to me."

"Verity was a good mother. She took care of me. She gave me everything."

Everything but love and protection, moral guidance, or a conscience.

CHAPTER FIFTY-THREE

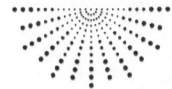

*Y*ou must really miss her," Reg repeated sympathetically.
He fixed his gaze on her. "You can't get inside my head."

She hadn't even been trying to read him, so she was surprised at the accusation. But maybe he wasn't referring to telepathy, just her attempt to understand and manipulate him.

"We can't let you go on as you have been," Corvin told John. "You can't destroy the wolf pack for your own gain. We need to live in harmony with the other communities here."

"Why?" John laughed. "They're just *dogs*. And even if they were human, I wouldn't care. If they were standing in my way, I would do what I had to. As it was…" He shrugged. "I only used them to get the coven to elect me. And I had to eliminate Jake so he couldn't spill anything about our plans and what we had done. Now… I don't care. They can go on and do what they like now, as long as they don't get in my way. They are not worth worrying about."

A wind blew in off the sea, making Reg shiver.

"You no longer lead the coven," Corvin told him. "I do."

John stood there with his mouth open. His face went pure white. He clenched his jaw and stared at Corvin with pure hatred.

"You cannot take it away from me."

"I didn't. It reverted to me because you were elected by fraud. You broke the rules of the coven in your attack on the townspeople and the werewolves. You have betrayed everything that we stand for. You cannot lead us in what you do not espouse."

"I was properly elected by the coven," John insisted. "You can't take that away from me."

"I wish there was another way to do this. You need to be stopped."

"The power you have drained from me is nothing," John boasted. "It is a mere drop in the barrel. You have no idea how much I have. More than you have ever had. You have been so careful to follow the rules and conventions that the *marginally* magical have set down; you have no idea what is possible."

"I have taken power from the Witch Doctor," Corvin reminded him. "You have not risen above the power he had. He was immortal."

"You took it, but you can't access it. You don't know how to use it all. I can use all my powers. I know exactly how to manage every gift I have. And you have been convalescing for weeks. You are out of practice."

Reg glanced at Corvin, wondering if it were true. He had been sitting around the house drinking, mourning the loss of his powers, refusing even to go out to get food. Had his abilities atrophied during that time? Was it going to take time for him to get warmed up?

Corvin smiled reassuringly at Reg.

This will not be a problem, he assured her.

"Why don't you make it easy for yourself?" Corvin encouraged John. "There is no need for it to be painful or traumatic. Let me help you like my father helped me."

Reg remembered the horrific stories Corvin had told her about how his father would come home drunk after a fruitless day of hunting and strip Corvin's power from him, sucking him dry and leaving him starving and in pain. The way that his father had repeatedly abused him had not been painless or helpful.

For Corvin to now do the same thing to his own son, stripping the powers from him so that he could not continue to hurt and kill others in his quest to take over the world, seemed like it would be almost as painful, bringing back those memories and deepening the trauma. He would know the pain he was causing his son. This son that he had only recently discovered, who he wanted to build a relationship with. He had hoped they would be able to be friends, that since they had things in common—the love of Verity, their insatiable hunger for power—that they would bond. That one person in this town would be able to understand Corvin completely.

"Just let you try to take my power?" John demanded, "You think I would do that?"

"Sometimes, it is necessary. You don't understand how this works. You grew up without a father, and Verity twisted up the natural order of things. You need the guidance of a father even though you are an adult now, especially because you were neglected growing up."

"Neglected?" John scoffed. "I was never neglected. Verity gave me everything I needed, and more. She nurtured and cared for me like a father never could."

Corvin took a small step toward John. He smiled, trying to make it all seem natural. "Even the love of a mother could never replace the guidance and direction of a father."

He raised his hands very slightly, in a movement that might have been the type of calming gesture one would use on a frightened horse, but Reg recognized it for what it was. He was pulling power from John. Trying to do it gently and so unobtrusively that John would not know it.

"How could you treat Jake like that?" Reg demanded, her voice strident, trying to provide a distraction. "Using him, collaborating with him to get what you wanted, and then killing him! And all those in the pack who were hurt or killed. Innocents who had done nothing wrong, and you just wiped them all out. Do you really think that the people of Black Sands and the rest of the wolf pack will tolerate that kind of behavior?"

"How will they stop me?" John countered smugly. "What will

they do about it? None of them have any power to speak of. They are all like you, with just one little speck of power they can call on from time to time. They think they are gifted, but they are…" he searched for words or a comparison and ended up just shaking his head. "They are morons. They have no real power. They are just like children playing house."

Reg had been told since she had come to Black Sands that she had considerable powers and, while she had always felt inadequate and like they didn't really know what they were talking about, she was irritated by John's words. Maybe because she was afraid they were true.

But like Corvin, she had stood up to the Witch Doctor. She wasn't the one who had defeated him, but Corvin hadn't done it alone. She had stood up to someone with much more power than she had, and she and the others had managed to overcome him together. She had since faced others who had power, sometimes much greater than hers and, while she had not always come off unharmed, she had survived and grown stronger and more confident in her own abilities.

"Maybe I don't have power like yours," she told him, "but I have friends and a good life here. What kind of life do you have? What's it going to be like when you are finished in Black Sands and go on to your next target? You aren't going to have any friends. You aren't going to have any kind of life. You'll never be happy."

John laughed. "I'm already happy," he bluffed. "I don't need friends to be happy. I don't need people propping me up. I have everything I need."

Aleph had moved around to flank John on the side opposite Corvin. Moving slowly and keeping low to the ground so that John would not see him. He was in the open, but Reg was being as annoying as she could to keep John's attention on her.

"People who can't make friends always say they don't need them. I think it is so sad that Verity did this to you."

"She didn't do anything to me! She was the best mother anyone could have. She was always there for me. I didn't need anyone else."

You don't need anyone else, Verity's voice confirmed. *Just me. Just do what I say, and you will always be happy.*

"She's lying," Reg said. "She wanted you to herself. She didn't want anyone to see what she was doing to you, so she kept you away from them. You couldn't have any friends because they might see how abusive she was. And now, do you think she wants to lose you? She wants to stay bound to you in spirit forever. Is that what you want? To be bound to someone who could never say a nice thing about you for eternity? To have her foul voice whispering in your ear for the rest of your existence?"

John's cheeks flushed. "You don't know anything about it!"

"I can hear her, John. You might think you're the only one, but I can hear every word she says. She's not a very nice person, is she?"

John's face was nearly purple with rage. A dark red aura swirled around him. "You are not allowed to say anything about her! You don't know anything about her! You're the reason he's dead!"

"But you're glad she's dead, aren't you?" Reg challenged. His eyes widened in shock. "While she was alive, she wouldn't let you keep any of your power. You had to keep feeding her so she was so powerful, and she barely let you keep any for yourself."

Reg took a step forward. She gave John a knowing look. "She kept you down. She kept you from becoming what you could have been. She made sure that you were weak and she was strong. You could never raise a hand against her. You could never choose to do anything that she disagreed with. She was in charge, and you couldn't have anything you wanted."

"You don't know anything about it."

"I saw. I saw the way she treated you. I saw how powerful she was and how she suppressed you. You could have been so much more, but she wouldn't let you."

John's eyes blazed. He shook his head and sputtered, seeming unable to find the words.

CHAPTER FIFTY-FOUR

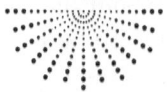

*V*erity's voice shrieked like a siren. Reg glanced at Corvin and Davyn to see whether they could hear her; she was so loud in Reg's ears. But they gave no sign they were aware of it.

She doesn't know anything about it. She doesn't know you. She doesn't know how I raised you. I did what I had to. I loved you. I made you what you are!

"You're like a kid who wasn't allowed to have any sugar," Reg said with a laugh. "And then, when you're away from her, you gobble up all the sugar you can, regardless of whether it is good for you and how cloyingly sweet it is. You want all the sugary treats, even if they make you sick."

"You're wrong. You don't know what you're talking about," John echoed Verity's words. He covered his ears as if that could shut her out. "Stop it, just stop it!"

"You see, even now, she won't let you be free. She can't do anything on her own, so now she wants you to do her bidding. I'll bet you didn't even want to take over the world. You probably just wanted to be an accountant or something like that. Or maybe a toy maker. Did she ever let you have toys when you were a kid, or did she keep those away from you too, so that you would pay attention to her? John couldn't play with toys. He couldn't play with the other boys. Because his mommy said. She only wanted Johnny to be with her all the time, sitting in her lap, being her puppet and doing and saying whatever *she* wanted him to."

"I loved her! I was a good, obedient boy because I loved her and wanted to make her happy. She took care of me. She gave me everything I wanted."

"Except power. And friends. And whatever else she held back for your own good."

"I should have killed you back when I first saw you," John growled. "But she said not to do anything that might attract his attention. Corvin left my mother for you, and I wanted to kill you."

"He left...!" Reg laughed. "He didn't leave Verity for me! I've only known Corvin for a couple of years! How old are you? I wasn't even *born* yet!"

"You're a witch. That's why you look so young. A lot of practitioners look much younger than they really are."

"No. I look my age. I'm not like Corvin or you. I haven't used any spells to keep myself looking young." Reg looked over at Corvin in his suave suit and cloak, his face unlined, all the marks of age that she had seen there the last few weeks erased. "I don't know how you do that, but I'm not sure I want to look this young forever. You might need your appearance to attract your prey, but I don't."

She's lying! Verity insisted, her voice slicing through Reg's brain. *Stop listening to her. Everything that comes out of her mouth is a lie.*

John held his head between his hands as if he might crush it. "Stop, please, I can't think."

You're not supposed to think, his mother's voice reminded him. *You are supposed to do what I say.*

"I can help you, John," Reg told him quietly, trying to be the voice of reason, even if Verity was trying to drown her out. "We used the Oathstone to heal Corvin. We can use it to heal you."

Corvin looked alarmed at this suggestion. John shook his head.

"There is nothing wrong with me. I don't need to be healed."

"Wouldn't you like to be released from this spirit? I could help you do that. I've done it several times before and, with the help of the Oathstone this time, it will be a cinch."

Corvin was clearly not on board with this decision. But as Reg thought it through, it seemed like the only thing to do. What else could they offer John? They couldn't give him more power or help him to become the most powerful warlock in the country. Corvin couldn't get close enough to touch John again, and who knew how long it would take, trickling off what little power he could, until it made a difference. Who knew whether Corvin was powerful enough to beat John in combat, even with the others there to help. It was all too uncertain.

But if she could gain John's cooperation, that flipped everything on its head again. The purpose of the Oathstone was to facilitate peace between the warlocks and the wolves. It was a powerful object. If they could use it to help Reg successfully separate Verity's ghost from John, maybe his attitude toward the wolves or the coven would change. He would no longer prevent their reconciliation.

"You can't—" John's protest was cut off when Corvin rushed him. John raised his arms to defend himself and put his foot back to widen his base. Unfortunately, there was a wolf behind his leg and he hit the ground with a crash.

Corvin moved his hands like he was tying John up with a long length of rope, but there was nothing between his hands. Muttering under his breath and weaving a spell, he bound John as tightly as possible.

John struggled and cursed. Reg wished she could put her hands over her ears to stop Verity's screaming and threatening but, instead, she pulled the Oathstone back out of her pocket and cradled it in her hands, calling upon its power.

Corvin and John struggled with each other, both growling and muttering curses, John unable to move, thanks to whatever spell Corvin had bound him with. Yet, still, Corvin was fighting his influence off, looking like he was shadowboxing or wrestling a ghost. John might not have the power necessary to escape the invisible binding, but he was still not helpless.

"Davyn, will you help me?" Reg asked. "And Aleph."

"I'm not the leader of the coven," Davyn reminded her.

"You have been, and maybe that's enough. Or maybe now that it has been activated once, any of us can access its power now, but let's try it. I don't know how long it will take Corvin to get control of him without it. If he even can. If we use the power of the Oathstone, it should work against him, since he was the one who was behind all of the trouble."

Davyn looked uncertain. Aleph sat beside Reg as she crouched down to John's level, waiting to do his part. Maybe he didn't believe it would work, but he was willing to try.

"What do you want me to do?" Davyn asked finally.

"Just touch it. Leave space so Aleph can reach it, too. Focus on John and Verity."

"We can't see Verity," Davyn reminded her.

"I don't think you need to be able to see or hear her." Reg took a deep breath and focused on the struggling man and Verity's howled imprecations. "I call on the ancients," she blurted, as Davyn and Aleph touched the stone and Corvin and John continued their struggle. "Your children have been betrayed and disrupted by this unholy union. Mother and son still bound in death. Free him from her influence. Let him stand for himself. Heal the breach between the clans by healing him."

"No!" John shouted, struggling with renewed vigor.

Verity's shrieks subsided to a hiss of whispered imprecations. The hair on the back of Reg's neck pricked. She stared at John, feeling the weight of the Oathstone in her hands, trying to keep herself focused on him, nothing wavering.

Suddenly, Verity's voice was gone.

Reg waited for her to start up again. Maybe as a ghost, she didn't need to take a breath in order to go on, but she might have decided to switch tactics when her pleas so far were not working.

But the whispers did not start again. It was suddenly quiet on the clifftop, other than John's whimpers.

Corvin was still, waiting. He probably thought the same thing as Reg: it was only a lull, and a further fight was coming. John was merely gathering his strength for a renewed protest.

CHAPTER FIFTY-FIVE

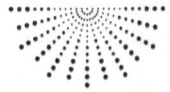

*W*hat have you done?" John demanded in horror.

Reg let her fingers curl around the Oathstone. Davyn removed his hand and Aleph his paw, and Reg carefully wrapped the stone again and put it into her pocket.

"Verity!" John shouted. His voice echoed out over the water. "Mother!"

There was no answer but his own voice. John sobbed. "Mama. Please."

"She's gone on," Reg told him. "Like she was supposed to do to start with. She's gone on to her eternal reward. Where she can be at peace."

Did Reg really believe that?

Verity had been an evil person. If she had gone on to her eternal reward, Reg imagined it was very much like the void she had rescued Davyn from. Lightless, formless. Filled with the fire Reg had ignited. But she wasn't going to tell John that. He was suffering already. She wasn't a cruel person. Some of her foster families had terrified her with visions of fire and brimstone.

Of course, they were not supposed to. They weren't allowed to even take her to church unless her guardian had approved, but they hadn't bothered to ask before explaining how she was going to...

that *place* if she did not correct the errors of her ways. Too often, the very people threatening her with eternal punishment were the ones who had committed the worst crimes against her. Somehow, they had to justify themselves, to prove that she was the sinner.

"How could you do that?" John whimpered. "How could you take her away from me? She belonged here, with me, always."

"When a child grows old enough, he leaves his parents and seeks his own way in the world," Reg told him. "That is the way it works. Even if they don't want to separate, they know they have to sooner or later. So the child can continue to grow and mature."

"No, that is for other people. For people who are not as special as we are." His voice was soft, childlike.

"She had to leave you for you to grow. And she had somewhere else to go. Somewhere you can't follow her. Not yet."

John rolled his body toward the cliff's edge, determined to follow her anyway. Corvin stopped his movement, not letting him get any closer. John bared his teeth at Corvin, snarling.

Reg aimed her thoughts at Corvin's mind. *How much power does he have left?*

Too much. Corvin put his hand on John's shoulder and started siphoning off his power much more quickly than he had been able to when he was standing several feet away and being unobtrusive about it.

"No!" John howled.

Reg hated the thought of doing this to him right after the loss of his mother yet again. But they needed to protect themselves. The last thing they needed was for him to transform into another shape which could escape the bonds Corvin had placed on him. It seemed like there was always a way to escape. Even the most secure prison or binding seemed to always have a loophole. If John could get enough people on his side or enough power, he could do anything. They had to be sure that he couldn't attack them.

And to figure out where to take him.

Just banishing him from Black Sands would not be enough. He could just turn around and come right back again.

For some time, there was near silence. Just the sound of John sobbing to himself. He opened his eyes and turned to look at Reg, his eyes blazing and full of hatred.

"It's so quiet," he hissed. "I can't stand the quiet!"

Reg had experienced the same thing when Corvin had stolen her powers. That sudden echoing silence inside her head. She didn't know how normal people dealt with not having any other voices in their heads. For years she had repressed them but, once she was faced with total silence inside her, she would have done anything to have them returned. She had been lucky, because power drinkers never returned what they had taken.

"You'll get used to it," she assured him, though she had no idea how. He had not grown up with voices in his head as she had. He'd only had Verity's voice after she had died, over the past year. He would, she was sure, adjust to the silence again quickly.

"Get used to it?" John wept. "How am I going to get used to her being gone? How am I supposed to deal with that?"

He clutched at his stomach. Reg looked anxiously at Corvin, worried that he would take too much of John's power. She recognized the emptiness John was feeling, the hunger gnawing at his middle, which wasn't hunger for food but for something else that could never be satisfied. The same hunger that Corvin had once shared with her to prove how much he was suffering. To explain why he could never stop preying upon people as he did.

"Corvin."

She had stopped him before when he had been too greedy, when he had been ready to consume someone until they were all used up. But his eyes were clear this time, and he responded to her rather than being so engrossed in his predation that he didn't even know she was there.

"He's so high on power," Corvin told her. "He feels the pain even though he has plenty left. He'll have to come down. Detox. I won't take it all, but I must take enough that you and the others are safe."

Reg studied Corvin's eyes once again, then nodded.

CHAPTER FIFTY-SIX

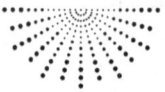

*R*eg looked around the room. It was a much smaller group than it had been for the Town Council meeting. The werewolf forces had been greatly reduced and the remaining members were reluctant to come into town or to attend anywhere there was likely to be a group of warlocks present.

Understandably.

The talks had resumed with a session led by the use of the Oathstone. There had been quite a stir about Corvin resuming public appearances, acting as though he had never been gone. He and Aleph had sat down with their hands on the Oathstone and promised to continue the talks in good faith. Reg didn't know how many others had been able to see the shimmering glow that emanated from the Oathstone, but she was satisfied that this time, the Oathstone had been activated and would power the talks and seal their oaths.

Aleph would be true to his word. Reg had no doubt of that. And although she knew Corvin to be treacherous in many ways, she did not believe that he would misrepresent the wishes of the coven and would not turn around and betray them with an attack on the wolves, as John had done. He shared many traits with John, but that was not one of them.

The talks continued behind closed doors, and Reg sat and paced around the lobby, wishing she didn't have to wait for hours for everything to be settled.

"You could go home," Sarah suggested. "You could go run errands or do something else to distract yourself. I'll let you know when they are finished."

"No. I want to be here when it happens. I have to know that it is real this time."

"I understand the sentiment."

"What is the latest on John?" Reg asked. She could not go to the hospital herself. Seeing Reg would set John off, triggering all kinds of problems with his treatment. So she had to let Sarah or others see him and report back. He didn't react to anyone else quite as strongly as Reg. Not even Corvin. But that might have had something to do with the power Corvin fed back to him. Very slowly, one precious drop at a time, allowing him to recover gradually.

"He is improving," Sarah informed her. "There are setbacks, of course, but he is getting better. Whether he will ever live a normal life, or what qualifies as normal for his kind, I don't know. But the grief and depression seem to be slowly improving."

And Jake? While Reg had told John that he had killed Jake, the wolf had hung in there and had begun to heal from his injuries. Reg didn't know what he would do when he was released from the hospital. Try to convince the pack that he had never meant them any harm by his actions, but had been negotiating in good faith? That he had not taken the leadership of the pack by deception?

Or would he leave town and start a new life somewhere with a new name? Maybe acting as a human or joining another pack somewhere they hadn't heard of him. Reg assumed that with modern communication systems, any other packs would have advance warning of who and what Jake was. But the wolf packs did not all use technology like humans did, so maybe there were a few where he would still be unknown.

Reg turned her head when a movement caught her eye, and she saw two boys approaching her. She immediately recognized the one in front as Fenris. His nose had healed and the bruises were already gone, thanks to the accelerated healing of a wolf. She thought in that first split second that the other boy with Fenris was his brother, Gerwulf, frequently abbreviated as Gerf, or a particular wolf bark that Reg recognized but could not adequately imitate.

But it wasn't Gerf at all. Though he was about the same height as Fenris and looked like a child, most people would have recognized him as something otherworldly if they saw him without his sunglasses.

"Theodore." Reg frowned and looked at her homunculus, who was apparently spending time with the young werewolf. "What are you doing here?"

"Witnessing the use of the Oathstone."

Of course he had an interest in the Oathstone being used. He was the one who had suggested it could be used to reverse Corvin's curse and facilitate the talks between the clans. He wasn't doing anything underhanded by being there. He was not trying to hide his movements. Though she wasn't sure she liked him hanging out with Fenris.

"You said we would celebrate," Theodore reminded her. "With marshmallows."

Reg vaguely remembered promising him something when he had been so upset about not being able to go to Corvin's to see if they could reverse the curse. She forced a smile. "Yes, of course. We'll do that soon. Maybe tonight."

They also needed to have a conversation about his withholding information about John's actions. Maybe that information could have prevented the ambush of the werewolves and some of the loss of life.

Sarah raised a questioning brow at Reg, and she nodded heavily.

It would not be an easy conversation.

Did you enjoy this book? Reviews and recommendations are vital to making a book successful.

Please leave a review at your favorite book store or review site and share it with your friends.

Don't miss the following bonus material:
Sign up for mailing list to get a free ebook
Read a sneak preview chapter
Other books by P.D. Workman
Learn more about the author

DON'T MISS A THING! GET THE LATEST NEWS AND A FREE EBOOK

Your First Taste

PDWORKMAN.COM/SIGNUP

PREVIEW OF GLUTEN-FREE MURDER

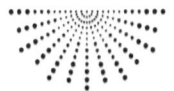

Reg Rawlins initially appeared as a side character in book 6 of the *Auntie Clem's Bakery* culinary cozy mystery series, *Coup de Glace*. If you haven't already sampled this series, give it a try!

Don't worry, I'm not yet done with Reg, but I need some time to get the next books written!

* * *

CHAPTER ONE

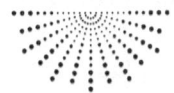

*E*rin Price pulled up in front of the shop and shut off her loudly-knocking engine. She took a few deep breaths and stared at the street-side view. She hadn't seen it since her childhood, but it looked just the same as she remembered it. Maybe a little smaller and shabbier, like most of the things from her childhood that she re-encountered, but still the same shop.

Main Street of Bald Eagle Falls was lined with red brick buildings, pasted shoulder-to-shoulder to each other, in varying, incongruous styles. Each one had a roofed-in front sidewalk to protect shoppers and diners from the blazing Tennessee sun they would face in the coming summer. All different colors. Some of them lined with gingerbread edges or whimsical paint jobs. Or both. Some of the stores appeared to have residences on the second floor, white lacy curtains drawn in windows that looked down at the vehicles, mostly trucks, nose-in in the parking spaces. There was no residence above Clementine's shop. She had lived in a small house a few blocks away that Erin had no memory of. She had spent most of her time at the shop and did not remember sleeping over at her aunt's when her parents had brought her for a visit.

A US flag hung proudly on a flagpole in front of the stores, just fluttering slightly in the breeze. It was starting to get dark and she knew she'd have to find the house in the dark if she were going to stop and take the time to explore the shop.

With another calming breath, Erin unbuckled her seatbelt, unlocked the door, and levered herself out of the seat. She felt like she'd been pasted into the bucket seat of the Challenger for three days straight. She had been pasted into the bucket seat for three days straight, other than pit-stops and layovers. She wasn't tall, so she wasn't crammed into the small car, but she'd been in there long enough to want to get out and straighten her body and stretch her legs. And to go to bed, but bed was still a long way off.

Erin walked up to the shop and put her key into the lock. It ground a little, like it hadn't been used for a long time. Maybe it needed a little bit of lubrication to loosen it up.

The air inside the shop was too still and too warm. She remembered when the little shop had been filled with the smells of exotic teas and fresh-baked goods, but Clementine had retired and closed it years ago. It had been a long time since anything had been baked there. It just smelled like dust and stale air. Erin left the front door open to let some fresh air circulate while she took a look around. There wasn't much space to explore in front of the counter. She would need a couple little tables, with a limited number of chairs, for the few people who wanted to eat in. Most of her business would just be stopping in to pick up their orders. She walked behind the counter. Everything seemed to be in good shape. A good wipe-down and some fresh baked goods in the display case and she'd be ready to go. Maybe a fresh coat of paint on the wall and a chalk board listing the daily specials and prices.

She walked into the back. A kitchen with little storage and a microscopic office that might once have been a closet. The back stairs led to a larger storage area downstairs, she remembered. And what Clementine had always called the commode. There was a second set of stairs from the store front down to the commode for customers. Not exactly convenient, but it was a small, old building. The arrangement had worked okay for Clementine. As a girl, Erin had always been a little afraid of the basement. She would creep down the stairs to use the bathroom and then race back up again, always drawing a warning from Clementine to slow down or she would trip and catch her death on those stairs.

All the old appliances were still there in the kitchen. Even a decades-old industrial fridge stood unplugged and propped open. There was no microwave and Erin was going to need a fancier coffee machine, but everything else looked usable.

* * *

"What are you doing here?"

Erin turned around and saw a looming figure in the kitchen doorway at the same time as the clipped male voice interrupted her thoughts. She just about jumped out of her skin.

She put her hand on her thumping chest and breathed out a sigh of relief when she saw that it was a uniformed police officer. But he wasn't looking terribly welcoming, jaw tight and one hand on his sidearm. There was a German Shepherd at his side.

"Oh, you scared me. I'm Erin Price," she introduced herself, reaching out her hand and stepping toward him, "and I'm—"

"I asked you what you're doing here."

Erin stopped. He made no move to close the distance between them and shake her hand, but remained standing there in a closed, authoritative stance. His tone brooked no nonsense. Erin couldn't imagine that she looked anything like a burglar. A little rumpled from the car, maybe, but she hadn't been sleeping in it. Was a slim, white, young woman really the profile of a burglar in Bald Eagle Falls?

"I own this shop."

He raised an eyebrow in disbelief, but he did let his hand slide away from the weapon and adopted a more casual stance. Erin allowed herself just one instant to admire his fit physique and his face. He was roguish, with what was either heavy five o'clock shadow or three days' growth, but his face was also round, giving him an aura of boyishness and charm.

"You own the shop. And you are...?"

"Erin Price. Clementine's niece."

"If you're Clementine's niece, why haven't we ever seen you around here?"

"It's been years since I've seen her. My parents died and I lost all my family connections years ago, living in foster care. A private detective tracked me down."

He considered this and took a walk around the kitchen, looking things over. His eyes were dark and intense. "You'll be selling the place, then? Why didn't you just hire a real estate agent?"

"No, I'm not selling," Erin said firmly. "I'm reopening."

The eyebrows went up again. "This place has been sitting empty for ten years or more. You're reopening Clementine's Tea Room?"

"No, I'll be opening a specialty bakery, once I get everything whipped into shape." She folded her arms across her chest, looking at him challengingly. "I assume you don't have a problem with that?"

"No, ma'am."

But he didn't give any indication of leaving. Erin swept back a few tendrils of dark hair that had slipped from her braid, aware that she was probably looking travel-worn after several days in the car. She had put on mascara and dusty rose lipstick before getting on her way that morning, but she felt gritty and sweaty from travel and would have preferred a shower before having met anyone in her new hometown.

Erin strode toward the front of the store and the policeman moved out of the doorway and then back around the counter toward the front door.

"You shouldn't leave the door wide open."

"I wanted some air in here. I've only been here five minutes. Do the police always show up that fast in Bald Eagle Falls?"

"I just happened by. Thought it was strange to see Clementine's door hanging open. Didn't recognize the car."

"Well, thank you for looking into it." Erin waited until he stepped out onto the sidewalk and then followed, pulling the door shut behind her. He watched as she locked it again. "You see? I have the keys."

"Where did this detective find you?"

"Maine."

"Is that where you're from?"

"I'm from a lot of places. Now I'm looking at settling back down here."

Erin looked at the German Shepherd, doing the doggie equivalent of standing at attention.

"I've never heard of a small town like this having a K9 unit."

"Well," he looked down at the dog, chewing on his words, "this is the extent of our K9 contingent."

"He looks... very well-trained. What's his name?"

"K9."

Erin cracked a smile. "Seriously?"

He kept a serious face, nodding once.

"Okay. Well, again, thank you for checking in on my store, Officer...?"

"Terry Piper."

"Erin Price." Erin offered her hand and this time Piper took it, giving her hand a brief squeeze as if he were afraid of crushing it.

"Pleased to meet you, Miss Price. Or is it missus?"

"It's Miss."

"Keep safe. Give us a call if you need anything." He produced a business card with a blue and yellow crest on it. "We don't exactly have 9-1-1 service but there's always someone on call."

Erin nodded her thanks. "I'll keep it handy. A lot of crime in Bald Eagle Falls?"

"No. It's a sleepy little town. Not too much excitement. Rowdy teenagers. Some of the drug trade trickling down from the city. The occasional domestic."

"Not a lot of break-and-enters?" she teased.

He didn't look amused. "You can't be too careful. Where are you headed now? There's a motel down the way..."

"No. I got the house too. I'll be staying there."

"You can't sleep there tonight. Won't be any water or power."

"They've been turned on. Thanks for your concern."

He looked for something else to say, then apparently couldn't find anything, so he nodded and walked down the sidewalk with his faithful companion.

* * *

Erin kept one eye on the GPS and the other on her rearview mirror to see if Officer Piper had any ideas about hopping into his car and following her home to make sure that she was properly situated. But apparently, he couldn't think of any laws she had broken and he never appeared behind her. Clementine's house was only a few blocks away. Erin parked on the street in front of it and took it in. It was a pretty little house with white siding and green shutters, roof peaks, and accents. The living room had big windows to let in the light and a window up at the top peak hinted at an attic bedroom or study. Beside and behind the house, beyond the fence line, were shimmering green, dense woods.

Erin got out of the car and grabbed her suitcase before walking up to the heavy paneled door and inserting her key in the lock. This one didn't stick, but turned smoothly like it was welcoming her home. Erin lugged her suitcase into the front entryway and closed and locked the door behind her. No point in inviting more visitors. She really didn't want to have to deal with anyone else until morning.

The AC was on, so the house wasn't stifling like the shop had been. Erin hadn't been sure what to expect. Burgener, the lawyer, had informed her that the house was furnished, but she hadn't known what kind of state it would be in. But it was neat and tidy. Furnished, but not cluttered. There were a couple of magazines on the coffee table in the living room that were months old, but other than that, Clementine might have just left it a few days before. Or still be in the other room just awaiting Erin's arrival.

She wasn't a believer in ghosts or restless spirits, but Clementine's smell and flavor still clung to the place.

Erin left her suitcase at the door and explored the house slowly. Living room, small dining room, kitchen, Clementine's bedroom, a guest room, and what Erin thought she might call a sewing room.

There was fabric, rolls of wrapping paper, partially finished crafts, and post-bound books of genealogy, painstakingly written in longhand.

There were pull-down steps to the attic. If there had only been a ladder, Erin probably wouldn't have explored any further, but the stairs were well-made and modern and raised her hopes that the attic had been properly developed and wasn't just a storage space full of boxes, bags, cobwebs, and dust.

She mounted the stairs. At the top, there was enough light from below to find a light switch. Erin switched it on and had a look around.

It was a beautiful, bright room. Erin knew she was going to be spending a lot of her free time up there. White paneling and built-in cabinetry, soft, natural-looking lighting; it consisted of a reading nook, a writing desk, a comfy-looking couch, and various other touches that would make it a paradisiacal oasis at the end of a tiring day of baking.

Or driving.

After exploring the attic, Erin shut off the light, descended, and pushed the stairs up until the counterbalance took over and raised them to snick softly into place in the ceiling.

Erin returned to the kitchen for a glass of water, not looking forward to the fact that she was going to have to go out and pick up groceries if she wanted anything to eat. She found a sticky note on the fridge on notepaper preprinted with the lawyer's logo and phone number.

Welcome home. You'll find some basic supplies in the fridge. JRB

Erin opened the fridge door and sighed. Milk, juice, eggs, bagels, jam, and some precut fruit and vegetable packs. That and the coffee maker on the counter would do just fine. If James Burgener had been there, she would have hugged him.

A quick snack and then she would be off to the guest room for some shut-eye. Ghosts or not, she wasn't going to be sleeping in the master bedroom until she had made it her own.

* * *

Never one to let moss grow, Erin set to work immediately the next morning. She found a sort of a general store which carried both the small appliances she needed and painting supplies. With the back seats folded down, she filled the cargo area of the Challenger with as much as it would hold. She went back to the shop, opened the windows, and prepped the walls to start painting. Best to get a fresh coat of paint on before installing anything new.

"Knock, knock?"

Erin was startled out of her thoughts. She yanked the earbuds out of her ears and turned to face the woman who was trying to get her attention.

"I'm sorry," the woman said, giving her a tentative smile. She had a pleasant face; a middle-aged woman with ash blond hair. Either she had the perfect figure, or her clothes were hand-tailored. "I didn't want to startle you, but you were pretty engrossed…"

Erin wiped her forehead with the back of her hand. "Yeah. A little caught up in my music and my work."

"My name is Mary Lou Cox. I heard a rumor that you were here. So, I just had to come over and extend a good old Bald Eagle Falls welcome."

"Erin Price. I, uh… Clementine was my aunt."

"Well, if you're kin to Clementine, you're kin to half the mountain. Welcome home."

Erin nodded awkwardly. "Thank you. That's very kind of you."

"So…" Mary Lou took a look around the kitchen. "A fresh coat of paint and then I hear you're opening up Clementine's Tea Room again? I'll tell you, this town has surely missed the tea room."

"Uh. No. I'm not reopening the tea room." Erin enjoyed a cup of tea at the end of the day as much as anyone, but she was much more interested in baking. The groove she got into while painting was nothing compared with the nirvana she would achieve while baking. "I'm opening a specialty bakery."

Mary Lou patted her hair. "We already have a bakery in Bald Eagle Falls."

Erin ran the roller down the wall, watching carefully for seams or drips.

"I'm sure the town can support more than one bakery."

"But we already have The Bake Shoppe. We don't need another bakery."

Erin gave her a determined smile. "I'm opening a bakery."

"Angela Plaint owns The Bake Shoppe and does a really nice business, I'm not sure any of us would go to another bakery. It wouldn't be a very loyal thing to do."

"You could go to The Bake Shoppe for... whatever Angela Plaint is best at and then come to my bakery for gluten-free muffins."

"Gluten-free?" Mary Lou echoed.

"I assume you don't already have a gluten-free bakery."

"No, we do not. If you want that kind of baking, you have to drive into the city."

"Well, now you'll be able to get them in town."

"There aren't that many people that want that gluten-free stuff in Bald Eagle Falls. I don't see how you could make a living off it."

"We'll just have to see. I do other specialty baking as well. Dairy-free, allergy-free, vegan."

"We don't have a lot of *those* kind of people here. We like our meat. Whoever put meat in muffins anyway?"

Erin studied Mary Lou for a moment, trying to divine whether she was teasing or being sarcastic. "You might not put meat in a muffin, but you would probably put eggs and dairy."

"And you could make it without all those things? Who would eat such a thing? It would be like eating cardboard."

"Not when I make it."

"I guess we'll just have to see," Mary Lou said. "I sure don't cotton to the idea of you trying to take Angela's business."

"I guess we'll just have to see," Erin echoed.

* * *

Mary Lou was the first citizen of Bald Eagle Falls to express her opinion and welcome Erin to town, but she wasn't the last. Next came Melissa Lee, a woman with curly dark hair and a wide, even smile. And then Gema Reed, with her long, steel gray locks and a girlish complexion.

Erin did her best to explain to them that she wasn't there to horn in on Angela's business and take money out of her pocket, but to offer a new service that hadn't previously been available. But it was like talking to the wall. Or yelling at an avalanche. It didn't stop them from dumping advice all over her, while smiling and telling her she was welcome in town.

She didn't feel welcome.

At least Terry Piper did not show up with his K9 to give his input on the matter.

It was a long day and Erin never did meet Angela, her competition. The end of the day, the walls were freshly painted. Everything looked fresh and new. Exhausted though she was, Erin spent a few more minutes in the tiny office, going through the papers and plans in the folders she had brought with her from Maine.

Then she locked everything up tight and headed back home.

CHAPTER TWO

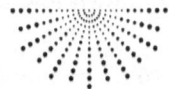

$\mathcal{T}$he day dawned bright and clear. Erin woke up earlier than she expected after her hard work of the day before. She was looking forward to each new day, rather than dreading another day of work.

Starting the day in her attic study, Erin wrote up lists of things she would need to get in the city. Not only did Bald Eagle Falls not have a specialty bakery, the general store did not carry any of the specialized flours or other ingredients that she would need. Erin had no intention of taking months getting outfitted. The store and the appliances were on hand and ready for use, so why wait?

It was late when Erin returned to the shop at the end of the day. Darkness was settling over Main Street and the streetlights were few and far between. As she juggled her first armload of goods while trying to unlock the front door, chiding herself for using the front door instead of the back—even though she would have had the same problem at the back—a voice spoke in her ear.

"Can I help you with those?"

The bag of flour she was pressing against the door with her body in an effort to hang on to it while unlocking the bolt was removed from its position. Erin laughed a little and unlocked the door, turning to get the bag of flour back from him.

She froze, looking into the dirty, sweaty face of a man she had never met before. He was white, though the word white did nothing to convey the color of his skin, dirt ground into it as if he had been working in a coal mine or living on the street for weeks. He had a fringe of a mustache and a few bristles on his chin, looking more like he was careless with his shaving than that he had intentionally trimmed his facial hair in a particular style. He had a filthy, army-green cap pulled down low so she could just make out his dark eyes.

"I can take this in for you," he offered. His voice was gravelly and low, but polite. He didn't have the drawl that would indicate he was native to the area.

"Oh, no, let me take it back," Erin said, encircling the bag with her arm and taking its weight.

He looked at her with a sullen expression that told Erin he understood that she didn't want him in her store. She turned her back on him to take the supplies into the kitchen, mentally sorting out possible weapons and escape routes. She was sure he was going to follow her in. Would a scream bring Officer Terry Piper or whoever else might be on shift?

When she went back out to her car for the next load, the man was still hanging around, as she had expected. He took bags out of her car and handed them to her.

"Really," Erin told him politely, "I'm okay. I don't need any help."

He didn't react with anger or violence, but his dark eyes glittered under the bill of his cap. "Just trying to be neighborly."

"I appreciate it. You're very kind. But you're making me nervous."

She surprised herself by telling him that. Was she acting like a victim? Encouraging him to menace her further? She knew from self-defense classes that predators looked for shyness and low self-esteem. Did she sound weak saying he was making her nervous?

But the man immediately backed off, shaking his head. "Not trying to make anyone nervous, miss."

"Then please leave me alone."

He stood there looking at her for a minute, then turned without a word and walked away. Erin blew out her breath, relieved. Here she had thought that moving to a small town in the South, she would be safe from crime and unwanted attention, but obviously nowhere was completely safe. She needed to be realistic instead of idealizing small-town living as being something it wasn't. Next time, she would not be unloading her car after dark. She would plan ahead and be better prepared.

Erin took the rest of the supplies into the kitchen and put them away. She stopped in the office to pick up one of her folders, frowning. She had a strange feeling of vertigo, like everything was slightly out of place. She couldn't identify any one thing that would make her feel that way, but couldn't help feeling like her things had been touched and moved around. She found the folder she was looking for on signage and took it home with her, locking up carefully.

* * *

Traffic was even quieter than usual in the sleepy town when Erin got to the shop to finish organizing her ingredients and to make plans for what she would make to kick off her opening and really wow her customers.

She was sitting at her desk in the tiny office, scribbling away and flipping back and forth between recipes when she heard the bells over the front door jingle. She didn't want anyone sneaking up on her today.

Erin reluctantly stood up from her work and went out to the front of the shop. It was Gema Reed, the beautiful gray-haired woman.

"I thought I saw your car outside," Gema declared. She couldn't very well have missed it. It wasn't exactly camouflaged. And it was one of the only vehicles parked on sleepy Main Street. "So, I thought I would drop in and make sure everything was okay?"

Erin tilted her head slightly, trying to figure out where Gema was going with the inquiry.

"Umm, yes. Everything is fine. Why wouldn't it be?"

"Well, being as it's the *Sabbath* and you're at work. I was worried maybe you had a water main break or vandals. Maybe even a fire. You never know what's going to happen."

"No, there's nothing wrong. I just wanted to get some work done. There's lots to do before I open."

They stood there looking at each other awkwardly for a few moments. Erin knew she was moving into the Bible belt, but she hadn't expected things to be that different from the way they had been in the North. Some people were religious and some people were not and everybody observed their beliefs as they wished. But apparently, things were not quite so straightforward in the South.

"Well, maybe no one invited you to Sunday morning services. You probably don't even know the schedule!" Gema proclaimed. "Now there are lots of churches to choose from, of course, but if you want to join us at First Baptist, just down at the end of Main Street and Garity, why, we'd *love* to have you!"

"I'm going to have to pass…" Erin said slowly, feeling her way through. "I'm not really the churchgoing type."

"Not the type? Why, bless your heart, dear, you don't have to be a type to join your fellow Christians at worship on Sunday! You… *are* a Christian, aren't you? Not one of these… other sects? I don't mean to put down Jews or Muslims or anyone else, but here in Bald Eagle Falls, we're Christian. Baptists, Catholics, Protestants, it doesn't matter, as long as you're Christian!"

Erin cleared her throat. She wished she had brought a cloth with her out to the front, so she could occupy herself with polishing the glass and chrome display case and counter. Just to have something to do with her hands and somewhere to look other than Gema Reed's benevolent Christian face. "Actually, Mrs. Reed. I'm not."

"You're not… what? You don't look like a Jew or one of those… pagan people. Not everyone goes to church every Sunday, but…"

"I'm… not Christian. I'm atheist."

"Atheist!" Gema was aghast. She held her hand dramatically at her throat, halfway to covering her mouth in horror. She stared at

Erin pleadingly, as if she thought it might just be a clumsy joke and Erin would change her tune. "You're not! Really?"

"Yes. I am. I'm sorry if that upsets you…"

"Well, Jesus loves every humble seeker of the truth. You are a seeker, aren't you? Not everyone can be converted, but as long as you're looking for the truth, you will find it in the end…"

Erin took a deep breath and let it back out again. As much as she wanted to smooth Gema's ruffled feathers, to just reassure her and send her on her way, she wanted to get it out in the open. Her real beliefs, not just rumors or half-baked explanations.

"Mrs. Reed—"

"Gema, sugar…"

"Gema. I am an atheist. Not an agnostic. Not an investigator or a seeker. An atheist. I'm not looking for something to believe in. I already have a belief system. And it doesn't include God."

Gema gasped audibly and this time she did cover up her mouth. "Oh, my dear…"

Erin forced a smile. "I'm not a witch or a devil-worshiper. And I won't try to talk you out of your beliefs. But I, myself, do not believe in God. Not a god of any sort. Not the universe, or Mother Nature, or a higher power, or Jesus. I'm sorry."

"Well." Gema looked for a moment as if she would flee without another word. Instead, she smoothed her waves of silver, took a calming breath and gave a polite nod. "Everybody is entitled to their own opinion, no matter how wrong. I'd better get on my way, or I'll be walking into service late. I just hope… that you won't be encouraging others to break the Sabbath by your blatant disregard for it. You won't have your bakery open on Sunday, will you?"

Erin gave a little shrug. "Didn't my Aunt Clementine have it open after services on Sunday?" she asked tentatively. Her memories of Clementine's Tea Room were startlingly clear in some respects and shrouded by fog in others. She was sure she remembered helping to serve the church ladies after Sunday services. They had all thought her such a cute, pretty young thing. She remembered her resentment over being treated like a puppy or a baby instead of a person with a mind of her own. She loved helping Clementine in the tea room, but she didn't like that part of it.

Gema made a noise of indecision, not wanting to admit that Erin was right and yet compelled by her Christian morals not to tell a lie. "Mmmmm… yes, it is true that she opened up for an hour or two after services on Sunday, so the ladies would have somewhere to go to discuss Christian services required in the upcoming week…"

"So, it would be okay, as long as I waited until after your worship services?"

"As an atheist, I'm not sure it would be the same…"

"I would be shunned for opening my restaurant, but a Christian would not? When it's against a Christian's beliefs, but not mine? Wouldn't it be worse for a Christian to do it?"

"I just don't know," Gema snapped, shaking her head in confusion. "I must get on now, but I'll… I'll think it over."

"Okay…" Erin gave her a little wave. "You be sure to let me know what you ladies decide. Someone mentioned that Clementine's Tea Room had been sorely missed and I thought that if I could provide a similar service…"

Gema Reed gulped. She shook her head and retreated. The bells tinkled behind her and Erin stood there, watching her get into her big red truck and pull out into the street. Then she was gone.

Erin went back to her office to continue working on her opening and marketing strategy. She added 'Sunday social tea' to her list with a wry smile and continued to look through her recipes.

* * *

After Erin finished her plans, she carefully filed her folders in the cabinet beside the desk. There was no reason to leave her lists scattered all over her desk and take the chance of losing something when she had a perfectly functional file drawer to put everything neatly away. She emptied the dregs of her cold coffee from her mug and washed it out, leaving it upside down on a towel to dry.

When she stepped out of the shop onto the sidewalk, she nearly collided with a woman coming the other direction. Sunday had been so quiet, she hadn't expected any foot traffic and hadn't even looked before stepping out the door.

"Oh, I'm sorry!" she apologized.

The other woman was ruddy, a redhead, on the plumpish side. Her hair fell in waves around her head, partially obscuring her face. She stepped back from Erin, folding her arms across her chest and staring at Erin as if she had just committed a mortal sin. Which, given Gema's reaction to Erin working on a Sunday, was probably the case.

"I didn't see you coming," Erin apologized. "That was my fault. I'm sorry."

The woman ignored the apology. "You're Clementine's niece."

"Yes, I am."

"You don't favor her, do you?"

"I don't remember her too clearly," Erin admitted. "And I don't really know what she looked like in later years."

"If you don't remember her, then what are you doing here? Why come to Bald Eagle Falls?"

Erin's mouth was dry. She tried to put together words that made sense, flummoxed by the woman's attack.

"I inherited the store and the house. I wanted to reopen the shop."

"Only you're not," the redhead hissed. "You're not reopening the tea room, you're opening a bakery."

"Well, yes. That's what I do, I bake. I'm still planning on serving tea after Sunday services each week, so the women can get together..."

"We don't need another bakery."

Erin sighed and shook her head. "It's a specialty bakery. It means people won't have to go into the city to get gluten-free or allergy-friendly baking. It doesn't directly compete with the other bakery."

"You are competing, little Miss Out-of-Towner. And you're not going to last a week!"

With that, the redhead marched on, shouldering past Erin with a force that staggered her and made her catch herself on the side of the building.

Looking across Main Street, she saw Officer Terry Piper watching her, K9 at his side. She considered calling him over to vent about the rude woman, but decided that would just be sour grapes. She didn't really want to charge the woman. There was no point in reporting the encounter to the police.

* * *

Erin yawned as she pushed open her door, sending the little bells tinkling in welcome. She was going to have to get used to getting up early if she were going to be running a bakery. She was going to have to get up while it was still dark and everyone else was sleeping in order to have freshly baked goods in the display cases when people started walking in for a little something to go with their coffees or office meetings.

Her day would start way before anyone else's and, if she were going to stay open past afternoon, she was going to need to find an assistant to split shifts with. It wouldn't have to be another baker, just someone who could answer questions about ingredients and work the cash register.

Taking into account the not-so-warm reaction she was getting from the women of the town, she might have to go to the city to find someone willing to work the bakery.

Erin juggled her keys and her bag of groceries to turn on the kitchen light and put her bag on the counter.

Her coffee mug lay on the floor, shattered. Erin frowned and looked around. A shiver ran down her spine. Had someone been there? Had her shop been broken into?

For a few moments, she just stood there, frozen, listening for any movement.

There was only silence. She considered the situation. Had she put the mug too close to the edge of the counter and it had fallen off by itself? Were there earthquakes in Tennessee?

The imprint of the mug was still in the towel she had left it sitting on. Close to the edge of the counter, but not over it.

She heard the bells on the front door ring and hurried out to see whether someone was leaving the shop. Had she actually walked right past an intruder? Maybe hiding behind the counter, below her eye level while she yawned and juggled her groceries in the morning dimness?

She stopped stock-still. Nobody had left the shop; wild-haired Melissa Lee had come in. She was all smiles and sweetness, launching into a long-winded description of some fundraiser that she and some of the other women were running. She cut herself off abruptly.

"My dear, you look like you've just seen a ghost. Are you okay?"

"I… I think someone has been in here."

"What do you mean, in here?" she asked doubtfully.

"I think someone broke in…"

"You have been burgled?" Melissa's voice rose, a mixture of disbelief and alarm. Such things were probably unheard of in sleepy little Bald Eagle Falls. "Honey, you stay right there while I get the police."

Melissa hurried back out the front door and, without a clue what else to do, Erin obeyed, standing there like a statue. It was only a few minutes before Melissa returned, Officer Terry Piper in tow with his K9. Melissa was babbling on about crime rates and burglaries. Piper ignored her and focused on Erin.

"The place was broken into?" he demanded.

"I don't know. I think someone has been here."

Feeling embarrassed that she might be overreacting, Erin took him into the kitchen and showed him the broken mug and where it had been sitting on the counter. Piper nodded and looked around, his brows drawn down.

"Anyone else have a key?" he asked.

K9 sniffed at the broken mug with interest, but didn't lead his master along a scent trail. He just sat back on his haunches and panted.

"No. I haven't given anyone else a key."

Piper looked into the small office. "Anything been touched in here? Anything missing?"

Erin hadn't yet had a chance to look. She gave a little laugh and slipped by him to see. The room looked untouched. Erin checked her file drawers.

"There was one other time… when I thought things had been moved in here. I put everything away in my drawers, this time…"

"Do you have petty cash in here? A safe?"

"No. Nothing like that. And no cash in the register yet, either. I haven't opened for business yet." She knew she didn't really need to add that part. Terry Piper was undoubtedly aware that she hadn't yet opened to the public. If there had been any doubt, the fact that there were no baked goods in the display case or in the oven would pretty much be a giveaway.

"When are you opening?" he asked. "Assuming you still are?"

"Yes, of course. I'm just putting together my plans for a small opening celebration right now. A few days…"

He raised an eyebrow. "That quickly? I thought it would take longer to get things up and running."

"Everything is already in place. I've bought supplies. I am still waiting on signage and a few little things like that, but for the time being, I'll just put a handmade sign in the window."

He pursed his lips and nodded. He and K9 went to the back door and examined it to confirm it was still locked and had not been tampered with. He looked at the steep stairs to the basement.

"What have you got downstairs?"

"Storage and the commode. I haven't been down there yet this morning…"

K9's ears pointed down the stairs curiously.

"Does he hear something?" Erin asked.

"No… not yet. Come on, K9. Let's go investigate."

The dog eagerly led the way down the stairs. Erin realized she was holding herself tense and she tried to relax. There wasn't anything downstairs. She already knew it. There had been no sign of forced entry at either door. No open windows somebody might have crawled in through. She was going to have to accept that there had been a tremor or something else that had made the counter shake and caused her coffee mug to go crashing to the floor. The shops were all connected; perhaps someone had dropped a pallet of books with enough force in the bookstore next door that it had shaken the shared wall and sent her mug on its kamikaze journey.

There were no sounds of conflict downstairs. No sign that the officer had found anyone lurking below them. He was back up the stairs in a minute.

"All clear."

They went back out to the front, where Melissa was anxiously waiting. Piper examined the front door and frame.

"There aren't any signs of forced entry," he said with a shrug. "Is it possible you left it unlocked last night?"

"No, I'm sure I…" Erin remembered colliding with the woman on the sidewalk as she left. Had she locked the door afterward? Erin knew she had unlocked the door in the morning. And it could only be locked from the outside. If she'd had to unlock it in the morning, then she had locked it the night before. "Yes. I'm sure I locked it. It was locked when I came in this morning."

"Maybe you knocked the mug down without realizing it, last night or this morning. Or maybe a crosswind or the building shaking for some reason?" Piper shrugged.

"It's a mystery!" Melissa said in dramatic tones.

Piper gave her a tolerant smile. "Yes, Mrs. Lee. It surely is."

"Maybe it's a ghost! The tea shop is haunted."

"Bakery," Erin corrected, aware she was nitpicking, but irritated about the community's opposition to a second bakery opening.

"We haven't had a ghost here before," Melissa enthused. "I wonder who it could be. There are a lot of civil war ghosts in the area. We have a rich civil war history, you know. Why, the library is practically famous in these parts. There are so many legends of lost and buried treasure in the hills around here, a person can hardly go for a hike without tripping over one!" She laughed.

"If there hasn't been a ghost here before," Piper said gravely, "then the ghost must be of a more recent vintage, wouldn't you say?"

Melissa stopped and considered. "Well, yes, I suppose. Unless you've somehow awoken a restless spirit. You haven't been digging down there in your basement? Or in the back?"

"No," Erin assured her. "The basement floor is concrete and so is the parking lot in back."

"Then we need to think of who might have died recently that would have a reason to haunt the store." Melissa pondered the problem.

Erin exchanged looks with Piper. He appeared to be suppressing a smile.

"Maybe... the owner?" he suggested.

"Erin?" Melissa said blankly.

"The... previous owner...?" Piper prompted.

"Oh, Clementine! Why, of course it would be Clementine! Silly old me!" She put her hand on Erin's arm. Her dark curls quivered with her movement. "You are being haunted by your Aunt Clementine. Did you have any unfinished business with her? Something that she would be expecting from you?"

"Just opening the bakery. And why, if there was such a thing as ghosts, would my aunt's restless spirit want to break my coffee mug?"

"She's trying to reach you, dear. Ghosts are very limited in what they can do. Move things, appear to you, maybe make noises. It's not like on TV, where they can just walk up and talk to you and explain themselves in words. All she can do to reach you is to move things around."

Erin nodded. "I see. Well, I don't believe in ghosts, so I'm going to look for more earthly explanations. You can... believe what you like."

"Oh, I do," Melissa agreed. "I am going to talk to the others and we'll see if we can sort this out. After all, we all knew Clementine. I knew her my whole life. We'll figure out what it is that she wants to reach you for. Mary Lou's sister-in-law, she's very good with spirits. We'll see if she can come here and make contact with your poor dead auntie."

Erin glanced over at Piper, widening her eyes, sure she was

being played. But Piper gave no sign that Melissa was joking. And Melissa continued to look earnest and excited about the whole ghost business.

"Isn't contacting ghosts considered sorcery in Christian circles?" Erin suggested.

"No, no! Mary Lou's sister-in-law won't be using a Ouija board or any other devil's tool. She just uses prayer. There's nothing wrong with that."

"Ah." Erin nodded. She looked at her watch as obviously as possible. Time was trickling by and she had work to do. "Did you want to leave me a flyer about your fundraiser, Melissa?" At Melissa's blank look, she indicated the woman's clipboard. "That was why you came in here, wasn't it?"

"Oh, yes!" Melissa pulled a fuchsia-colored page from her clipboard and handed it to Erin. "Of course, no one is required to donate or put time into it, but every little bit is appreciated! I'd better get on my way! If I stop to yap at every store, it's going to take me all day! I'm already busier than a one-armed paper hanger."

Erin nodded and gave a little wave, and Melissa went on her way. Erin sighed and looked at Officer Piper. He had a gorgeous smile, when he let it show.

"Miss Price, I'm sorry I couldn't be of more assistance. You feel free to call on me if you have any more troubles. Hopefully, your ghost won't cause any more trouble."

"Thanks," Erin said dryly. "Just tell me... everyone in town doesn't believe that, do they? In the existence of ghosts, I mean? And that they can just... be contacted?"

"Not everyone is quite as literal as Mrs. Lee, but... I do imagine most of them will agree that your shop might be haunted. They might not be willing to say that it is, but they won't say that it isn't..."

Erin shook her head. "I suppose it's harmless, as long as they aren't demanding to hold séances in here."

* * *

Gluten-Free Murder, Book #1 of the *Auntie Clem's Bakery* cozy
mystery series by P.D. Workman
can be purchased at pdworkman.com

* * *

ABOUT THE AUTHOR

P.D. Workman is a USA Today Bestselling author and multi-award winner, renowned for her prolific output of over 100 published works that span various genres. With a knack for crafting page-turners, Workman captivates readers with everything from cozy mysteries like the Auntie Clem's Bakery series to gripping young adult and suspense novels.

A prolific reader and writer since childhood, P.D. Workman crafts emotionally powerful stories that don't shy away from hard topics. Her books tackle mental illness, addiction, abuse, and trauma with raw honesty and compassion, giving voice to the often unheard. If you crave authentic, character-driven page-turners that hit deep and stay with you long after the final page, you're in the right place.

With each new release, fans eagerly anticipate another thrilling blend of thought-provoking storytelling and relatable characters that define P.D. Workman's brand as an author of unforgettable page-turners—gripping tales that leave a lasting impact long after the last page is turned.

> P. D. Workman, does not shy from probing the deep psychological scars of childhood trauma, mental illness, and addiction. Also characteristic of this author, these extremely sensitive issues are explored with extensive empathy, described with incredible clarity, and portrayed with profound insight.
>
> — —KIM, GOODREADS REVIEWER

Some of Workman's titles have been translated into Spanish, French, Portuguese, German, and Italian.

Workman began writing at an early age and is a prolific reader as well as writer. She is also passionate about teaching and learning, expresses her creativity through art and cooking, and loves exploring the Calgary parks and green spaces where the Parks Pat Mysteries are set. She was a legal assistant for many years and has done extensive charitable work.

Workman was born and raised in Alberta, Canada, and is married with one adult son.

* * *

Please visit P.D. Workman at pdworkman.com to see what else she is working on, to join her mailing list, and to link to her social networks.

* * *

If you enjoyed this book, please take the time to recommend it to other purchasers with a review or star rating and share it with your friends!

tiktok.com/@pdworkmanauthor

facebook.com/pdworkmanauthor

x.com/pdworkmanauthor

instagram.com/pdworkmanauthor

amazon.com/author/pdworkman

bookbub.com/authors/p-d-workman

goodreads.com/pdworkman

linkedin.com/in/pdworkman

pinterest.com/pdworkmanauthor

youtube.com/pdworkman

Find P.D. Workman's books at

PDWORKMAN.COM

Scan the QR code below

www.ingramcontent.com/pod-product-compliance
Lightning Source LLC
Chambersburg PA
CBHW030934260626
47169CB00002B/468